FINDING HER HEART

FINDING HER HEART

A Christian Romance Novel

HEART OF A FAMILY SERIES

DONNA WITTLIF

This is a work of fiction set in the present. Some of the places are real, but not all. All the characters and events portrayed in this book are fictional, and any resemblance to real people or incidents is purely coincidental.

ISBN: 978-1-63161-054-7

Published by TCK Publishing
www.TCKPublishing.com

Again, thanks to my husband, Edward, for his constant encouragement. This book is dedicated to all those who are lonely and don't know how to make friends, especially all those suffering from Asperger's Syndrome.

But as many as received Him, to them He gave the right to become children of God, even to those who believe in His name.
– John 1:11 (NASB)

CHAPTER 1

HIDING THE TRUTH

June 20

MY NAME IS ALLISON, OR Allie, and today was my thirteenth birthday, but it wasn't fun. Nope, not a bit. I woke up to Aunt Harriet and Uncle Deb fighting.

"We've got to get Allison into town near people. She's not thriving here!"

"Allie's fine here. If you keep naggin' at me, I'll leave!" Uncle Deb shouted.

I buried my head under my pillow so I couldn't hear them fight and they couldn't hear me crying. The older I got, the more they fought. The house shook as Uncle slammed the back door on his way out.

I got up and dressed. Peeking out of my bedroom door, I asked Aunt Harriet, "Where'd Uncle Deb go?"

"Out back. Guess he had to smoke."

"I'm going out to the woods." I smothered a biscuit with jelly, and with my art bag in hand, went out the front door. After making sure Uncle Deb wasn't where he could see me, I sneaked out to my place in the woods. I wasn't in the mood to talk to him.

My little squirrel friend, Wee Ears, scampered down a tree and sat at my feet. I handed him a piece of my biscuit. He hopped up on the fallen tree trunk where I was sitting to nibble on it.

"Wish me happy birthday, Wee Ears," I said as I painted his portrait. He flipped his tail at me, and chattering, scrambled up a tree.

When I finished, I stuck the painting into my art bag and headed home for lunch.

"Happy birthday, Allie," Uncle Deb said when I came in. "Here's your present."

"What is it?" I asked, looking at a flower-covered book with a lock and key on its front.

"A diary," Aunt Harriet said. "You can lock it so no one can see what you write. The counselor at school said it would help you learn to communicate better."

"Thanks. Every day I'm going to write down what I did to become a famous artist." *Why didn't they give me art supplies? I never have enough.* Inside the art bag Aunt Harriet gave me last year, I tuck special things I need. I slipped my diary inside my bag.

"Who's comin' to your party tonight?" Uncle Deb asked when I joined them at the table. "Who did you invite?"

"Mary. She can't come because her family is going on vacation. Doris said she wasn't coming, but she didn't tell me why."

"Come to your party, Dandelion? No way!" was what Doris said. I don't care. At least I asked her.

"Did you invite any boys? How about George Benton?" Aunt Harriet asked.

"That the banker's son?" Uncle Deb asked.

I nodded. "He said he would like to come but didn't think he could. Something's going on at home."

"Anyone else, honey?" Aunt Harriet placed her hand on mine.

"Lots of kids, but they all had other plans," I lied.

"Well, we'll have a happy little party then," Uncle Deb said. "Just us."

"That's the trouble. It's always *just us.*" Aunt Harriet glared at Uncle Deb.

I held my breath. *No more fighting, please.* I gulped down my hotdog, grabbed my art bag, and headed back to the woods to paint.

Most everyone called me Dandelion. Everyone in school and in town, that is. Probably because my hair was so blond it was almost white. It was kinky-curly and flew all over. My real name is Allison Bainsworth Cooper. Least that's what it said on my birth certificate down in the county courthouse in Puttersville, West Virginia. I never heard my mama say my name. Not once. Aunt Harriet told me she passed after I was born. And my daddy ran away. My only other living kin were Uncle Deb and Aunt Harriet, and they took me in.

I knew Uncle Deb and Aunt Harriet loved me. When I was little, they let me run loose among the trees in the holler. Uncle Deb showed me where the wild strawberries grow, and the may apples with their soft mellow fruit, and the morel mushrooms that soaked up spring's silvery showers. Aunt Harriet let me reach under the hen's feathers to gather her eggs. In the spring, she hoisted me up to smell the apple blossoms and in the fall to reach the reddest apples on our tree.

No one knew what made me tick, not even Uncle and Aunt. Sometimes I cried because the kids at school and the teachers didn't like me. The school counselor told Aunt Harriet that I have a condition called Asperger's Syndrome. Mrs. Bunker, my first-grade teacher, had me tested. I remembered, like it was an hour ago, the day when we learned the results of the test.

"Allison is very intelligent," Mrs. Williams, the school counselor, had said. "She has an IQ of one-forty-five, but she shows signs of Asperger's Syndrome. Allison needs to be in the city where she can make friends and play with other children."

"She has plenty of friends," Uncle Deb had said, scowling. "Half the animals in the woods will let her pet them."

"Mrs. Williams means children her own age," Aunt Harriet said. "I agree. We need to move into Puttersville."

"Harriet Gray, if you want to live in Puttersville, you can take Allie and go. But don't expect me to support you!" Uncle Deb shouted, right in front of the principal, Mrs. Bunker, and Mrs. Williams. He'd stalked off.

"I'm sorry," Aunt Harriet said, shaking her head.

"Allison is falling behind in her school work," Mrs. Bunker said. "Every time I check on her, she is drawing and not doing her assignments. She won't look at me when I speak to her."

"Allison's social skills are not commensurate with her age," Mrs. Williams had reported. "She doesn't play well with other children. She needs friends to play with."

"I do want friends, but the other kids don't want to play with me," I said. "So I draw. Someday I'm going to be a famous artist."

"Allison is a great little artist. You should have seen her snow sculptures of animals last winter," Aunt Harriet said. "They looked so real."

"Mrs. Gray, I'll ask our special education teacher to write an Individualized Educational Plan for Allison. She'll call you when it is ready, and you and your husband can come and sign it. It will contain goals for Allison getting her work done in school and socializing with other students."

That was six years ago. Did the goals work? Maybe I did a little more schoolwork because my teachers gave me extra time to draw after I finished my assignments. But did I make more friends by my thirteenth birthday? No one was coming to my party.

That night, I wrote my first entry in my new diary:

> *Uncle Deb and Aunt Harriet fight all the time. About me. Aunt Harriet wants to move so I can have friends. But will I? The same kids who live in town go to school with me, and they're not my friends. So, I don't think moving will change a thing. They won't play with me, so why should I play with them? Sometimes I'm sad because I don't have friends at school. But other times I don't care. I don't need them if they don't want me.*
>
> *The fire that burns within me drives me to draw and paint. Someday I'm going to be a famous artist. I'll have my own art gallery and charge other artists to display and sell their paintings. Everyone will want his picture in my gallery, and I will be the artist everyone talks about.*

"Allison," Aunt Harriet yelled through my bedroom door. "Come get your socks and put them away like I asked you to."

"Sorry. I forgot." I locked my diary and put it on the shelf in my closet, then went to get my socks.

CHAPTER 2

ALL MY FAULT

JUST BECAUSE UNCLE DEB SAID I was doing fine doesn't mean I was. I just started the seventh grade. Today at school, Janie passed by my desk.

"Hi, Dandelion, you look just like your namesake in that green skirt and blouse," she said. Some of the girls near me snickered.

"Allison, is that you talking?" the teacher asked, giving me the evil eye.

"No, ma'am."

"I hope not. I'd hate to have to give you detention the first week of school."

The other students rolled their eyes and smiled as they worked. I didn't cry because I didn't want anyone to know how sad I was.

After dinner, I helped Aunt Harriet with the dishes. She brought the book we were reading together to the table, and I plonked down beside her and buried my head in my arms.

"What's wrong, Allie?" She rubbed my back, then put her arm around me.

"I don't know," I mumbled, keeping my face hidden.

"I think you do know. You can tell me."

"I don't have any friends." The words opened the flood gates holding back my tears, and they rolled down my face. "No one really talks to me except George. He's the only one who's ever said anything nice to me. All through school."

"I remember that day when you were in third grade. The school secretary called us to come meet with Mr. Wheyton and talk about you and George. You said he put his hand on you."

"Yeah, when he was in grade school he sat and picked his nose when he couldn't figure something out. Like a math problem. All the kids called him Snotty Georgie and I didn't want him to touch me."

"So you hit him with your book." She laughed. "You reminded me of a feisty little blue jay."

"He pestered me. He always wanted to see my pictures. I hid them in my desk, but the teacher found them and took them after I went home."

"I think he likes you."

"George? No way. Besides, he's a silly old boy. I want some girlfriends."

"I know. I hate having to live in isolation from the rest of the world. And at school you isolate yourself more. You paint all the time and don't play with the other kids."

"The girls think I'm weird. They don't say much to me, and I don't talk to them."

"How are you weird? What do they say?"

"They laugh at my clothes. They think I'm weird because all I ever wear is skirts. Please, Aunt Harriet, I want some jeans. And some sleeveless blouses for when it's hot."

"You will dress modestly, Allison," Uncle Deb said as he strolled through the door. "I won't allow any woman in this house to wear jeans so tight every inch of her behind shows."

"Jeans for a skinny little girl aren't immodest, Deb. What we should do is move to the big city so Allison can have some friends and get special tutoring in art."

"She's getting more learnin' here than she would at any special school. You know how she takes to the outdoors. It's a natural tool for teachin' art."

"Sometimes I feel like a hermit shut up in our little house with no neighbors," Aunt Harriet said, scowling at him. "We don't have a television, nothing."

"It's the devil's tool for leadin' people away from God."

After Uncle Deb stepped into the bathroom, Aunt Harriet said, "So why did I marry Deb? I guess I saw him as a man given to spiritual devotion who had a love for things holy. At the time, I was searching for God, and my heart yearned for any wisdom leading to heaven. I thought he knew where he was going with his philosophy of back-to-nature and back-to-God, and I looked up to him. Now I wonder. I certainly haven't found what I was looking for."

When Uncle returned to the room, Aunt Harriet pursued the subject of moving us to Puttersville. "Allison needs more guidance and training than you and I can provide. A lot more. She's really smart. But smart doesn't always mean she's able to cope. Seems like every day she comes home crying."

"Harriet, take her into the city if you want, but don't expect me to go with you."

"I wish I'd finished my college degree," she fumed. "I wouldn't have married a stick-in- the-mud who can't even hold down a job. And I would've had a job teaching."

"You know I ain't well enough to work." Uncle Deb's face was red and sweating. He took two quick steps toward her and raised his hand.

I held my breath, sure he was going to hit her.

"Every time I go to do somethin' physical, my leg gives out. And a crowd bothers me," he said, snatching his cap from his head and hurling it past her. "People might as well be that enemy soldier standin' behind me, rifle raised to shoot me!"

"Well, I should go back to college. Finish my degree. Get a teaching job."

"Go. Just don't expect me to support you on my veteran's disability pension."

"If you don't get medicated for your PTSD, I'll leave you. And take Allison with me." Aunt Harriet started crying as I ran into my room. I was shaking, and my stomach was churning. It was all my fault they were fighting.

CHAPTER 3

THE WOODS

"WHAT ARE WE GOING TO do for fun today?" Aunt asked several months later.

"I want to go to the woods to paint something special. I'm entering an art contest for kids thirteen to sixteen years old."

"How did you learn about the contest?"

"From a magazine at school. It's the McCabbock State Young Artist's Competition. First prize is five thousand dollars. And there are other prizes." I reached into my art bag and pulled out the clipping. "Will you help me send my painting in when I finish it? It has to be there by the end of July, but I'll have it painted way before then."

"You paint it, and I'll help you mail it. It'll be our little secret."

"Thanks." I kissed her cheek and headed out the door.

Bits of dried corn, crusts of bread, apple cores, nuts, and lettuce bounced in my pocket as I ran to my spot. Rumple Tail, my little rabbit, hopped out from behind a bush and nibbled the lettuce leaf I brought him from our garden. The top of a sapling rustled as Wee Ears climbed down the tree to eat the bread crusts and nuts I scattered at my feet. The chickadees and cardinals lit on my knotty bench and pecked at the seeds I tossed them.

I sank down on a tree trunk and retrieved my drawing materials from my bag. With quick strokes I sketched a pond with cattails on one side and lily pads on the end. Just for fun I pictured a frog sitting on one of the lily pads, his long tongue streaking outward to catch a dragonfly. Then I drew an outline of Rumple

CHAPTER 4

TALKS

UNCLE DEB FOUGHT IN THE Middle East during the 1990s, but he didn't talk about it much. Shrapnel hit him in the leg, damaging the bone, muscle, and nerve. Most of it healed. He still limped when he was tired or when the weather was cold and damp. Aunt Harriet said it hurt at night and he couldn't sleep.

One afternoon, thunder boomed and streaks of lightning sizzled outside the window. Uncle Deb grabbed his Bible from its special shelf and sat down at the table.

"Come sit with me, Allie. Let's read some Bible." He opened to Psalms and read, "O God, hasten to deliver me: O Lord, hasten to my help."

Thunder crashed, shaking our little house. Uncle Deb jumped from his chair and ran to the windows, pulling the curtains closed. When he sat again, he turned a page and read, "Save me, O God, for the waters have threatened my life."

I didn't like loud noises either, but they didn't frighten me. I reached over and held his hand.

"God will take care of us, Allie Girl. Remember that all your life," he said.

I nodded, but I didn't understand. If God will take care of us, why was he so afraid? Why was his Bible so special? One time I got his Bible from the shelf. Its dried leather cover crackled as I opened it. A hand-written note filled the bottom of the first page, and as I started to read it, Uncle Deb stepped in front of me.

"What do you think you're doin'?" He snatched the Bible off my lap. "No one reads this Bible except me." He placed it on the shelf like it would break.

The sun shot its rays through the small cracks between the curtains, and Uncle Deb placed his Bible back on the shelf. We went outside to check on his flowers to make sure they were okay. Some special plants grew behind the backyard near the woods, and we looked at them first. He took out his pen knife and cut one off near the bottom. We walked onto the back porch, and he lopped all the leaves off the plant and laid them to dry on a sunny shelf. He picked up some of the dry leaves and rolled them in a thin square of paper, making a cigarette, which he lit as we walked into the house.

"Get that stinking weed out of the house!" Aunt Harriet yelled.

Uncle Deb left in a hurry, and I grabbed my art bag and walked with him out to the barn. We sat down on some hay while he puffed. The smoke from his cigarette swirled around us, creating a cozy tent. Maybe his smoking was his escape, like my art was for me.

"God's perfect medicine," he said. "Don't understand why Harriet doesn't try some herself. Sure does help my leg." He smiled. "You know, Allie Girl, God gives us lots of good gifts. The flowers and plants, for example, they're tons better for what ails you than those bottles of pills in the drugstore."

Sometimes it was better just to listen while I sketched, so I didn't say anything. Wasn't like Uncle Deb expected me to.

After taking a few puffs, he let loose. It was like some giant key unlocking the door to the thoughts that built up inside of him. Like a gust of wind sweeping a pile of leaves and driving them down a road, his words tumbled out.

That day he told me, "Don't like bein' around a lot of people. Don't like the cities where people run all day and work themselves to death. Smoke, dirt, loud noises, beggars on the streets, stench, trash, and nothin' but poverty. They even have pitiful little girls dressed skimpily, roamin' the streets at night lookin' to make a dime."

I nodded. I'd never been to a big city, but I could only imagine. Uncle Deb had traveled around the world, seen things. What he said was bound to be true.

"Government's bad," he said. "Politicians are nothin' but rich crooks. They pass laws that put money in their own pockets. Always exactin' more taxes, thinkin' up new ways to get your money. They rob us poor folks to make themselves rich. That's why I don't vote. Doesn't matter who gets elected, they're all the same. Out for themselves.

"Don't care for churches," he said, rolling and lighting another cigarette. "Mom took me to a little community church. It was okay, but don't believe in goin' to church now. They're all hypocrites. Go to church on Sunday and act like pious saints. Hold themselves up as God's people leadin' others to Him. But look at them. They'd just as soon cheat you as greet you. Don't trust any of them."

I smiled up at him. I'd never been to church, so I didn't know. But Uncle Deb had been there. And he saw everything when his mom took him, so he should know. That night I wrote in my diary:

I'm worried about Uncle Deb. Twice that day we went to the barn so he could smoke. Those cigarettes calm him, but after smoking, he isn't himself. That morning he left the gate to the pigpen open, and I had to chase the pigs through the garden to get them back in. Then he started his truck and revved the engine until the fenders shook and black smoke poured from the tailpipe. And he's smoking more and more.

CHAPTER 5

FIRST PRIZE

TWO WEEKS AFTER THE STORM I came home from school carrying a load of books. Lots of homework this evening, and I accosted Aunt Harriet as soon as I plopped my books down on the dining table.

"Why can't we get a computer? I have to write out all my papers by hand. I get a lower grade because my writing isn't pretty."

"We can't afford hundreds of dollars for a computer," Aunt Harriet said. "Let me see one of your papers."

I slid a folded paper from between the pages of my science book. "See," I said, opening it up. "Look at all these marks."

Aunt Harriet stared where I pointed to all the smudgy erasure marks on the page. "Why did you erase so many times?"

"As soon as I write an answer, I think of a better way to say it." Tears brimmed in my eyes as frustration filled my chest. "It's never good enough."

"I understand." She put her arm around me. "Your handwriting is fine. The problem is your sense of perfection. Everything has to be just right, doesn't it?"

"Yes. And I can't get it the way I want it. If I had a computer, I could fix it until it's the way I want it."

"I wish I could get us a computer. I could use it too." She sighed. "Deb and I had another argument this morning. I told him I was going to go into Puttersville to look for a job. He said we had everything necessary. Same old story about God taking care of us. Then he left and hasn't been back. I think he's out in the barn smoking, but I'm not going to check on him. He's a big boy. Just wish he wouldn't smoke that weed so much."

"I'll check when I go out to milk the cows."

"Thanks. Oh, something came for you in the mail. I put it on your bed."

"For me?" With two skips, I entered my room and picked up a large envelope from my pillow. The return address read *McCabbock State Young Artist's Competition*. My hand trembled as I tore the end from the envelope and pulled out the letter. It started with my name, Allison Bainsworth Cooper, and my address. The letter read:

Dear Miss Cooper,

We are pleased to inform you that you have won first place in this year's McCabbock State Young Artist's Competition. We received more than 200 entries. Your entry titled Woodland Friends is one of the best depictions of animals that the Judging Committee has seen.

Enclosed is your winning prize check for $5,000. Our annual book depicting our winners and their art will feature your painting on its cover. Congratulations on winning first place in this year's competition.

I reached into the large envelope and pulled out a sealed business envelope with my name on the front of it. Inside was a check made out to me. Five thousand dollars! All mine.

"Aunt Harriet! Aunt Harriet!" I screamed as I jumped up and down and ran out of my bedroom. "I won! I really won!"

"What's all the commotion?" Uncle Deb stood in the middle of the living room, his cap in his hand. "What's goin' on?"

"Allison entered an art contest and she won. Oh, Allison, I'm so happy for you." She hugged me, and I ran back and retrieved the letter and check.

"Here, look at these," I said, handing them to Uncle Deb. "I won five thousand dollars! Now I can buy me a computer."

"Not so fast, Allie Girl," he said, giving them back to me. "Tomorrow mornin' we're headin' straight to Puttersville First National Bank and investin' that money for you. We'll have the bank put it in some big investment company so it can grow fast. That's your college money."

"*The Puttersville Daily Times* should write a story about Allison," Aunt Harriet said. "Nothing's ever happened like this around here. I'll go talk to them while you're in the bank." She hugged me again. "Good for you, Allison. See, you're a very smart girl with a lot of talent."

"I will be a famous artist someday. I know I will."

"Come on, Allie. Time to do the milkin'." Uncle Deb put his cap on and headed for the door, and I gathered the milk buckets and followed him.

"A computer would cost only a few hundred dollars. I can put the rest in the bank for college. Please, Uncle Deb, let me get a computer. All the other kids have one."

"If all the other kids jumped off the bridge and drowned in the river, does that mean you'd do it? We'd have to pay Internet fees every month. And computers have all sorts of bad things on them," he said. "There will be no computer in our house. If you need one for homework, use the school computers."

I glared and stuck my tongue out at him as he disappeared into the pig house. It didn't make me feel better, and tears filled my eyes as I put the milk bucket under our cow Betsy and started milking her. I was going to ask Mrs. Williams to write having a computer as one of my special accommodations. Then Uncle Deb would have to let me get one.

CHAPTER 6

TROUBLE AT SCHOOL

"WHAT'RE YOU DRAWING, DANDELION?"

"Hi, Janie." I stopped to look up at her, following one of the goals on my eighth-grade Individualized Educational Plan that says *Always look people in the eyes when you're talking to them.*

"A picture of the fawn I saw in the woods yesterday," I told her. "It's for the McCabbock—"

"See you later," she said, turning and walking to a group of girls on the other side of the lunch room.

How nice it would have been if she'd said, "Come show the other girls" or "Why don't you eat with us today?" I ate my last bit of sandwich, folded my brown paper lunch bag and put it into my art bag, and walked outdoors.

I headed toward what I thought of as my private art bench, a wooden bench with most of its green paint worn off. The bench was nestled under a towering pine tree near the school yard fence. Sharp-pointed pine cones littered the ground beneath it, repelling those kids playing games and insuring a bit of privacy.

After pulling out my drawing pad, I closed my eyes, trying to recapture the spots on the fawn's sides, the subtle rippling movements of the muscles under his skin as he walked with his mother, and the twitch of his tail when the doe nuzzled him. Every detail had to be perfect.

A gasp and a half-smothered sob, followed by sounds of weeping, drifted to my ears. I opened my eyes, searching the nearby school yard, but saw no one nearby. *Maybe I'm hearing things.* I retrieved my drawing pencil and made a couple light strokes to begin the fawn's hind quarters when the unmistakable sound of crying came from behind the pine tree's broad trunk. Laying down my drawing, I crept around to the back side of the tree. George stood there, his hands covering his face, his body wracked with sobs.

I stood there for a few seconds, not knowing what to say or do. Then I put my hand on his shoulder and said the only thing that came to my mind. "George, it's me, Allison."

He turned to face the tree trunk, folded his arms across its rough surface, and buried his head in them. "Go away. Please, just go away," he mumbled.

"Tell me what's wrong. Maybe I can help."

"No. You can't. No one can." More sobs shook his body. "Please go away."

I don't know what made me do it. Maybe his aloneness, his hurt, his wretchedness. I put my arms around him, and he turned and put his head on my shoulder.

"I'm sorry. So sorry; I don't want anyone to see me like this."

"It's okay, George. Please tell me. Maybe I can help."

The noise of scuffling feet made me whirl around. Janie, accompanied by Kim and Mary, dashed around the tree.

"Dandy's kissing George, Dandy's kissing George," Janie shouted. "Come on, let's go tell the teacher." Off they flew, giggling.

"I hope you're not in trouble," George said, wiping his eyes.

"Don't worry about it. We weren't doing anything wrong."

The bell rang. "Better get to class," I said. "Are you okay?"

"Yes. I have a study period next. You?"

"Language arts." I gathered my bag, and we entered the school building and went in different directions.

Poetry by e. e. cummings, algebra problems, and a science test dispersed my thoughts of George for the rest of the afternoon. As I left science class, the teacher pulled me aside.

"Mr. Horton wants to see you in his office before you leave," he said. "Some kind of meeting with your aunt and uncle."

"Okay." My heart jumped to my throat as I made my way to the principal's office. Did Janie and her friends really go tell a teacher that George and I were kissing? Was I in trouble for trying to help him? In grade school Mrs. Williams said children with Asperger's Syndrome lacked empathy, but I had felt sorry for George and had just wanted to comfort him.

I plodded down the steps to the first floor and trudged down the hall leading to Mr. Horton's office. Through the floor-length windows, I could see Uncle Deb and Aunt Harriet sitting in front of his desk. Sighing, I walked through the open door and sat in the chair between them.

"Hello, Allison," Mr. Horton said. "How are you today?"

"Fine," I said, running my finger along the seam in the chair upholstery.

"Please look at Mr. Horton when you speak to him," Mrs. Klat, the school counselor said as she scooted a chair in beside the principal's. "Remember, that is one of your goals."

"Yes, ma'am." I looked up at Mr. Horton.

"I'm sorry I couldn't notify you sooner about this meeting," the principal said to Uncle Deb and Aunt Harriet. "I received this just this morning. I think it's a great opportunity for Allison, and we'd like to change her schedule for next year to include her." He handed a printed brochure to them. "If Allison wants to participate."

I exhaled in relief and looked over Aunt Harriet's shoulder as she studied it for a moment, then passed it to Uncle Deb. "Allison's too young to go to college," Aunt Harriet said. "Besides, we can't afford it."

"As you know, Mrs. Gray, Allison will start high school next year. This is a scholarship for high school students to take special art classes at West Virginia University in Morgantown. That means it's free. Allison can take it as her elective, and it will count as a college credit."

"We need to think about it," Uncle Deb said. "We've already scheduled her classes for next year."

"That's why we're holding this special meeting. I have to give them an answer by this Friday, and I have to be out of town that day," Mr. Horton said. "The university plans to offer this program every year. By the time Allison finishes high school, she can have four college classes taken, all for free."

My heart pounded in my chest, and I jumped to my feet. "Please, Uncle Deb, this is something I really want. Please, please, please."

"Is it during the day?" Aunt Harriet asked.

"It's after school, from five until six-thirty on Monday and Wednesday," Mr. Horton said. "You would have to pick her up from school and take her to Morgantown on those days."

"We'll talk about it on the way home," Uncle Deb said.

"Please call and let me know by noon tomorrow," Mr. Horton said.

Uncle Deb and Aunt Harriet rose to leave and I followed. Before I got to the door, Mrs. Klat laid her hand on my shoulder.

"Were you and George Benton kissing during lunch break?"

"No, we weren't." My cheeks burned, and I broke into a cold sweat. "I promise."

"I hope not," she said. "We don't do those things on the school grounds."

"No, ma'am."

I fled to the truck, and as I climbed in, Aunt Harriet asked, "Everything okay?"

"Yes. Can I go to the class? Can I?"

"Two trips into Morgantown a week," Uncle Deb said. "Sure would use up the gas."

"I'll get a job," Aunt Harriet said. "These classes will give Allison a jump start on her career."

"You're needed here, Harriet."

"Not all day."

"If you take the truck, what'll I do if I need it?"

"The only time you need it is when we go for groceries. We can do this. I'll call Mr. Horton tomorrow morning and let him know Allison can take the class next year."

Yes! We pulled up to our house, and I jumped out of the truck and ran into my bedroom before Uncle Deb could say another word. I was writing the good news in my diary when Aunt Harriet opened my door and stuck her head in.

"Homework first, young lady. You'll have to develop good work habits if you add another class."

"Will do," I said. After she closed the door, I added a line to my diary entry:

I'm never going near George Benton again!

CHAPTER 7

EXCUSES

I WOKE UP THE NEXT morning to a loud roar. Acrid smoke seeped into my bedroom through the cracks around the window sills and burned my throat. I got out of bed and scurried into the kitchen, where Aunt Harriet was scrambling eggs.

"What's that noise? What's that terrible smell?"

"Deb's out working on the truck. Says the engine's not running the way it should."

Just then he opened the door. A cloud of black smoke blew into the living room and drifted into the kitchen. "Couldn't get the truck to start, took a long time, but she finally ran. And all that black smoke she's pourin' out. Somethin's gotta be wrong, and it'll probably cost a pretty penny to fix it." He sat down and propped his elbows on the table. "It's gonna take every dime of our savings," he moaned, looking at Aunt.

"What's wrong with it?" she asked.

"Don't know. Mechanics was never my thing."

"So what are you going to do?"

"Take it in town to the garage, if it'll make it." He sighed. "Better call the school and tell them we don't have the money for that art class."

"It's free," I said. "How can we not have the money?"

"Gotta get you home two nights a week, don't I? Who knows? By then I may not have a truck if I can't get it fixed." He looked at Aunt, who had her back turned, scraping eggs from the skillet.

"After breakfast, I want you to call the school and tell them. Can't do the class."

"Uncle Deb, you can't do this to me!" I stated, stamping my foot. "It'll hold me back forever!"

"Can't help it if the truck don't run," he said.

"Deb, you'll have the truck fixed by then. I won't deny Allison this opportunity," Aunt placed the eggs on the table. "Let's eat our breakfast."

"You can keep your breakfast." He shoved his chair against the table as he headed for the door.

"He can't...do this...to me." I choked back tears. "Mr. Horton was talking about next year. When I'll be a freshman. I haven't even finished eighth grade yet."

"I know, dear." She pulled out my chair. "Come have some eggs and biscuits."

I let her put the food on my plate even though I didn't feel like eating.

"Let me tell you a story I heard once," Aunt said, putting a spoonful of strawberry jam on her biscuit. "A man asked a farmer if he could borrow his pitchfork. The farmer said, 'No. I have to eat my soup with it.'"

"Then you think he's just making excuses?"

"Yes. Truck probably needs an oil change." She winked at me. "Don't worry. I'm calling Mr. Horton this morning and telling him you're going to be in that art class."

When I arrived at school, I went straight to Mr. Horton's office and barged in through the closed door.

"Allison, I'm talking with a teacher," Mr. Horton said. "Please wait outside on the bench."

"Sorry." I backed out, closed the door, and sat down.

"Everything all right?" George asked as he passed on his way to class. When I nodded, he said, "Great. See you in class."

Mr. Horton opened the door. "Come on in, Allison."

"I just wanted to say I can take the art class." I remembered to look him in the eyes. "Thanks for telling us about it."

"I forgot to tell you that the class is free, but there is a one hundred dollar fee for the book and supplies," he said. "I hope that's okay with your uncle and aunt. You need to send the money in by August. Here's the form."

My knees shook, and I sank into a chair. A hundred dollars, on top of getting the truck fixed. Uncle Deb would never give me that much money.

"A hundred dollars is nothing for class supplies," he said. "Surely your uncle and aunt can come up with a hundred dollars."

"Thanks," I said as I left. All day long I worried. When the bus dropped me off at our lane, I raced into the house.

"Well, Deb got the truck fixed," Aunt Harriet said. "New oil filter and new oil. Truck wouldn't start because the battery was almost dead. Add all that to the cost of labor…"

"How much?"

"Almost two hundred dollars."

"I need one hundred for the art class book and supplies," I said. "By the first of August."

CHAPTER 8

ENTERPRISE

SCHOOL WAS OVER FOR THE year, and one morning Aunt Harriet said, "I'd go get a job, but I'm afraid of what will happen to Deb if I leave him. You're too young to get a job. But I know how we're going to get the money for your art class supplies."

"I have money for college. Five thousand dollars at the bank."

"Deb would never let you use it until after you graduate. But don't worry, we'll earn it."

"How?"

"We're going to plant a large garden so we'll have some to sell. We'll sell tomatoes, peppers, onions, and sweet corn. And we're going to pick raspberries and blackberries and sell them."

"Where can we pick berries? We don't have any."

"They grow wild everywhere. Way in the back of this property there's a big patch of blackberries. I see them growing along the road, raspberries too. All we have to do is find them and pick them. And we'll ask nearby farmers if we can pick the berries in their fields."

"Planted the onions and potatoes in March," Uncle said when we told him. "The tomato and pepper plants I started from seed are comin' along. Big enough to set out."

"We'll plant more onions," Aunt said. "That way we'll have a second crop to harvest when we've sold the first. And this year I'd like to try some pole beans."

We made a trip to Walmart to buy seeds for beans, corn, beets, carrots, and peas. Uncle added a new hoe to our cart. As we checked out, he told the cashier, "Too bad you're out of onion sets." He handed her a twenty and a five. "May you return to us a hundredfold," he said to the bag of seed packets as he handed them to me.

After lunch, we all went out to the garden area. Uncle handed Aunt and me each a hoe. "I'm going to dig up the soil with the shovel, and you two come behind me and break up the clods."

The sun beat down on my head, and after a half hour, sweat trickled down my face, stinging my eyes and dripping from my chin. I glanced at Aunt. Perspiration covered her beet-red face. She wiped her brow with her sleeve.

"Didn't think it would be so hot this early in June," she said.

"'Cursed is the ground for thy sake: in toil shalt thou eat of it all the days of thy life. In the sweat of they face shalt thou eat bread. That's what God told Adam, and it's true today,'" Uncle said. After we worked another half hour, he said, "Time for a break. Let's go to the house for a drink."

After drinking water, we headed back to the garden. We stopped a minute to gaze at the row and a half we had upturned. "Let's hit it," Uncle said.

The second hour we finished only one row. When we stopped for drinks, I held out my hands to show Aunt. "I've got three blisters."

"Wish we'd bought some gloves." She found an old pillow case, tore it into strips, and wrapped them around my hands. Then I helped her wrap her hands.

Clouds gathered as we returned to work, and a strong breeze cooled us off. The breeze was a curse and a blessing. As it blew, it caught up the loose soil and whisked it onto our faces. The dirt mixed with our sweat, covering us with a layer of grime.

We quit near dinner time. My back and legs ached as we walked to the house for dinner. "A little work never hurt anybody," Aunt said. "You'll get used to it." She put leftover beans and cornbread on to warm.

"Come on, Allie. Cows to milk," Uncle said after dinner.

Every muscle in my body screamed for more rest as I followed him to the barn. I milked while he fed the pigs and chickens.

Thunder rolled and lightning flashed through the sky, but when I returned from taking the milk to the house, Uncle was in the garden.

"I think it's going to rain," I said as I approached him.

"We need to get these seeds in." His voice trembled.

I knelt to help him, covering the corn seeds he dropped, three to a spot every six inches. The warm soil slipped through my fingers as I pulled it from the sides of the indented row he had made and patted it on top of the seeds.

"The next row will be the pole beans," he said. "It's close to the corn so they can climb up the corn stalks. It won't hurt the corn."

In the last three rows we planted peas, carrots, and beets. Huge drops of rain hit us as we finished, and by the time we ran into the house, my hair and blouse dripped.

"Least we got most everythin' planted," he said as we hurried through the door and shed our muddy shoes. "We'll plant the tomatoes and peppers tomorrow."

It rained for two days, turning our garden into a sea of mud and obliterating the rows. Three days later we dug holes and set out the tomatoes and peppers, carrying water from the house to give them a good start in the clay soil that was already drying.

A week later the corn and bean plants poked their heads through the soil, and the other seeds soon followed. Spaces where no seeds emerged pocked each row.

"Seeds probably got washed away in all that rain," Uncle said. "Or the crows ate them. They'll eat the corn seed every time."

The next week, he handed me a hoe after breakfast. "Weeds growin' faster than the plants."

We pulled the weeds growing close to the plants, then hoed out the ones between the plants and the rows. The sun beat down on us without mercy. I could feel the sweat running down my neck and sliding along my arms underneath my long sleeves.

"Oomph," Aunt said as she straightened up. "I feel every muscle in my back and legs."

"Me too." I stood, put my hands on the small of my back, and bent backwards, stretching, then bent over to pull more weeds.

It didn't rain again the whole month of June. Every morning, we carried water by the bucketful from the house, but the tomatoes, peppers, and beans dropped their blossoms.

"Have it your way," he said, shrugging. "But are you sure this is God's plan for you?"

"It's my plan for me."

"Better ask God about it," he said, rolling another cigarette. "I'm sure God doesn't want you movin' so far away and leavin' your Uncle Deb and Aunt Harriet when they're getting' old and feeble."

That night I wrote in my diary:

Uncle Deb doesn't want me to go to Denver. He's not going to stop me this time.

CHAPTER 10

THE DRESS

"WE'RE DRIVING INTO PUTTERSVILLE TODAY," Aunt Harriet announced one Saturday morning. "You're finishing your senior year, and you need some new skirts and blouses for college. We'll go to the new Walmart and pick out some materials and patterns."

"I've worn most of my outfits the last two years, and they're wearing out," I said, pulling up my skirt so Aunt Harriet could see the frayed hem.

"Let's get one of those patterns that makes different styles. We'll have time to look while Deb picks out seeds for the garden."

We climbed into Uncle Deb's Ford pickup and bounced in our seats as it traversed the muddy, rutted corduroy roads through the woods into town, where he parked in the grocery store parking lot between the hardware store and Walmart.

As we walked to Walmart, we passed Judy's Special Occasion Dress Shop on Main Street. I'd never gone inside, but that day a dress hanging in the window caught my eye. I stopped and gazed. It was floor length and made of sky-blue satin with wide puffed strap sleeves, an empire style waist, and dainty buttons dancing from the waist to the top of the bodice. I'd never seen such a gorgeous dress. I stood breathless and transfixed.

Aunt Harriet walked ahead, but I barely noticed. Then she came back and laid her hand on my shoulder.

"Do you like that dress?"

"Oh, yes…it's, it's…" Tears sprang to my eyes, and unable to express how I felt, I choked out, "Can I have it, please?"

Aunt Harriet's eyes met mine in surprise. "Do you want it for the prom?"

"The prom? No." I shook my head. "George asked me, but I don't want to go."

"Why not?"

"All the girls will laugh at me. We'll both be miserable."

"Allison!" Aunt said, her voice sharp. "Life will never have any meaning if you keep yourself isolated!" She joined me at the window. "If you're not going to the prom, why do you want the dress?"

"It's so beautiful, so wonderful." I looked up at her, my eyes pleading. "Please let me go try it on."

A momentary look of panic swept across her face before she gathered her composure. "No, I don't think you better do that. Come on. Let's go buy the material for your new clothes." Turning toward Walmart, she quickened her pace.

Tears stung my eyes as I followed her. I couldn't stop thinking about the blue dress and how it would fit me perfectly. Visions of myself walking down the streets of Puttersville in that dress popped into my mind. With my long hair in curls secured on top of my head by sparkling combs and the blue dress swirling around my feet, I'd feel like a princess or movie star. I imagined George Benton strolling down the street, then stopping dead in his tracks to stare at me as I smiled and waved at him.

"Allison!" Aunt Harriet yelled, "Come on!"

I hurried to catch up. Aunt Harriet was right. It would be foolish to buy the dress just to show off in, not practical at all. Then another thought hit me. That dress was probably very expensive.

"Are we poor?"

"We manage. But we don't have money for frivolities."

We entered Walmart and went to the craft and sewing section. Aunt Harriet pulled roll after roll of material off the shelf and held it up to me for my approval, and I shook my head at each one. Before I saw the dress, I probably would have been thrilled with all of them, but now they were dull and lifeless.

"We'd better pick out something or Deb's going to be in here saying it's time to go home. Here, let's go look at the patterns."

I swallowed deep disappointment as we headed for the racks of patterns. If I couldn't buy the dress, I wished to make something different from what I'd been wearing. We settled on a new skirt pattern that made two kinds of long skirts and a blouse pattern with three variations. I found six bolts of material for the skirts and blouses. The person working there measured and cut the yardage, and we walked up to the check-out stands. On the way, we passed jeans and summer shirts on sale. I didn't dare even eye them. I could hear Uncle Deb say, "Christian girls don't wear skin-tight jeans, short skirts, and frilly blouses with no sleeves."

Maybe Uncle Deb wasn't always right after all.

CHAPTER 11

THE ACCIDENT

TEARS STREAMED DOWN MY FACE and splatted onto my diary page as I wrote. I couldn't stop them. "Uncle Deb, oh, Uncle Deb," I said, and my words came out entangled in my sobs. That day was a day like any other, and it started out so well. Up until right before dinner.

"Aunt Harriet, I'm going out to help Uncle Deb with the chores," I said as she sat writing. I grabbed the clean milk pails and headed out the door to the barn. A warm rain had fallen all day, and black clouds dulled the summer evening light.

The smell of Uncle Deb's cigarettes greeted me at the open barn door. He was spending more time in the barn lately. I knew why he was out here, but I tried not to think about it or ask him not to do it. He had to live life the way he wanted. Besides, I would be gone in a few weeks, attending Watson Academy of Arts in Denver. The thought scared me, mostly because I'd never been away from home. And I would miss the woods and the animals, but fulfilling my dreams was within my reach.

"Uncle Deb, I'm going to start the milking," I yelled as I picked up the stool and placed it beside Molly, our Guernsey cow. She turned her reddish brown head toward me and mooed, and I gave her rump a pat and checked her udders. Seeing no cuts or scratches, I squeezed downward, sending a stream of rich milk into the pail. In ten minutes I finished, and I grabbed the other pail and moved the stool to Betsy, our black and white Holstein. When I had stripped every squirt from her udders, I turned the cows back out into the pasture.

After taking the full buckets of milk to the house, I went to join Uncle Deb and help him with the pigs. I picked my way through the wet grass and tried to avoid stepping in the mud that filled the path. I didn't hear or see Uncle Deb, and I raised my eyes toward the pig house. A dark form lay across the cement blocks leading up to the door.

"Uncle Deb!" My scream shattered the air as I rushed to him and knelt at his side. A deep gash split the skin across his forehead and ran down to the top of his ear. Blood covered his ashen face and mingled with the mud and rain on the block step.

"Aunt Harriet! Aunt Harriet," I screamed and gathered his head into my arms. "Aunt Harriet!" Uncle Deb's eyes stared up at me vacantly. "Uncle Deb!" Sobs strangled my words as I sat and rocked him. "Aunt Harriet!"

She couldn't hear me. My befuddled mind cleared, and I knew I must get help. Putting him down as gently as I could, I ran to the house. Reaching the door and pushing it open, I screamed, "Aunt Harriet, Uncle Deb's hurt! Come!"

"Where?"

"By the pigpen! Call for help!"

She dialed 911 and gave brief details, and then we ran to the pig house together. She bent over him and felt for a pulse on the side of his neck. She said nothing, but her frightened eyes told me.

Sitting down, she put his swollen head on her lap. "Deb, oh my Deb, don't leave me. Please, Deb." She rocked back and forth, tears streaming down her face. "Deb, I'm here. Please don't leave me."

The ambulance arrived, and they hoisted Uncle Deb onto a gurney, and with sirens wailing, the ambulance headed for the small hospital in Puttersville. Aunt Harriet and I arrived a few minutes later in the Ford pickup. We sat in the foyer that doubled as a waiting room.

Mud and blood covered our clothes, and our shoes tracked mud all over the floor. People coming and going stared at us as if we were from another planet, but it didn't matter. We waited for the emergency room doctor to tell us about Uncle Deb.

After what seemed hours he came. He reached out his hands to Aunt Harriet. "Mrs. Gray, I'm Dr. Hudson. I'm sorry, but your husband didn't make it."

The room swirled around me. I couldn't get my breath, my stomach churned, and I wanted to vomit. Aunt Harriet covered her face with her hands and sobbed. We fell into each other's arms. Her body trembled, and all I could do was wrap my arms around her.

The receptionist approached us. "Mrs. Gray, the police are coming to talk to you. They just want to know what happened. Please wait for them here."

I looked up at the receptionist. How could she know what he meant to us? Aunt Harriet and I clung to each other. All we had was each other.

The next morning I wrote it all down, but I still couldn't believe it. Oh, I yearned to be sitting out in the barn, him smoking and telling his stories, and me drawing and listening. And Aunt Harriet was not herself. Oh, she got up, dressed, and mopped the floor, but she didn't talk to me. I could tell she was lost without Uncle Deb. What would we do without him?

CHAPTER 12

AUNT HARRIET'S DECISION

"WE'RE NOT HAVING A FUNERAL for Deb," Aunt Harriet said. "No one here knew him, and only a few people know us. So there's no use."

Maybe it's no use to you, but I would like a funeral. I dared not say it. Uncle and I didn't always agree, and sometimes we didn't get along, but I missed hearing him say, "Come on, Allie Girl, let's go talk." Maybe someone out there would understand, and their arms around me and their words of comfort and offers to help would assuage the deep wound within.

"How will I remember Uncle Deb?" I asked. "Can I have something of his? Like his Bible?" I looked up at the shelf. It was empty. "What happened to Uncle Deb's Bible?"

"I got rid of it," she said, disappearing into the bathroom.

I followed her. "Got rid of it? How? Why?"

Tears streamed down her face. She took hold of my shoulders and gently pushed me back through the open door, then shut it.

It was a relief to milk the cows and feed the pigs and chickens. They were someone to talk to. I brought in the milk, strained it, and put it in jars to store in the refrigerator. I slid into a chair at the table, and Aunt Harriet joined me.

"We're moving next month, Allison," she said, her voice like steel. "My stepdad said we could live with him in Chicago. You will soon go to college, and I can't stay here alone."

"We're going to Grandpa's?"

"Your step-grandpa. My mother married him after she divorced your real grandfather. You met him when you were eight. We weren't at his house very long."

"What about Molly and Betsy? And the pigs and the chickens? And this place?"

"Do you think I can afford to pay the rent? We don't own this place, you know. We'll sell the livestock and use the money to move. That's all we can do."

The news slashed through me like a knife, releasing all my pent-up grief, and I buried my head in my arms and sobbed.

"Don't cry, Allison. You should be excited about going to college. You sent in your registration papers? And the five thousand dollars for the first year?"

"Yes," I said. "Remember the acceptance letter that came in the mail?"

"Uh-huh," she said. "But that was before..."

I could have finished her sentence, but I didn't. "I'll miss it here... my animal friends."

"I know." Her smile was as thin as I've ever seen. "Tomorrow we'll go into town and look for packing boxes. I want to talk to Mr. Bryant at the hardware store and see if he knows anyone who might buy our livestock. We need to be ready to move in two weeks.

"But you said next month. Next month, not two weeks."

"August is next month, and it'll be here in two weeks. We have to be out then as I can't afford another month's rent. You need to spend some time going through your things to decide what you want to take."

My meager wardrobe would take about fifteen minutes to pack and my precious art supplies were already in my bag, but I was glad for the chance to escape to my room. As I closed the door, tears flowed silently down my face. I lay down and buried my head in my pillow, and my body shook with wrenching sobs that dared not make a sound.

In my closet hung five skirt and blouse sets that I'd worn forever, one newer set in blue for good, and my new clothes that Aunt Harriet had made me for college. That plus my underthings and socks and two pairs of shoes, one pair of tennis shoes that I wore around the house and one nicer pair that I saved for when I'd go to Watson Academy and of course, my precious art supplies.

Three days later, a truck pulling a big trailer backed up to the barn. Two men got out and loaded up all the livestock. I stayed in my room, so glad Aunt Harriet didn't make me go out and help. If I had been out there, the dam would have burst. They took most of what reminded me of Uncle Deb.

The day after the animals were gone, I went out to the back yard. In my mind I could see Uncle Deb walking around the flower beds, stooping to pull weeds poking through the mulch, watering the base of the flower stems with his watering can. I stared at the flowers drooping in the hot sun. His medicine plants hid in the weeds at the back of the yard. All the plants needed some TLC, but you know what? I didn't water anything. They belonged to Uncle Deb, and he took care of them. Watering them would have kept them alive a few days longer, but Uncle Deb was gone. I struggled with that reality. Saving the plants was like thinking he was still here.

We finished packing and put everything in boxes except the few pots we needed for cooking. Aunt Harriet bought a package of paper plates and some plastic forks and spoons. She always was brave and businesslike. But last night I heard her crying after she went to bed.

CHAPTER 13

THE MOVE

"CHICAGO IS A LONG WAY from West Virginia," Aunt Harriet said on moving day as she pulled the tarp over the pile of boxes in the back of the pickup and tied it down. "It's going to be a long drive. Wish you had your license."

I wished so too. I'd planned to get it this summer, but it didn't happen. She climbed behind the steering wheel and motioned for me to get in. A huge lump of sorrow throbbed in my chest as we drove down the dirt road for the last time. I looked over my shoulder at the house and my beloved woods as long as I could, all the way until we rounded the bend and entered the paved highway to town.

My angst hung over me for a while, but I felt a tinge of excitement as we drove through Puttersville and onto the interstate. All of a sudden I didn't care if I never came back here. College and the world waited for me.

Aunt Harriet stayed in her own thoughts until we were on the freeway. As she left the slower right lane for the middle lane, she broke her silence. "I'll have to get a job, you know. I doubt three people can live on Trag's veteran's pension."

"That's Grandpa's name? Trag? How strange."

"That's what everyone calls him." She glanced at me. "It's been a long time since I've seen him or talked with him."

Her anxiety didn't ease my apprehension. "You've never said much about Grandpa Trag. What's he like?"

Aunt Harriet's brow furrowed, and she pursed her lips. "When I last heard, he wasn't doing too well. We'll see."

The countryside passed us as we wove our way around eighteen wheelers and past large farms with stately homes, red barns, and fields of waving grain.

"Farmers here grow mostly corn and wheat to sell," Aunt explained.

"Well, I know the corn, but I never saw wheat except in pictures. I better remember how wheat looks in case I have to draw it."

We stopped in a small town and bought some hamburgers, fries, and a drink. Aunt Harriet paid from the wad of bills she carried in her fanny pack. She had all the money we got from selling our livestock, over a thousand dollars, in that fanny pack. A heavy lump stuck in my throat as I remembered Molly and Betsy and our pigs and chickens. I dipped a couple fries in ketchup and swallowed them, forcing the knot back into my stomach.

That evening, we had dinner at a cheap Chinese restaurant, and when we finished, Aunt Harriet found a hotel. Nothing big and fancy, just an older one where we could park in front of the door to our room. I helped her unload the suitcases. The room had one queen-size bed and a television in it.

"Up and at 'em," Aunt said the next morning when the alarm went off at six. It's the first of August, and we have to be at Trag's today, so we better get on the road."

In twenty minutes, we were in the truck, heading for a fast-food place on the edge of town. She bought breakfast sandwiches and coffee, and we ate them on the highway.

About mid-afternoon we got to the outskirts of Chicago. I watched in fascination as the freeway widened to six lanes and we took exits to get on different highways. Aunt Harriet knows how to drive in such traffic and how she can find her way around, but not me. At last we got off onto a two-lane road, and after about twenty minutes, she pulled onto a street and drove slowly.

"Look for twelve forty-one," she said, following the numbers with her eyes.

I spied the house before she did, and she parked on the street in front of it.

"Not much of a house," I said, disappointment swelling in my chest as I stepped out of the truck onto a broken sidewalk running by a gate leaning on one hinge. "Smells like new-mown hay." Looking through the wood fence slats, I saw long stalks of weeds scattered on the bare spots in the yard and grass and weeds a foot high lining the dilapidated wooden fence. The weather had stripped the outside of the house bare of paint, leaving its boards gray and splintered.

The screen door opened with a creek. An old man in a wheelchair propelled himself through the doorway and onto the porch. His back was so humped that his head hung over his enormous belly, and a couple upright beer cans filled the space between his side and the side of the wheelchair.

"Harriet, is that you out there?" he croaked. "I hope you brought some dinner. I fired the help soon as I learned you was comin'."

CHAPTER 14

GRANDPA TRAG

AUNT HARRIET AND I ENTERED the house and stood in the middle of the living room floor, our suitcases at our feet while our eyes adjusted to the dim light. Green shag carpet covered the floor, and navy blue paint darkened the walls. Two completed jigsaw puzzles in frames hung over a fake fireplace, and a black, empty vase about eight inches tall occupied the spot between them on the mantle. A dark brown sofa with thread-bare cushions sat under a window covered by heavy gold curtains. Against the opposite wall was a small wooden stand holding a thick, boxy television set. A path made by Grandpa Trag's wheel chair rutted the carpet from the door on one end of the room to another door on the other end and cut the room in half.

Grandpa Trag's eyes traveled from my toes to the top of my head in one piercing glance that transmitted neither warmth nor approval. He turned to Aunt Harriet. "Is this the brat you told me about?"

"This is Allison, Trag. She'll be headed off to college in a few days."

He frowned and jerked his head toward the hallway. "You can put your bag in there, last door down the hall on the left."

"Thank you," I said, picking up my suitcase and escaping into the dank hallway. I was sure Aunt Harriet did not call me a *brat* to Grandpa, but it didn't matter. I wouldn't be here long. The last door on the left was closed, and I grabbed the doorknob, and giving it a twist, pushed inward. The door didn't open. I held the knob and leaned in on the door, pushing it with my shoulder. It flew open, and I turned the light on.

A stale gust of air crossed my face. In one corner sat a single bed with a stained mattress and a narrow, dark dresser with four drawers stood beside it. The room had no closet, no place to put my clothes, and only one window covered by a wooden blind. I set my suitcase down beside the bed and walked to the window. Dust filled the air as I raised the blind and tried to push up on the lower window, which didn't budge. Running my fingers along the bottom sash, I felt nail heads protruding from the wood. Nails sunk into the sash kept the window locked.

I walked out of the room, closing the door behind me. A light shined into the living room through the door on the other end, and I followed it into the kitchen, where Aunt Harriet was emptying the sink of a mountain of dirty dishes.

"Sorry about the mess. I'm just not up to doing much these days," Grandpa Trag said as he wheeled himself to the refrigerator and opened the door. "Nothing much in here to eat," he said, rolling his eyes at Aunt Harriet.

I peered in over his shoulder. Three cans of beer sat on the top shelf. The only food was the dried stains from long-gone dishes.

"There's a grocery store three blocks down that way." Grandpa Trag jerked his head to the right.

Aunt Harriet's face was void of emotion except for her eyes, and you'd have to really understand her, like I do, to see the anger and despair in them. She handed me a dish towel.

"You'll have to do these dishes while I make a run to the store. Don't drop the last clean dish towel," she said and headed out the front door.

Grandpa Trag did not give her any money. He sat in his wheelchair and watched my every move as I scrubbed at the hardened food on the plates. I wished he would go away, but he began to talk.

"Sally Mae was my last help. She did a pretty good job with the laundry and dusting, but she didn't like doing dishes. But that's okay. She was a fair cook, and she made herself handy in other ways." He chuckled. "They'll never be another Sally Mae. Too bad I had to let her go." He backed up and wheeled himself into the living room, where he turned on the television.

The dish towel was soaking wet before I finished drying the pots and pans. I left the largest pot in the drainer and hung the towel on the oven door handle as Aunt Harriet walked through the door.

"Not much of a store." She set a couple bags of food on the table. "Come help me get the rest."

We walked out the front door. She made sure it was shut, and as we hurried to the truck, she said, "They have a job opening for a cashier, and I applied. The hours are six until midnight. They said they would call and let me know in a day or two. I may be working soon."

I gulped. That meant I would be alone in the house with Grandpa Trag at night. Even though he was in a wheelchair, I didn't like the way he looked at me. He was the embodiment of dirty old man, and I stayed as far away from him as I could.

CHAPTER 15

BOOTS

THE NEXT DAY, I ATE a bowl of cornflakes for breakfast and headed outside, determined to do some exploring. I walked to the side of the house and pushed open a squeaky metal gate into the backyard. A soft cry greeted me, a call for help, and my eyes surveyed the foot-tall grass covering the yard.

In the corner under the only tree in the yard I could see the roof of a small doghouse. The grass near it swayed, and yips of joy rose to my ears. I ran to the doghouse. There on a heavy chain attached to a thick collar around his neck sat a scrawny brown puppy. He appeared to be part cocker spaniel, but I couldn't tell since he was so tiny. The chain was about four feet long, and he could barely lift it to move.

He cowered as I reached for him. My gathering him into my arms and running my hand from the top of his head down his back to his tail sent spasms down his thin frame. All the while his pink tongue licked my hand as he snuggled against my chest.

"What's your name, little fella?" I looked him over. He was all tan except for his two front feet, which were white.

My eyes searched the tamped down grass in front of his doghouse. I could see no water, no food dish, no indication that he had anything to eat and drink. His sides quivered as I passed my hand over them, feeling his sharp rib bones.

He whimpered, and I rocked him in my arms. "Shh, little one," I said as he whined and smelled my hand. Cuddling him close, I carried him into the house.

Grandpa Trag looked up from his television, a scowl crossing his face. "Get that cur out of here before I throw you both out!"

I stepped back, and in spite of his menace, I didn't run. "Is he your dog?"

"No. Young man next door went to try out for a job, and I promised I'd watch after him. If he's not back in a couple days, I'll shoot the stupid thing. Now get him out of here."

I took him back to his doghouse and clipped the chain onto his collar. "Sorry, fella. If I let you run loose, you might run away, and I wouldn't blame you."

He lay down and put his head on his front feet, then looked up at me and whimpered. I ran into the house and found a couple empty pint cottage cheese containers. A quick search through the closet yielded no dog food, so I poured a cup of corn flakes in one container and covered them with milk. The other I filled with water, and I carried them out the back door so Grandpa wouldn't see me.

He wolfed down the cornflakes, his tail wagging with every bite. I knelt beside him and stroked his head, but he didn't growl, a good sign. He licked up every drop of milk, then turned and lapped up the water. When he finished, he placed one white paw on my leg as if to say thanks.

"I'll call you Boots. And I'll draw a picture of you to hang in my room." I ran into the house to get my art supplies.

Aunt Harriet was at the kitchen table folding a load of towels. "I got the job," she said. "You'll have to help with Grandpa and other chores, at least while you're here."

"Okay, I will." I picked up a towel and folded it. "You won't believe what's in the back yard."

She kept stacking towels. "What?"

"A little dog. He's tiny and brown with white paws and I named him Boots and he already likes me."

"You're talking like a six-year-old. Is it Grandpa's?"

"No. Grandpa said he's watching him for someone." I picked up another towel. "But he's hungry, and there's no dog food here." I gazed into her eyes. "He's really hungry, Aunt Harriet. Could you please buy him a small bag of dog food? Please, please, please? His owner will be back in a couple days."

She smiled, but it was the kind of smile that ended in a sigh. "I'll see what I can find at the store this evening."

I gathered the towels and headed for the bathroom, where I packed them into the narrow linen closet. When I returned, Aunt Harriet was sitting beside Grandpa Trag, and they were discussing something in low voices. I couldn't hear them, an indication that they didn't want me to hear, so I walked out the back door to Boots' doghouse. He yipped and tried to run toward me, his heavy chain dragging him down.

I scooped him up and snuggled him against my chest. We were both captive in a place we didn't want to be. My escape to college was coming soon, but I wondered what would happen to him.

CHAPTER 16

GOODBYES

WITHIN A WEEK SINCE I found Boots, we'd become fast friends. As he was so skinny, each morning and each evening I gave him a cupful of the dog food Aunt Harriet bought him.

"His owner better pick him up soon," Aunt Harriet said as I poured his food into the cottage cheese container. "I won't get paid until next week, and I can't afford more dog food."

"Mail came yesterday," Grandpa Trag said as he came into the kitchen. "Electric bill is here. I'll let you take care of it." He handed the envelope to Aunt Harriet.

Her eyes narrowed and a frown crossed her face. When Trag left the room, she motioned for me to come near. "I bought you a going-away present," she said, reaching into her purse and placing a small bag into my hands.

A narrow box slipped out of the bag into my hands. "A phone!" I squealed. I'd never had a phone of my own, and I opened the box and pulled it out.

"It's one that you have to buy time for. Look in the bag. There's a card with sixty minutes on it. Make sure you copy down Trag's phone number."

"Aunt Harriet, thank you, thank you." I gave her a hug.

She laid her head on my shoulder and held on, seeming reluctant to let go. "Tomorrow morning I'll take you to the bus station. Be sure and call me as soon as you get to the academy." She looked up at me through teary eyes. "Here's the number to call at the store." She handed me a slip of paper. "Put it in a safe place in your bag."

"I will, Aunt Harriet. And thank you for everything."

"I'll miss you." She turned to finish the dishes. "You better get packed."

I was packed, at least as packed as I could be and still have clothes for tomorrow. But I knew Aunt Harriet needed a few minutes, so I headed toward the bedroom to give my things a final check.

Trag was in the living room cleaning his .22 rifle, pulling a small cloth attached to a wire through its barrel. The sweet odor of his rifle cleaning fluid wafted past my nose. "Got some business to take care of tomorrow," he said, pointing the gun toward the backyard and peering through the sights.

I gasped. No doubt he meant to keep his threat of shooting Boots, who had been here longer than the few days his owner had promised. The little dog's fate was in my hands.

That's why the next morning when Aunt Harriet helped me put my suitcase and bag of art supplies into the bed of the Ford, Boots frolicked at my heels tied to a piece of rope. Aunt Harriet raised an eyebrow when she saw him, but she said nothing. She knew why I was taking him.

A sign across the bus stop door caught my attention. *No Animals Allowed on Bus.* I had to think quickly. I stuffed Boots into the bottom of my bag and gave him a chew strip Aunt Harriet had bought him.

"I'm sure you'll have to get some kind of part-time work when you get there. You'll have to work hard with a job and going to school, but hard work never hurt anyone," she said, her eyes following what I had done with Boots. "I made you an egg salad sandwich for lunch. Some cookies and a bottle of water in there too. Here's some money for dinner and breakfast tomorrow morning." She handed me a bag and slipped a twenty into my hand. "Take care of yourself, and be sure and call me at the house as soon as you get there. I'll be waiting."

"I'll call you. I love you, Aunt Harriet." The words came out even though it was something we seldom said to each other. But I knew I wouldn't be seeing her for a while, and I wanted her to know.

"Here comes the bus. Have a good trip."

I picked up my suitcase in one hand and bag with the other and climbed the steps into the bus. The driver looked at my bag with suspicion, but he didn't say anything.

I spied an empty seat in the back of the bus and made a beeline for it. A man showed me how to put my suitcase in the rack over the seat, and I sat down and put my bag and Boots between my feet on the floor. Feeling for the half empty bag of dog food nestled in the bag, I pulled it out. Aunt Harriet was right. I'd have to get a job to take care of my little friend.

As the bus pulled out, I thought about high school graduation. Of course Uncle Deb and Aunt Harriet had been there for me, but no one else. The only classmate who spoke to me was George Benton.

"I hear you're going to Watson Academy of Arts in Denver," George had said as we were leaving the graduation ceremony.

"Yes, I got a good scholarship, and a government grant. I feel so fortunate."

"I really like your pictures. Good luck."

"Thanks." Through the years, I had fantasized about having George for a boyfriend, but only a little. After all, his father was president of the Puttersville First National Bank. In Denver, I could make new friends, get a boyfriend who was as interested in art as I am, and make a new life.

The brochure for Watson Academy of Arts was in the top of my art bag. I pulled it out for the tenth time and ran my fingers along its glossy front cover showing a beautiful white building surrounded by a manicured lawn with a cascading fountain. I would soon be there.

Boots squirmed in the bag between my feet. Afraid he'd hop out, I put my hand on his soft back. "It'll be okay, little one. I'm going to be a famous artist, and we'll buy us a house with a yard for you to play in."

His body relaxed and I stroked his back until I guessed he was asleep. The bus schedule I had copied showed we would be stopping in three hours for a lunch break. My plan was to high-tail it until I was out of sight from the bus station and find a place to walk Boots and feed him while I ate the lunch Aunt Harriet packed. A half hour wasn't much time, and I'd have to be careful to be back at the bus on time.

CHAPTER 17

WATSON ACADEMY

I WOKE UP THE NEXT morning cramped and stiff. Spending all night on a bus was no fun, but the dorms at Watson Academy opened that day, and I was excited to get there. The bus's air brakes whooshed as we pulled into the station.

Boots whimpered softly. As I retrieved my suitcase, I could feel his whole body wiggling and hear his tail thumping the sides of the bag so fast it could have been driven by a motor. I held my breath and hoped he would be quiet until we got off the bus. He did, almost, but as I stepped off the bus, he let out a yip.

I perused the map on the other side of the Watson Academy brochure. Ten blocks away was 2900 Stewart Avenue, the place of my dreams. My heart pounded in excitement as Boots and I headed up the street.

Older, two-story brick homes with yards bearing stately maple trees and flowers lined the street, which became steeper as I climbed uphill, and as I walked, I took care not to trip on the cracks in the sidewalks. The houses in the fifth block brought back memories of early twentieth century style brick homes I had seen in magazines. Out of breath, I stopped and surveyed my surroundings. It was hard to imagine a famous art school here.

A small shopping center lined the next street. Boots and I needed breakfast. Spying a small cafe, I spent five dollars on food. The night before I'd spent ten of the twenty dollars Aunt Harriet gave me for a sandwich and Boots a water dish and food dish and another chew strip. A bench on the street made the perfect place to eat, and Boots enjoyed some of his dog food while I ate my breakfast sandwich.

Five blocks to go, so I renewed my climb, then I spied the house, an old, rambling brick and wood structure, 2900 painted on its mailbox. No sign, nothing but a worn porch, its floor covered by bare, broken boards, its roof supported by straight columns half naked of paint.

I climbed the porch steps and rang the doorbell. No one answered. I rang the bell again and waited. No one came. I knocked until my knuckles hurt. I had just about decided that I was at the wrong place when the door opened a crack.

"Who's out there?"

"Is this the Watson Academy of Arts? I'm a new student."

"Hi, I'm Lettie," a woman said, opening the door a few inches more. She stood there in blue jeans and worn sneakers, her brown hair tucked behind her ears. "I'm the only one here," she said, "but you can come in and wait in the sitting room until Master gets here. I'm sure the rest of our students will be here soon."

"Thanks. This is the Watson Academy?"

"It is. I'm the do-everything help around here." She eyed Boots. "Make yourself at home."

I sat down in a stuffed chair and traced the pattern of its faded upholstery with my fingers while Boots huddled at my feet. *Was this really a school for aspiring artists?* Boots looked up at me and whined, as if he also had questions.

Remembering my promise to call Aunt Harriet, I dialed the house number and she answered. "Aunt Harriet, it's me, Allison. I'm here at the academy."

"I'm so glad you made it. How is it?"

"Okay. Just not exactly what I expected. How are you?"

"I'm tired. Trag went on a rant last night because you took the dog. I won't tell you what he said, but it wasn't pretty."

"Sorry. I hope you got some rest."

"A little. He sure tries my patience."

"Well, I'd better save some minutes for later."

Lettie was standing in the doorway. "Master just got in, and he said to tell you he'd see you soon."

Master? What kind of person wanted to be called Master?

"Hello, miss," a man said from the opposite side of the room.

I whirled around as a small man stepped through a door and into the sitting room. He wore a black beret and a black jacket with gold buttons. His black handlebar moustache curled up to form a circle on both sides.

"I am Master Ancel Granville. And you are?" He walked toward me, and his beady eyes purveyed me and my few belongings with one swift glance, then settled on Boots.

"Allison Cooper. I paid to be a student here this fall." I stared at the brochure in my hands. "It's not...not what I expected."

"Oh, that." He snatched the brochure from my hand and stuck it into his jacket pocket. "That's our mother school in Paris. Surely you weren't expecting that here."

I *was* expecting that here. Because of the way he addressed me, eyes glaring, acting as though he owned the world, all I could say was, "No, sir."

"Good. Come into my office, and we'll get you completely registered."

I followed him through the same door he had come from and sat in a chair in front of his desk. Rifling through a file of folders, he pulled one out.

"You've had some training?" he asked as he glanced over my application.

"Just what I've taught myself."

"Ah, I see you've paid your tuition fees, all five thousand dollars. How about your housing costs?"

"My scholarship will pay for housing."

"Very well. Welcome to the Watson Academy of Arts."

"What classes will I be in? Will I take a class teaching me how to do digital art?"

"Classes?" He donned a pair of glasses with small lens and peered at me. "Our classes don't have a name, Allison. We learn freestyle. Is that okay with you?"

I was under his scrutiny, as though I were a rabbit about to become a fox's dinner. I nodded, although I had no idea what he meant.

He stood and opened the door into the sitting room. Like magic, Lettie appeared.

"Take her to C-1."

"Come on, I'll show you where to stow your things," Lettie said, leading the way with a big smile.

These people are nice, and I'm going to get along with them just fine. It's not going to be like high school.

We walked down a long hallway that ended at a doorway. Lettie opened the door and ushered me inside a room that must have been forty feet square. Bunk beds lined every wall and formed a row in the middle of the floor. A single letter decorated each wall—the letter A above the door we had just come through, B on the wall to the left, C on the long wall with windows, and D on the end wall.

"You're lucky," Lettie said. "You get a corner bed and a window. Master must like you." She led me to the first bed in the corner between walls B and C. A drawer eight inches deep helped support the mattress, and pulling it out, she extracted a sheet, pillow case, pillow, and blanket.

"They don't give us a desk?"

"No. After you make your bed, you can unpack your suitcase and put your things in this drawer."

"Where do I put my hanging clothes? My skirts and blouses?" I asked.

"Over there." Lettie opened a door in the wall and showed me a closet. "You share this with the student in bed C-2. The bathroom is over here." She led me through the doorway in the middle of wall C into a common bath with six stalls on one side, six sinks on the opposite side, and four showers on each end.

"Come, let's go see the kitchen."

I followed her down the hallway. Turning right, we walked into another long room. Two gas cooking stoves and sinks lined one wall. On the other side were three refrigerators bearing signs, one for breakfast, one for lunch, and one for dinner.

"Master keeps the breakfast refrigerators stocked with milk and orange juice, the lunch one with sandwich meat, bread, and fruit, and the dinner one with things we might need such as butter. You may buy your own things and keep them here, but your name must be on them. Over here in the pantry is plenty of cereal."

She pointed to the other end of the room that held two long tables and chairs. "Here's where we eat, of course. Let me show you something else." We walked to a small desk in one end of the dining area. "Here is a sign-up sheet for kitchen duty."

"Kitchen duty?"

"Yes. You must sign up for cleaning up after three meals each month. One each of breakfast, lunch, and dinner. Someone else will be working with you. For breakfast, you must have the dishes done and the tables wiped off by nine o'clock, as that's when classes start." She handed me a pen. "Sign up now and get the good spots."

My heart sank. I didn't know any good spots. How unfair to pay all that money and have to work. Then Lettie dropped another bomb.

"Here is our bulletin board." She pointed to the wall above the desk. "Check it every morning to see what you need to bring to class."

"Bring to class?"

"Yes. The academy supplies some of your art supplies, but not all. Beginning students need to purchase this book listed here. It costs one hundred dollars, but it's the only book you need for the first year. The academy gives you your paints, but each student buys her own canvases. You won't need the book or the canvases until near the end of September."

My heart pounded. Where would I get enough money to buy an expensive book and canvases? All I had in my purse was $4.55.

CHAPTER 18

FIRST CLASS

CLASSES STARTED MY FIRST MONDAY there. During the weekend, I had finished a drawing of Boots. It showed him sitting looking up at me, his eyes full of adoration and love. I planned to hang it on the end of my bed, but I was anxious to show it off in class.

The students gathered in a large room at the other end of the building. Master pulled a cart piled high with wooden easels, and he stopped in the middle of the room and began unloading and standing them in rows. "Find yourself a work station," he said as he emptied the cart and hauled it out of the room.

I picked an easel near DeeDee, the girl who had bunk C-2 next to mine. The day before she had sashayed into the dorm room holding up a bag of dog food. "Just bought a few things," she said as she plopped down another bag. "Some new clothes. And after I saw your little dog, I thought I'd get him some food."

"Thanks." She didn't know how much that meant, as a half cup of food was all that was left.

"Come get it, little puppy. What's his name?"

"Boots. See his two white paws?"

"Here, Boots, come here, boy. DeeDee has a treat for you," she said, letting him eat from her hand.

She was sweet, and I hoped we could be good friends. I smiled at her as I leaned my bag and painting against the easel stand.

"I hope you saw the note in the dining room that you were to bring a sample of your work," Master said as he came back into the room. "If you didn't, please go to the dorm and get one of your works. The rest of you, please place your work on your easel."

My heart pounded with pride as I displayed my picture of Boots. The painting was the image of him sitting at my feet. I turned to look at the paper on DeeDee's easel. A weathered building sketched in dark pencil filled one corner of the paper, and above it rose foreboding trees that cast a shadow in front of the building.

"My best work," DeeDee said. "My parents paid for lessons for me before I started."

"Uh-huh," I said, nodding. Out of the corner of my eye I spied Master coming toward us.

"What have you?" he asked, approaching my easel. Picking up my portrait of Boots, he grunted, "Not bad, but where's the feeling? What meaning? What are you trying to show?"

"He loves me. Can't you see the adoration on his face?"

"In the Academie de l'Art, we explain with the strokes of the brush. I will show you what I mean." He stepped to a bookcase and returned with a large volume.

"Concentrate on Marc's work called *Tiger*. See how its shape and outline suggest the animal in a hiding place? Here the lines in its muscular body remind us of the surrounding shapes of rocks and plants." He flipped the book's pages. "Study this painting by Ed Morgan. See how the silhouette of this horse is brown while other horses are white and blue? Explain to me. What does that tell you?"

I stood in silence and shrugged. I'd never heard of Marc and Morgan.

"Go back to the dorm and paint something worthwhile that shows you understand symbolism. I want to see it next class." He glanced down at Boots. "Take that mutt with you and don't bring him back in here."

Shaking, I led Boots out of the room and exited the building into the backyard. How could he say that my painting was not good, that my art had no meaning? Wasn't my artwork good enough to win me enough money to be here?

I returned with Boots to the dorm to contemplate my assignment. Nearing my bed, I heard crying. DeeDee lay across her bunk on her stomach, her body enveloped in wringing sobs.

"What's wrong, DeeDee?" I sat down beside her and rubbed her back.

"Master hates me," she said. "He said my sketch was the worst thing he'd ever seen. He said he sees no talent in me."

Boots jumped onto her bed and nuzzled her arm.

"Oh, Boots!" She sat up and wrapped her arms around him, and he wriggled with joy. "You love me, don't you? You're my little buddy."

"He didn't think much of my picture of Boots," I said. "He wants me to paint something with meaning. Trouble is, I have no idea what he's talking about."

"This is my third day here, and already I hate it," DeeDee said, blowing her nose. "Let's go down to that little shopping center and look around."

"I don't have any money." My cheeks burned. "And I need to work on that picture for Master."

"Well, you don't need money to look." She put on her jacket. "Come on, we'll be back for lunch, and we can work after that."

"Okay." I grabbed my jacket and picked up Boots' leash. "Want to go for a walk, boy?"

The Aspen Grove Shopping Center consisted of the small cafe where I ate the day I arrived on the bus, one of those five-dollar pizza places, a small dress shop, a drug store, and some kind of store on the other end. The minute we arrived, DeeDee headed for the dress shop. I didn't want to go in, knowing that I'd see things I couldn't buy, so I told her I'd just look around outside.

To my surprise, the last shop bore a sign, Artistic Horizons. I ducked inside. Art work, sculptures and paintings of all sizes lined the walls and shelves. As I walked over to the wall across from the door to examine the art, an acrid odor stung my eyes and made me cough.

"Maybe the incense is a little strong. I'll put it out."

I whirled around. An older woman of small stature, her gray hair tied in a bun, smiled as she came around the corner.

"I burn it after some of the academy boys come here. They smoke. I think some of them even use the weed. You know."

"Yes," I said, nodding, for I had caught the whiff of a familiar smell. Uncle Deb's cigarettes.

"How can I help you?"

"I'm a student at the academy. Can you tell me how to show meaning and symbolism in my painting?"

"I'll try. You won't find any famous artists here, but I believe I can show you some examples. Come with me."

Boots and I followed her through the shop as she pointed to one art piece after another, explaining the symbolism she saw in each. I didn't care for most of them, for they were dark and grotesque representations of electronic devices, weapons, and fantasy monsters.

"I can see these don't impress you. What do you think of this one?" she asked as we stopped under a painting of a girl who looked to be five or six. She reached up to caress the lines of the girl's dress and the brown curls falling on her shoulders.

"I like it. She appears to be very happy. Do you know the artist?"

"David Hammond." She lingered and straightened the painting. "Oh, by the way, I'm Gertie."

I shook her hand. "And I'm Allison. But friends call me Allie." Then I thought about DeeDee. I thanked her for her help and left Artistic Horizons with a warm feeling. Gertie and I were going to be friends.

CHAPTER 19

BETRAYAL

FRIDAY MORNING, A LOUD THUMP jarred me from dreamland. I sat up with a jerk, and Boots jumped off my bed. The first thing I saw was boxes and two suitcases covering bed C2.

"I've had it with this place, and I'm going home," DeeDee announced in a voice loud enough to wake everyone in the room. "My parents will be here in an hour to pick me up." She checked her phone. "They're on their way."

"I'm sorry you can't stay," I told her, and I really was, but her decision didn't surprise me. I had hoped she would last a while longer as I talked to her more than anyone else, and she was the closest friend I had.

"Not can't, *won't*. I'm tired of being put down every day because Master can't see the good in my art. Yesterday I really tried to put some meaning into my painting, and he held it up and told everyone what a terrible job I did. I won't be the object of his ridicule any longer."

How many times had I felt like that? Does she think she's the only one whose work is put forth as a bad example? "Where will you go?" I asked.

"Home, of course." She stared at me like I'd just asked her the dumbest question. "My parents will find me an art school more famous than this one where my talents will be recognized."

Home. Envy twisted through my gut like a knife. Trag's house would never be my home. I was stuck here, and I didn't have enough money to buy Boots' next bag of food.

I showered and dressed, then took Boots outside. When we returned, DeeDee's bed was stripped and her suitcases and boxes were lined up in front of her bed. I tied Boots to my bedframe and went to breakfast.

DeeDee was eating a bowl of cereal. Pouring a bowlful for myself, I joined her. "I'll miss you."

"I won't miss this place." She laughed. "It's been good knowing you. Don't let Master get you down."

Fine advice from her. She didn't know how many times I struggled not to go inside my secret world, but I had made a vow to myself. My secret world was part of my past. This, for bad or for good, was my new life. I was not going to run from Master.

"Parents should be here soon," DeeDee said, rising from her seat and taking her bowl to the sink. "If I don't see you again, have a happy life." Then she was gone.

Have a happy life. Tears welled up in my eyes. She had dismissed me and what I thought was our growing friendship as easily as she said good-bye to the academy. I didn't matter to her. I probably didn't matter to anyone except Boots. I drank the milk left in my bowl and headed toward the dorm to get my art bag for class.

DeeDee and her luggage were gone. How could I have missed seeing her and her parents pass by the dining room and out the door? Then I realized that Boots was missing. He wasn't curled up on my bed or beside it. I had tied him securely to the bedframe, and he couldn't have pulled his rope loose.

"Boots! Boots!" I called, my eyes frantically searching the room. "Boots, where are you?" I grabbed my art bag and ran through the house, screaming his name as I went.

"What's wrong with you?" Lettie asked as I passed through the dining area and kitchen.

"My little dog. Have you seen Boots? I can't find him anywhere."

"DeeDee had him. She said she was taking him for a walk. I thought you let her."

"Not this time!" Like a mad woman I dashed out the back door. No one there. Running around to the front, I surveyed every corner, every bush, yelling for them. No DeeDee and no Boots. I flew down the street, looking everywhere for two blocks. Nothing. No one.

Panting for breath, I stopped. Reality set in. DeeDee had stolen Boots. She had a home with loving parents and everything she could ever long for. All I had was Boots, and now he was gone.

An emptiness filled my body from my head down to my toes, leaving me numb and aching, and I sat down on the curb, took out the picture I had painted of him, and cried. After a few minutes, I realized how ridiculous I appeared, and I climbed the hill and up the steps to the academy. As I walked through the front door, I saw Master and Lettie talking in the sitting room.

"You okay?" Lettie asked.

"No. DeeDee took Boots. I'll never see him again." Tears I couldn't hold back slid down my face. "If it weren't for me, Boots would be dead. I rescued him. He loved me and was my friend." Remembering his soft fur and warm snuggles, I sat down and sobbed.

"I'm sorry," Lettie said. "If I had known, I would have stopped her."

Master stood there, shifting his weight from one leg to the other, a bemused smirk on his face. "You shouldn't have brought him here anyway. He just got in the way of your classes."

"Could you give me DeeDee's phone number and address so I can go get Boots?"

"No." His smirk turned to a frown. "It is illegal for me to give out another student's address." He turned and walked through his office door.

"I'm sorry about your dog," Lettie said as she turned to go. "Don't forget. You have to buy your book this week."

"Lettie, wait!" Fear pounded in my chest as I ran to catch her. "Lettie, how can I pay a hundred dollars for a book when I don't have any money?"

"You should have gotten a job." She thought a moment. "Some of the students go down and paint in front of the little art shop. Sometimes they sell one of their paintings. Why don't you try it?"

I dragged myself to the dorm to get my coat so I could go stand in front of Artistic Horizons and paint. "Sometimes they sell one of their paintings," Lettie had said. What if I didn't? How could I return to the academy if I couldn't buy my supplies? I hurried through the door so no one could see me crying.

CHAPTER 20

A NEW FRIEND

I HAD BEEN SITTING ON the sidewalk painting for hours when the wind began blowing cold and a drizzle of rain started falling. The rumbling of my stomach told me it was past lunch time. Looking at my painting of Boots, done in Master's style of darker lines showing muscles, I shuddered. In disgust, I tossed it in my bag. It was not my Boots, soft, wiggly, and warm, but some monster I had created just to please Master, whom I despised. Opening my art bag, I pulled out my first painting of Boots.

"Goodie, goodie. I like that one better."

In my anguish I had not heard anyone come up behind me. Startled, I looked up into a face sporting a blond goatee and laughing blue eyes.

"You're getting wet. Why don't you come into the shop and have some coffee with me?" He held his hand down to clasp mine, and I allowed him to pull me up and followed him into the shop.

Gertie smiled as we came through the door. "Hello. I saw you sitting out there in the rain and was just about to invite you in. But I see David asked you first."

"Any coffee?" he asked.

Gertie must have read his mind, for she had already filled two cups with the steaming brew.

David took them from her. "Let's sit over here," he said, leading the way to a small table around the corner. "Hang on a minute. I'll be right back. I want to talk to you."

I wondered what he had to say to me, a nobody want-to-be artist who had no money and no friends. Maybe he had some tips to offer me.

"Thought you might be hungry," he said, coming around the corner with a paper plate that he put on the table between us. One side of the plate held two sandwiches, and the other side, a pile of oatmeal raisin cookies. "Mind if we say grace?"

"No." I felt the red blush creeping up my cheeks. I never said grace, and I was hoping he didn't want me to say it. He held out his hand like he wanted to hold mine, but I had tucked both hands neatly on my lap. Bowing my head and closing my eyes, I listened to him thank God for the food.

"My name is David." He took a sandwich and some cookies and placed them on his napkin, then handed me the plate. "What's your name?"

"Allison. My friends call me Allie. My uncle called me Allie Girl."

"May I call you Allie?" His eyes seemed bluer as the smile lines around them creased.

"Yes." I took a bite of the sandwich. "Thanks for the food. Why did you want to talk to me?"

"I've seen you before."

"You have? Where?"

"The academy. I teach in the men's house."

"The men have a house? Where is it?"

"Up the street two houses from the main building. One day I came to ask Master a question, and you were putting your painting back into your bag."

"I didn't see you."

"I didn't think you did. But I saw you this morning, sitting on the curb with the painting of the little dog, crying."

"You saw me then?" I tried to swallow as my throat closed up and tears sprang into my eyes. "He was my dog. Someone I trusted stole him." A tear slid down my cheek, and I wiped it with my hand.

"I'm sorry. But I want you to know you have talent. You're better than any of my students, and Master says you're better than any of the other women."

"Master said that?" I stared at him, dumbfounded. "All he does is criticize everything I do. I thought he hated me. In fact, I was about ready to quit. But I can't because I don't have anywhere else to go."

"Tell me about yourself."

He was easy to talk to, and like Uncle Deb when he smoked his weed, I let the words rush out unchecked. I told him about Uncle Deb and Aunt Harriett, and of course, my problems at school, my animal friends in the woods, and about our move and Trag. He never took his eyes off me the whole time I spoke.

"I want to buy the painting of your little dog," he said when I finished.

I gasped. I could never sell my only picture of Boots. "I, I don't know," I managed.

"I know two little girls who would love it. Do you happen to have another painting of an animal?"

I fingered through my file of artwork and found one of my little gray squirrel friend Wee Ears sitting beside my rabbit Rumple Tail. Hesitantly, I handed it to him, holding my breath as I waited for his perusal.

"When did you paint this?"

"When I was about twelve."

"I love it. And I know Diana and Lilah will too. Can I buy both of these from you for a hundred dollars?"

"I guess so." My heart was pounding so hard I couldn't breathe. Those two paintings portrayed some of my dearest friends. To be without them…

"I'm sorry I can't offer more, and I'll understand if you don't want to let them go," he said, gazing into my eyes. "I think they're very good."

I remembered the book I had to buy. "One hundred dollars is okay." An emptiness took residence in my chest as I handed them to him. I was losing pictures of my best friends. He pulled five twenties from his billfold and passed them across the table to me.

"I hope we'll see each other again," he said. "Don't let Master wear you down. He doesn't know everything."

"I hope to see you again, too." The warmth of his smile filled my heart, and I told him good-bye and headed for the academy book store.

CHAPTER 21

MYSTERY MAN

TWO IMPORTANT THINGS HAPPENED THE next Saturday. Jenny Lou moved into C2. She had long black hair and an infectious laugh. It took her about fifteen minutes to get unpacked, and when I offered to show her around, she accepted. After we returned, she opened a large sketching pad and tore out a drawing that she hung between her bed and her clothes peg.

"You did that?" I asked as I studied the drawing of a mountain range covered by pine trees surrounding a glen where two moose grazed. They appeared so real, I reached out to touch them.

"Like it?"

"It's very nicely done," I said. "Have you taken lessons?"

"A few classes at my high school. Everyone always said I had a gift, and I want to stretch myself. I hope to do that here. What do you think of this school?"

I was torn between my desire not to influence her opinion before she started and telling her the truth about my disappointment with the academy, its forcing the students to work after they paid so much, and my increasing dislike of Master. "Oh, it's okay. It depends on what you came for."

"Hmm...you sound a bit ambivalent. Care to fill me in?"

"Wait and tell me what you think at the end of next week." I laughed as I said it, knowing she was perceptive enough to already have guessed how I felt.

"What do you do for fun around here?"

Fun. I didn't think that word was in my vocabulary or my life. Maybe when I was painting my forest friends or talking with Uncle Deb. But that was a long time ago.

"I like to go to the small shopping center about five blocks that way," I said and pointed down the hill. "Want to go to the art shop with me this afternoon?" *I hope we can be good friends, but it isn't her company that excites me. Maybe David will be there.*

"Might as well."

So we went. Neither Gertie nor David was there, but Laura was. I guessed her to be in her upper twenties. She wore a silk blouse, tan skirt, and high heels. Jenny Lou and I introduced ourselves, then walked along the walls, discussing the paintings.

"I like this one," I said as we reached the portrait of the little girl.

"Oh yes, David Hammond. Everyone likes his art."

"Do you know him?"

"I know *of* him. I've never met him, but I follow the art news in the papers and magazines, and he is gaining recognition in Denver. Especially this last year."

"Oh."

"Let's go see a movie," she suggested. "There's a movie theater not too far from here. We can take the bus."

"I don't know if I have time," I protested. I wanted to wait around a while to see if David would come into the shop, and I had less than twenty dollars left after buying the art book. It was on sale, twenty percent off. I had never been to a movie, and it didn't take long for her to wear me down. We watched a spy thriller, *Tale of the Doomed Man*, and I enjoyed it, but I don't think it was worth having only ten dollars left.

We were walking up the hill to the academy when my phone rang.

"Hi, Allison, this is Harriet," she said when I answered. "How are you doing?"

"Fine, Aunt Harriet." Her tone told me she had something on her mind. "How are things going with you?"

"Trag's drinking more, acts a little crazy. Sometimes I'm afraid of him."

"I was afraid of him, too," I said. "Only I didn't want to tell you. What's he doing?"

"Got drunk, tried to make a move on me." She paused. "I know we're not blood related or anything, but if I were picking a man, it'd never be him."

"What are you going to do about it?" Cold shivers ran down my spine. "You have to protect yourself."

"I'm working full-time now and putting a little money aside. In a few weeks, I'll have enough to rent a place of my own or maybe find someone to rent a room from."

"Are you already looking for something?"

"Sure am. I found some apartments on a bus route that would take me right to the store."

"Why don't you start looking for a different place to work? Trag knows exactly where to find you."

"I thought about that. Finding a job's not easy. Maybe I'll buy the Sunday paper and look at the want ads."

"How will Trag get by without you there to pay the bills, cook, and clean?"

"Oh, he's not as helpless as he lets on. Almost every day when I get home from work, I find things that he's done. Like the other day when I came home a little early, a large box of beer sat on the table. I stepped into the bathroom, and when I went back into the kitchen, it had disappeared. You know a box of thirty cans of beer has to be heavy. And he went somewhere to buy it, but not where I work as they don't carry large boxes." She laughed, a low, guttural sound I had never heard. "He's using me, and I'm not going to do all the work and pay the bills and be treated like a slave. Or worse."

"I don't blame you. Let me know what happens."

"I will."

She hung up abruptly. I can only guess that Trag interrupted our conversation. I worried about Aunt Harriet. Oh, how I wish I had an apartment and could ask her to come live with me.

My fun day turned gloomy, and I walked into the academy with the weight of a hundred-pound bag on my shoulders. I turned down the hallway toward the dorm and ran into Lettie.

"You had a visitor while you were out," she said. "A gentleman."

"Did he give his name or leave me a message?"

"No. He said he had to talk to you and he would return. But he didn't say when."

CHAPTER 22

WHERE TO GO?

WHOEVER WANTED TO TALK TO me last Friday did not return. He could have found me at the academy all week or he could have called the academy, and Lettie would have taken a message or summoned me to talk to him. But he didn't, so I quit thinking about him.

Something terrible happened that morning, and that's why I sat on the flower planter in front of Artistic Horizons writing in my diary. I shook as I pondered the injustice of it all.

All the girls were awake, and a few were taking showers, but most of us were deciding what to wear and talking to each other. The door to the dorm room opened and Lettie came in, followed by another woman. She was tall and wide, dressed in what looked like a man's suit, her blond and purple hair cut like a man's. Three two-inch circular gold earrings hung from each of her ears, and what looked like diamond rings flashed from the fingers of both her hands. What caught my attention was the size of her thighs and arms. She looked as muscular as a man who was into body building, and when she walked toward us, her thighs and arms strained to escape the confines of her suit. We moved out of her way in a hurry.

"This is Madam Kay," Lettie said. "Perhaps you have seen her art in galleries and art shops. She's Master's friend, and he has hired her as an instructor. He wants us all to make her welcome and comfortable."

Several girls stepped forward and held out their hands to shake. Madam Kay either didn't care or didn't see them as her eyes took in the whole room in one glance.

"That bed," she said, pointing to my bed. "Whoever has clothes on it, get them off and change the sheets. Lettie, bring my suitcase and bag up from my car." She handed Lettie her car keys, and poor Lettie hurried off to do her bidding.

"Whose bed is that?" she roared, stomping her foot. "I said get your junk off it and change the sheets!"

"That's my bed, and I'm going to keep it," I said in a calm voice as I sat down on it. I don't know why I thought I could stand up to her, but it was a mistake. The next thing I knew, she grabbed my hair and threw me onto the floor, sending terrible pain through my head and down my spine as I hit.

I managed to get to my knees, then stand up. Grabbing my suitcase from the closet, I shoved my clothes from the drawer under the bed and the closet into it. Then I picked it up and gathered my art bag and left. With tears stinging my eyes, I opened the door to Master's office. He looked up at me in surprise.

"Madam Kay took my bed. Where am I supposed to sleep?"

He stood and sauntered toward me. An evil sneer spread across his face and a cunning look gleamed in his eyes. "Well, my dear, you can sleep with me. You wouldn't mind that, now, would you?" He came up behind me, wrapping his arm around my waist, putting his hands where he shouldn't. "Just come with me, and you can leave your things in my room."

Anger flashed through me, and I reacted with a kick that landed where it would hurt him most. I fled through the front door as his scream echoed through the academy. Where would I go? Not here, no, never again. And certainly not back to Trag's. I didn't stop running until I passed through the door of Artistic Horizons. Laura was sitting at the small table where David and I had eaten. I put my suitcase down beside the table and sank into the chair across from her.

"Are you going somewhere?" she asked without looking up.

"Is Gertie here? David?"

"Not today. Can I help you with something?" She ran her fingers along a line of numbers and sighed. "No art sales for two weeks. Something has to change."

"Why don't you put some of the art in your display windows? People will see it and want to come in and look at pictures. Maybe buy."

"You know, I get so wrapped up in other things I forget to change the displays." She closed the book and looked up at me. "Want to help me do it?"

We went into a back room, and she unpacked a box full of artwork of different sizes and handed me four while she took another three. I helped her take the dusty statues and worn dolls from the table behind the display window. Then I washed the windows and dusted the table while she packed the things we had removed.

I stood back while she arranged the art. "It looks bleak. Doesn't have any life," I told her.

I spied a large crocheted afghan draped across the back of a sofa. Tiny red and white threads danced in and out of its blackness. It would be the perfect backdrop. I removed the pictures and placed the afghan on the table, then arranged the artworks at different angles. Two vases of flowers completed the array.

"It's perfect!" Laura said. "You did that so fast. Have you studied interior decorating?"

"No. But that looks better than the barren table."

She offered me sandwiches and cookies, and not having eaten breakfast, I devoured them. Then I said goodbye and went outside to paint. The only painting I had to offer for sale was the monster dog with heavy lines, drawn to please Master. I pulled it out of my bag and stared at it, then averted my eyes in disgust for what it was and who it stood for. The image of my little Boots flashed before me, and I sat down on the curb, removed my last piece of heavy water color paper and began to sketch with my art pencil. I dared not make a mistake.

So absorbed was I in my work that I did not see Laura leave. A couple stopped to watch me, then left. No one else noticed me. The sun sank into the horizon as I finished.

I bought a sandwich and asked for a water at the small café around the corner, then sat down on the planter wall to eat. I had no money when I came to the academy, so I had no local bank account. How long would it take me to open an account so I could have my money transferred? I decided I would do it first thing tomorrow. Wish I'd thought of it sooner. I fished in my art bag for my billfold and counted my money. Five dollars and forty-five cents. How could I live on that? My scholarship and grant were paid directly to the school on a schedule, and I had no access to that money. I'd probably have to go back to the academy and beg Master's forgiveness, but I'd rather go back to Chicago and live with Trag.

A cold wind blew through my jacket, and I picked up my suitcase and my bag and headed toward the bus station, a warm place where I could be safe for the night. As I walked through the door, I could hear Uncle Deb saying, "Just remember, Allie Girl. God will always take care of you."

CHAPTER 23

MY VISITOR

THE MAN AT THE TICKET counter in the bus station raised his eyes and watched me as I passed by him and headed for a chair in a corner. Others bought tickets and sat down to wait on their buses, and the two rows of chairs in the center filled up. I studied the people's faces, some young and carefree, some creased with lines of worry.

My eyes flew along the line of chairs to a chubby young man wearing a suit so wrinkled he must have slept in it. His eyes met mine, and I recognized him about the same time he saw me.

"Allison! I thought I'd never find you!" He hurried toward me and held out his hand. "Remember me? George Benton from Puttersville?"

"Of course I remember you, George. What are you doing here?" His suit jacket lacked three inches shy of his being able to button it, and his brown hair was greasy and disheveled.

"I've been hunting for you for a week. You weren't at the academy."

"Well, I've been there most of the week. Why are you looking for me?"

"We've had some problems at the bank." He sat down, breathing heavily, blowing into my face. "You know, my dad was president of the bank."

Was president? Those two words set my brain's alarm bells off. "Is everything okay at the bank?"

"No." He stared out the window across the room. "It was until a month ago, well, I guess it's been more like two months. Some of Dad's major investments fell through." His voice trembled. "His fund went under. I'm so sorry."

"So everyone lost all their money?"

"Just the people who invested with Dad. Your uncle was one of them. Dad thought he could double everyone's money, but instead, the overseas company he invested in went under and lost it."

"There has to be some of my money left."

"No. I'm so sorry to have to tell you, but those investments were not covered by the FDIC. They weren't deposits, they were investments…so there's nothing."

"So all my money from winning the McCabbock for three years is gone?"

"I'm afraid so. I've been here for a week, begging banks and institutions to loan us money so we could at least give the people some of their money back. I talked to my dad's old friend who runs his own business here, too, but he wouldn't loan us a cent."

"Then I don't have any money? Nothing?" My head was spinning, and what he had just said wasn't sinking in.

"No money left." He lowered his eyes and refused to meet mine. "I'm so sorry," he whispered. He reached into his shirt pocket and took out a twenty dollar bill, which he handed me. "That's all the money I have left. Here, take it."

"All aboard to Pittsburgh," the man at the ticket counter yelled.

"That's my bus." George stood and picked up his suitcase. "I'll make it up to you, Allison, I promise," he said as he turned and hurried toward the door.

I stared at him until he disappeared, then turned my attention to the bill in my hands. Never had twenty dollars looked so small. The odor of George's cheap cologne wafted from the bill to my nose, and its repugnance reminded me of everything he and Puttersville stood for. That small town had never welcomed me nor believed in me. Now, it had stolen the only thing I had left, my hope of being an artist and earning a living with my art. With shaking hands I pushed the bill to the bottom of my art bag.

The street light outside the building, buffeted by the wind, flickered for a few seconds and then went black as the wind rose to a gale. October in Denver could be cold. I shivered and pulled my light jacket around me. The man at the counter called for passengers to board another bus. I sat there for what seemed forever as the rows of chairs emptied. At midnight the call came out for another bus, and the last passenger left the station.

"This station closes at twelve thirty," the station clerk said. "If you're not catching a bus, you need to leave."

Shame at using the bus stop for shelter and worry at having no place to go, wrestled inside me as I picked up my things. The wind buffeted me and my suitcase and bag as I passed through the door as if it were trying to rob me of the few possessions I had left. To my relief, the street light came back on, and I walked toward Artistic Horizons, just in case David or Laura was there, but it was dark inside. The small cafe was open, and I lugged my things through the door.

Worry took over. Where was I going to live? How long could I survive on the little money I had? Unless I sold another picture, I couldn't even buy a bus ticket to go back to Trag's. Laying my head across my arms on the table, I dozed off.

"We're closing, miss."

"What?" I sat up and rubbed my eyes, trying to remember where I was.

"We're closing at twelve thirty. In just a few minutes."

"But I thought you were open all night."

"We're not a free motel, either."

"Sorry." My face burned in shame as I gathered my things. "I didn't mean to fall asleep," I said on my way to the door.

A gust of wind nearly knocked me over when I stepped outside. Its coldness pushed me on. I looked for a light inside a store, any sign that some shop was still open. Not this late. Somewhere nearby a door squeaked, and I slipped behind a tree.

A dim light shined through the dusty laundromat windows. Someone must be in inside. I banged on the locked door. No one answered. A narrow alley ran between the laundromat and Artistic Horizons, and in the scant light, I could make out a wooden gate at the end of the alley.

The alley would give me shelter from the wind. It could also be a trap, but in desperation I felt my way inside. Warm air spewed out against my skirt, driving it against my bare legs, and I reached down to investigate its source. A dryer vent blew welcome heat to the outside, and sinking down, I planted my cold back to its mouth. With my belongings piled at my left side toward the gate, I put my head on my knees and drifted into a restless sleep.

CHAPTER 24

GLORIOUS DAY!

SATURDAY MORNING, WRAPPED IN WRETCHEDNESS and driven to paint and sell a picture before the day was over, I sneaked into the bathroom at the little café shortly after seven, washed my face, changed clothes, combed my hair, and then ordered pancakes and sausage. After eating, I sat down on the brick planter in front of Artistic Horizons to paint. While I was riding the bus, I had seen the rising sun bathe the mountains to the west in splendor. I tried to capture the magnificence of the early morning sun coming up behind the mountains.

"Good, good morning, Allie Girl."

I knew the voice. David. How did he know I had slept in the alley? Tears sprang to my eyes and started down my burning cheeks. Oh, to be able to melt into the ground.

"Did I say something wrong? Aren't you even going to speak to me?"

"You called me 'alley girl'." The words came out in a squeak as I wiped the tears away.

"But I thought that was your name. At least you told me that's what your uncle used to call you, and I supposed you liked it."

"It's just that you're...you're a stranger," I said, covering up for my stupid misunderstanding.

"I'm sorry to hear that. I thought we'd met, been introduced, talked. How am I a stranger?"

I dared glance up into his deep blue eyes, those beacons that never left my face, smiling with kindness and understanding and peering into my soul. They disarmed me in two seconds.

"Sorry. I meant that I'm a stranger. It's been a stressful week."

"I know what you mean." His eyes swept over my baggage, and he picked up my suitcase and art bag. "Come in. The shop doesn't open for another thirty minutes. I'd like a few minutes of your time."

He held the door open, and when we were inside, he put my things down on a chair and went to the checkout counter. Turning on the computer, he motioned me to stand beside him.

"Laura told me how you helped her build the display in the window. Look what happened." He clicked on a ledger. "See here where the cursor is? Two paintings sold the day after, one from the window and one from inside the store."

"It was a simple thing. People can't buy what they can't see."

"You have talent, and I need your help. I mean, I want to hire you to work in the store."

"You own Artistic Horizons?"

"My family does. You see, Laura has the children and doesn't want to work weekday afternoons after they get out of school or on Saturday. And Grandma is not well."

"Grandma?"

"Yes." He paused. "You met her. You know, Gertie."

"She's your grandmother?"

"Yes. But back to this job. I'd like to hire you to run this shop from one until six in the afternoons on weekdays and from nine until one Saturday mornings, or whatever amount of time you can give me on Saturdays. Do you think you could work that many hours and keep up with your work at the academy?"

"I'm not at the academy," I mumbled. "I'm never going back there."

"Allie, why not? What happened?"

"Madam Kay came. She took my bed. And Master said—"

"Say no more!" Fire flashed in his eyes, and he put his hands on my shoulders. His gentle touch sent shivers through my body. "You're cold," he said, taking off his jacket and wrapping it around my shoulders. "I understand. She also took my job."

"Will you be okay?"

"Don't worry." He smiled. "I already have another job at an art school across town. That's why I need you. I won't be available to work here much."

"I don't know anything about running an art shop."

"No problem. I'll be here today to teach you everything, and after that, if you have questions, just call Laura. Will you accept?"

"I'd like to work here."

"As you know, we don't sell a lot, so we can't pay you a wage. But there's a small apartment in the back of the shop. I was staying there, but I have made other arrangements. The utilities are paid for. All you would have to pay for would be television cable if you want it. Does that work for you?"

"Yes. May I see it?"

He glanced at his watch. "We have a few minutes, so I'll give you a quick tour." He led the way through a door in the back of the display room, down a narrow hallway, and through another door. We entered a large room with a kitchenette on one end of a living area.

"It's not much, but you won't be sleeping in the street."

I felt the red creeping onto my face, giving away my thoughts.

"Sorry. I forgot to show you the bathroom. It's in the hallway, and like the rest of the place, not big, but it has a shower and linen closet. And the couch in the living room makes into a bed."

As we walked back down the hallway, he popped open the bathroom door and let me take a peek inside. "It's not modern, but it works," he said. "So do we have a deal?"

"Yes, David. I feel like I've died and gone to heaven."

"Talking about heaven, I liked what you were painting outside. Why don't you put it in our window display to sell when you finish it?"

"Really? How much do you think I can ask for it?"

"With your talent, I'd say a hundred." He winked. "You can charge more when you become famous."

That afternoon, I talked with several customers and sold another painting from the window display, as well as a vase with flowers painted on it. David taught me how to enter the sales into the computer, and when there were no customers in the shop, he showed me where they kept the money. We ate a late lunch, more sandwiches from the refrigerator in the apartment. The shop closed at six.

"Just in case you have questions Monday," he said, handing me Laura's card. "We're closed on Sundays." Then he leaned over and kissed me lightly on the forehead. "Take care. And sleep well."

David kissed me! Oh day, glorious day! Maybe he likes me. My mind whirred, thinking of future possibilities.

CHAPTER 25

ART FOR SALE

MONDAY MORNING, I DARED SPEND some of my money at the laundromat, and wearing my best clothes, went down the hallway to the shop at one. Laura was at the counter, staring at the computer, a frown on her face.

"Hello, Allie," she said. "We have a problem."

"We do? What happened?"

"Come here and see." She stepped over so I could see the computer monitor. "Look at these paintings that we have in our inventory. I just checked, and they're so new they're still in our storeroom, waiting to be hung and displayed."

"So what's wrong?"

"An elderly couple who have been customers for several years were here this morning. They showed me photos of art work they had just purchased and asked if we had any more by the same artist. We do. The problem is, their photos show art identical to two works we have in our storeroom, and they're signed by the same artist. He's a talented student at the academy."

"So either someone is copying his art, or he's selling multiple copies of the same picture? Is it a crime to make copies of your own pictures and sell them?"

"No, but…" She thought a minute. "Artists sell copies, but they're just that. Copies on good quality paper. They don't sit down and repaint the same picture over and over. This couple said the paintings they purchased were oil on canvas. And if they were copied and sold as originals, that's a crime."

"So what are we going to do about it?"

"I called the police this morning. They came out and took photos of the copied art and said they would talk to the man who painted them. We can't hang those paintings or put them out for sale until their authenticity is verified and they find out who is copying art."

"What should I do? Is there a way I can help?" I asked.

"Be on the lookout for anyone acting suspicious. Anyone coming and standing in front of a painting studying it, and especially be on the watch for anyone taking pictures with a phone." She shook her head. "It would be so easy for someone to take a quick shot with his phone camera and be out of here."

Laura left to pick up her children. It was drizzling outside, and only a few students came in to buy art supplies, but I wasn't bored. The shop contained so much art to study, so many books to read, and still, I had a lot to learn, things David showed me how to do but I hadn't done. I kept busy.

It was almost six, closing time, when Jenny Lou, who'd had the bed next to mine at the academy, came in. I rushed to her and said, "Hi. So glad you came."

"So this is where you are!" she exclaimed as she came around the counter. "Everyone is asking about you. Are you coming back to classes?"

"Definitely not. How are things going?"

"I don't like Madam Kay." A frown crossed her brow. "She hates everything I do. She hates everyone's drawings. No one likes her. She teaches the women two days a week and the men three days. They don't like her, either."

"I'm sorry. Did you come here to buy something?"

"No. Remember the drawing I showed you when I first came to the academy? I would like to leave it here on consignment. Madam Kay thinks it's ugly, but I like it." She pulled it from her bag and handed it to me.

"I think it's beautiful." I turned it around to examine every detail, feeling a twinge of envy at its exquisiteness. "Can you bring it back tomorrow morning when Laura is here? I don't know if I can accept art pieces for consignment." *No, that didn't sound right.* "I mean I don't know how. This is my first day here by myself."

"Okay, no problem." She put the drawing in her bag. "Well, have to go study." She pulled the door open and stopped. "You know, call me sometime, and we can go shopping or to another movie. Oh, my phone number is..."

I grabbed a piece of paper and scribbled it down. "Thanks. I'll call you sometime."

I was shutting down the computer when David came in.

"Just checking to see how your first day alone went," he said. "Anything strange happen? Different?"

"Some students came in to buy art supplies, and a girl I know from the academy wanted to leave a painting on consignment. I asked her to come back when Laura is here."

He was shuffling through drawers beneath the counter, and I didn't think he heard a word I said until he turned toward me.

"That's okay." He pulled open a file and handed me a sheet of paper. "If anyone comes in here with a piece of art for consignment, have them fill out one of these. Just make sure all the spaces are filled in completely and they understand that we charge thirty percent of the price for selling it." He was hunting through drawers again, thumbing through files, searching frantically for something.

"Can I help you find something?"

"Here it is! I knew it was here somewhere!" He extracted a drawing from a drawer and laid it on top the counter.

A smaller version of the portrait of the little girl smiled up at me. "You're the David who painted this? I love this picture."

"Thanks." He took out his handkerchief and blew his nose.

"Who is she? Why did you paint her?"

"Her name was Nancy," he said, wiping away the tears wetting his face. "My little girl. She died of leukemia."

CHAPTER 26

A VISIT WITH GERTIE

MY HEAD AND MY HEART reeled when David told me about his little girl. How could I possibly think he had an interest in me as anyone more than an employee? So he was married, and he was one of those friendly guys who hugs and kisses everyone. He bought my pictures of Boots and my forest friends for his little girls. I hadn't seen him or heard from him since he left four days ago. But every day that week a little thought spun in my head. *Maybe David will be in today.*

Laura wasn't busy when I arrived on Friday, so I asked her, "Why isn't Gertie here anymore? Is she okay?"

"She has severe arthritis that flares up, especially if the weather is inclement. Sometimes she can hardly walk." She stopped dusting the counter top. "I wish David and I had more time to spend with her."

The way she spoke, it sounded like David and Laura were married. But I liked Gertie, and I wanted to see her. "Do you think she'd mind if I came for a visit? Is she up to it?"

"I think she'd love a visit. I'll call and ask her when I get the kids home."

Several customers came in after she left, and I forgot about Gertie, but Laura called me around two thirty. "Mom says she'd love to see you," she said. "Can you go around seven tonight?"

"Yes."

"I'll call her and tell her you'll be there. And thanks, Allie. We appreciate your help. Oh, let me give you her address."

I wrote it down, and when six came, I had a quick dinner of soup and crackers, then pinned my wild hair back with hair clips to keep the wind from blowing it over my face. Gertie's house was a few blocks away, a ten-minute walk. I knocked on her door and waited, then knocked again. In a few seconds, the door opened with a slight creak, and Gertie's smile met me.

"Come on in, Allie. Oh, I was hoping someone would visit today, and when Laura called, I was so glad to hear you wanted to see me." She turned her walker around and led me into her small living room. "Please come sit down, dear, and I'll get us some tea."

The odor of cinnamon and spices wafted into the living room. "When I heard you were coming, I managed to make some snicker doodles. They're just the break-apart-and-bake kind you buy at the store, but I had them and figured it was time to get them in the oven."

"Let me help you," I said, joining her in her kitchen. She handed me a bowlful of cookies, which I put on the coffee table in the living room, and then I went back to help her with the tea.

"Laura told me what a good job you are doing at the shop," she said when we were seated. "I'm sorry I can't be there to help, but my feet won't take all that standing." She pulled up her skirt and showed me her swollen ankles covered with purple blotches. "You see, I not only have arthritis, but my heart is giving in."

"I'm sorry," I said. She pushed a bejeweled comb deeper into her gray hair, and I noticed her gnarled fingers. "I wish you felt better."

"Have a cookie." She pushed the plate toward me and sipped her tea. "I really want to be at the shop helping. You see, art was my husband's love. After he passed, the children and I had to take over. With Laura's little ones growing up, they keep her busy helping with homework and running to school. David works full time teaching. I'm so glad they hired you."

"I am too." I took another cookie. "How many children do David and Laura have?"

"Don't know if David will ever get married, but Laura and Don have two girls, seven and nine."

"Oh. David told me about Nancy, and I just thought that he and Laura…"

"No, no. Laura is David's sister."

So David wasn't married. During the next hour she told me of her family's plans to make Artistic Horizons a hub for talented young artists. Then, noticing the time, I promised to come for another visit, said goodbye, and walked home.

I had just stepped inside my small apartment when my phone rang. Aunt Harriet's name showed on the screen.

"Allison," she said, "I'm so excited. I've found a new job at a large grocery store. The pay is more, and I'll have insurance and other benefits after my probationary period."

"That's great. Have you found a different place to live?"

"Yes, that's another wonderful thing. A new apartment building is going up near the store, and I've secured a one-bedroom on the ground floor, already made the security payment."

"Awesome. When do you move?"

"I gave a week's notice where I work, so two Saturdays from now. So the first Saturday in November. I'll be so glad to get away from Trag."

"Don't tell him," I warned. "Not until the last minute. No, the last second."

"I'm not that stupid. I probably won't tell him at all. I'll be up that Saturday long before he is, and I'll just take my few things and leave him a note with no forwarding address."

"Good. I'm so happy for you."

"When I get my own place, maybe I can pay to fly you here for a visit."

"I'd love to come. Just stay away from Trag until you can move."

CHAPTER 27

A SURPRISE

SATURDAY, LETTIE CAME TO BUY art supplies for the academy. "You going to be back at the academy? You're really getting behind."

Not as long as Master's there and Madame Kay. I should sue them for taking away my place. "No. I can't come back. I hope everyone understands." Lettie had tried to help me while I was there, so I gathered the things on the list she handed me while she browsed. I had finished my painting of the mountains last night, and before she left, I showed it to her.

"Very nice," she said. "Do you have a website, anything online to help sell your art? If not, you should set something up."

The more I thought about getting a website, the more I liked the idea. I didn't have a computer, but maybe David would help me set up a site on theirs when he came in.

But Laura came for the afternoon shift. "Don's taking the girls to their school fair," she said, "and I have things I need to take care of." She sighed. "A young man who brought his painting to us a couple days ago called me at home last night. His friend told him he saw his work at an art show. The same painting, he left with us to sell."

I followed her into the storage room, and she showed me the painting, a blue vase holding pastel flowers. The painter outlined each petal in such a way that it shimmered in the light.

"Whoever painted this is very talented," I observed. "Was it painted by another student?"

"Yes. That technique takes practice. If someone is able to copy it, he or she should be painting his own pictures. Mom enjoyed your visit last night," she said as we went back into the main room.

"We enjoyed chatting, and I learned a little more about your family and the history of the shop."

"Oh? I suppose she told you about my dad. The shop was his idea."

"Yes. Does your husband ever come to the shop?"

"Once in a while. But Don can't draw stick figures. He works in a lab at a hospital."

I showed her my painting of the mountains. "David said I could display it in the window if it was okay with you. If only I had a frame."

"On top of the filing cabinet in the store room is a pile of frames we're not using. Go see if there's something that will work."

I flashed her a smile of appreciation and went to look. One of the frames suited my piece perfectly, and it came with a mat I could use as a background. Going back into the main room, I thanked Laura and went to my apartment.

Hungry, I opened the refrigerator. One slice of bread. No meat or cheese. I counted my money. With the twenty dollars from George at the bus stop, I had $29.45. As I walked to the grocery store, I noticed a crack in the toe of my best pair of tennis shoes. The soles were coming loose from the fabric in several places. I needed new shoes, and I hoped to afford some made of leather or maybe some boots for winter. But I had to eat. I bought the least expensive loaf of bread, a package of lunch meat, and a small jar of peanut butter instead of cheese.

Back in my apartment, I spent the rest of the afternoon cleaning the frame Laura gave me and setting the mat and painting inside it. It was almost six o'clock when I finished, and I ran through the hallway and into the shop to show Laura.

"Looks pretty good," she said when she saw it. "What are you calling it?"

"*Mountain Sunlight.*" I thought of that day, waking up from sleeping in the alley, seeing the sunlight shining through the tall buildings downtown, and the hope it gave me. Then David hired me, gave me the apartment, and kissed me on my forehead as he left that Saturday. Was that kiss a sign he liked me? Even just a bit?

"What price do you want on it?" Laura's voice brought me back to reality.

"I showed it to David, and he said he thought a hundred."

"Well, we can put a hundred on it. Can I sell it for less?"

I stared at my holey shoes. "Guess we can go down to seventy-five, but I'd really like to get more." *Especially if Artistic Horizons charges me thirty dollars to sell it.*

"I'll put one hundred. We'll see." Laura wrote the title and price in fancy letters on a strip of white paper edged in gold, which I placed under my painting as I sat it in the window display. Standing back to admire my work, I caught sight of Jenny Lou's drawing.

"I see my friend Jenny Lou brought in her landscape."

Laura raised her eyebrow. "*That* was your friend Jenny Lou?"

I turned to leave, but Laura stopped me. "A letter came for you today," she said, handing me an envelope.

The return label was an address in Puttersville. No name, just an address, 4040 Stanton Court. I hurried down the hall, and as soon as I hit the kitchen light switch, I opened the envelope. As I pulled a sheet of folded lined paper out, a twenty dollar bill floated to the floor. In letters so neat they looked like they were typed were the words:

Dear Allison,

I received some money for my birthday, and as promised, I'm sending you part of it. I have an interview for a better paying job this week. If I get the job, I will send you some of every paycheck until I have paid you back every cent of your money my dad lost.

Your friend,
George.

The words *Your friend* sent my head spinning, for I didn't want to be his friend or to have anything to do with his dad or Puttersville. But his vow to pay me back every cent touched me. I was grateful for what he sent.

CHAPTER 28

AN INVITATION

WEDNESDAY, I WENT TO THE shop as usual at one. Laura greeted me as I entered. "Mom would like you to come to dinner Friday night. Here's her telephone number so you can call and let her know."

Joy and gratitude swept over me, sinking into my whole being and lifting my spirit. I would have something to eat besides sandwiches. Gertie liked me and Laura did too or she wouldn't have trusted me with her mother's telephone number. I felt like I had a place in the world among people I loved, something precious and beautiful.

Around two-thirty, a couple came into the shop. "We'd like to look at one of the pieces in your window," he said. "The one with the mountains and the moose."

I took Jenny Lou's drawing from the display and handed it to them. They held it up to the light and examined every inch of it before giving it back to me.

"We'll take it," the woman said. "Can you put it in a box and wrap it for us?"

I hunted for a box the right size and wrapped it as best I could in some blue paper and a white bow. The man handed me a hundred dollars in twenty dollar bills, which I put in the secret money drawer.

I was so excited that I called Jenny Lou from my phone instead of the store phone. "Jenny Lou, your picture just sold!"

After a moment of silence, she spoke. "My picture sold? You don't have my picture."

"Yes, we did. Your picture of the mountains and the moose."

"No. I told you I would bring it, but I've been sick this past week, and I haven't even gone to class. You don't have my picture."

Panic struck like a bullet in my chest. "Okay, maybe I was mistaken. I'll call you back." I ran outside and looked up and down the street, but the couple was nowhere in sight. I called Laura and told her what happened.

"Call the police," she said. "Give them the best description of the picture you can."

I did as she instructed, but the police were neither helpful nor hopeful that they would find the person copying and selling art. They took the paper that the artist filled out, but before I gave it to them, I made a copy. Jenny Lou's address was correct. The phone number was not. Fifteen minutes after the police left, Jenny Lou stormed through the shop door.

"Here's the picture I painted. How can I have it in my hand and you declare I gave it to you?"

"I'm sorry, but someone who is a very good artist must have copied your drawing and sold it as theirs. I wasn't here when the person brought it in."

"Did they fill out anything when they left it?"

"Everyone who displays a piece here on consignment fills out a form with all their information." I retrieved it from the drawer. "Here it is. Take a look. I know that's not your phone number."

"And definitely not my handwriting. Who was minding the store when that person came in? I want to call him."

"I believe it was Laura." I handed her Laura's card. "Why don't you call her?"

She dialed the number, but Laura didn't answer. "Has this kind of theft happened before?" she asked when she hung up.

"I'm afraid it has. Monday some customers showed us paintings they bought at another art shop. We had just been given the same pieces to put on consignment. Laura notified the police, and I called them about your painting this morning. Problem is, they said thieves like this are hard to catch."

"It makes me very angry." Her eyes blazed, and she jerked the door open. "I had just put it on my new website, but now I'm taking it off. I really need the money I planned to get from the sale of that painting." She slammed the door shut as she left.

What happened wasn't my fault, of course, and I felt like Jenny Lou blamed me, Laura, and the shop. Had I lost her friendship? I hoped not. The thought bothered me through the rest of the afternoon, and I couldn't shake it even after I closed the shop and retired to my apartment.

I made myself another peanut butter sandwich and a cup of coffee, and as I ate, I thought about my life. Except for my animal friends, I couldn't remember ever having anyone to talk to except Uncle Deb and Aunt Harriet. We had no neighbors, so no little playmates lived nearby. We didn't go to church. The only classmate I remembered from school was George.

A wave of loneliness swept over me. I had to talk to someone. I picked up my phone and turned it on, knowing my card had only ten minutes on it. Whom should I call? Not David, as I didn't feel comfortable calling him. Not Laura. She was probably too busy with her family. Gertie might be in bed by now. I dialed Aunt Harriet.

Her phone rang six times before she answered. "Harriet here."

"Hi," I said, chuckling. "It's Allie."

"Sorry, I didn't recognize your number. How are you?"

"Did I tell you I have a job? And a nice apartment? I'm not staying at the school anymore."

"I'm glad for you. I'm excited about starting my new job next week. I'm moving a few things into my new apartment. Got the key today, and I'm already feeling like a free woman."

"My work is at an art store. They're letting me sell one of my pictures. I have a hundred dollars on it."

"Do you need anything, Allie? I'll be able to help you some."

"No, I'm fine. Have a warm place to live, and enough money to buy food. But I'd better go as my phone is almost out of minutes. Love you so much, Aunt Harriet."

"I love you too. Maybe you can come see me sometime."

I told her goodbye and my minutes ran out. The warmth of her voice made me forget Jenny Lou's anger for a little while. And Friday night I was having dinner with Gertie. And Saturday David should be here.

CHAPTER 29

PIZZA NIGHT

I SHOWED UP FOR WORK early Friday to find David minding the store.

"No classes today," he explained. "The students are working to finish projects that are due Monday. Laura needed a break. She worries so much about this place, and now, with all the art theft going on..."

"It worries me enough to want to take my painting from the display," I said. "If it's not where anyone can see it, no one can copy it."

"I have the same thoughts. The only thing the artists who've had their work copied have in common is that they all have websites."

Remembering Lettie's suggestion, I gathered my courage. "I'd like to have a website, but I don't even have a computer."

"I'm coming in tomorrow. If we're not too busy, I'll help you build a simple site. That's all you need."

"Thanks." I wished I could at least hug him, but he seemed too busy posting sales on the computer.

"Happy, happy, joy, joy, we've done pretty well this week," he said. "Four paintings sold, several hundred dollars' worth of art supplies, two vases, and three of the frames I made last week."

"And the week's not over," I said, laughing at his repetition of words.

"Well, I have errands to run, so I'll leave this place in your capable hands," he said, handing me the keys. "Until tomorrow, honey bunny."

For once my brain whirled, and before he was out the door, I yelled, "See ya, funny bunny."

"Hey, not bad." He gave me a thumb's up before he closed the door behind him.

I sold another student's painting, and when I called him, learned he was the real artist. That, plus David's offer of help in making a website, on top of his teasing and camaraderie, and I was fairly dancing down the street to Gertie's house after I closed the store.

"Come in, Allie," Gertie said as she opened the door. She smiled, but I could tell she was in pain. "Old legs not doing too well today. Must be a cold front coming through."

"I'm sorry, Gertie. If this isn't a good time, I can come another day."

"Heaven's no! Come, have a seat. David's bringing pizza for dinner, so I don't even have to cook."

My heart skipped a beat and thumped more loudly, and I hoped she couldn't hear it. In a few minutes he waltzed in, carrying a large pizza in one hand and a bag of salad in the other.

"Well, hello, Allie Pally. Imagine seeing you here. Hope you like pizza with everything."

"Of course I do." I inhaled the odor of meats and spices as he carried it past me into the kitchen.

"Just a minute and we'll be eating."

I walked beside Gertie, who leaned on her walker and limped slowly into the kitchen. As we arrived, David was cutting up some tomatoes for the salad, and he gathered them into his hands and tossed them into the bowl on top of the lettuce.

We sat down at the table. David put a large slice of pizza on my plate, then one on Gertie's and his. Gertie handed me the salad bowl, and after taking a generous helping, I passed it to David. I picked up the slice of pizza and guided it toward my mouth.

"Wait a minute, we'd better ask the blessing," Gertie said. "David, will you?"

I was so hungry I hadn't even thought about saying grace and I was glad David closed his eyes so he couldn't see me blush, but not before he reached for one of my hands and Gertie reached for the other. Sitting there holding their hands, listening to his deep voice give thanks to God, and again feeling a part of a family brought tears to my eyes.

As soon as David said "Amen," I devoured everything on my plate before Gertie had eaten more than a few bites.

"Would you like another piece?" David asked, sliding one onto my plate.

I ate it more slowly, savoring the rich flavors. Uncle Deb and Aunt Harriet never bought pizza, even at the grocery store, and I had no money to buy it since I left Trag's. It was a real treat, so I enjoyed every bite while I listened to Gertie and David reminisce about his grandfather.

"It's been ten years today since Arno passed," Gertie said. "That's why I had to have some company tonight. Thank you both for coming."

"So glad to," I said. "I know that must have been hard for you."

"I remember how you both worked on building Artistic Horizons," David said. "It was just a shell of a building when Grandpa bought it. He constructed walls, laid down flooring, and you helped him paint."

"Arno could do anything," Gertie said. "You were just getting old enough to help. I can still see you holding the nail bucket for him."

Their reminiscing went on for another fifteen minutes. David rose and wrapped the last two pieces of pizza in plastic wrap. "I'm putting these in the refrigerator so you can pop them into the microwave tomorrow, Grandma. And the rest of this salad goes into a smaller bowl."

He rinsed our plates and utensils and handed them to me to put into the dishwasher. *We make a great team.* I thought it, but I was too shy to say it. I didn't want to sound pushy.

"I'm tired. Think I'll get to bed early," Gertie said when we finished.

David kissed her good night, and we said our goodbyes. It was only seven-thirty. The street lights were sending their halos onto the sidewalks and yards, and the wind whistled, swirling my blue skirt around my legs.

"Your grandma's right, must be a storm coming," I said.

He wrapped his arm around my shoulder and walked me to his car. Opening the door, he tossed some papers from the front to the back. "Get in and I'll take you home."

We didn't talk much, and even though when we pulled in front of Artistic Horizons all he did was open the door for me and wish me good night, my heart was singing.

CHAPTER 30

TRAGEDY STRIKES

SATURDAY, I OPENED ARTISTIC HORIZONS at eight-thirty instead of nine as shoppers were already in the streets searching for a place to spend their money. Besides, David would come in at one and I wanted time to clean up. I swept the floor and dusted the shelves, then wiped off vases, the frames of pictures, and the frames David made to sell. Last, I emptied all the trash cans, dumping them into one can and taking it outside to the Dumpster.

A few minutes after nine the door opened, and Madam Kay stalked in like she owned the place. "I'm looking for a book," she said and thrust a notecard in front of me, all the while glancing around the store, but never seeing me. "It would make my life a lot easier if I don't have to go running all over town to find it."

One part of the store I hadn't spent much time at was the book shelves, and I headed to the far corner, all the time trying to keep one eye on Madam. As I guessed, the books were in alphabetical order by author, and it didn't take me long to find the book and take it up to the register.

"That'll be $49.89 with tax," I told her.

"That's outrageous! I'm sure you added twenty dollars to what you paid for it."

"You can look for it around town if you'd like," I said, acting like I was going to take it back to the bookcase.

"I'll take it." She stared right past me as she handed me her credit card. When I gave her the bag, she walked out as if she were in a huff over some imagined mistreatment from me.

She didn't even recognize me, the girl whose bed she stole, the student she caused to drop out. Maybe it's better that way. I shook off the morose feeling that had settled on my shoulders like a black vulture and thought about my night with David and Gertie. Once again I felt his arm around my shoulders and saw the intensity of his blue eyes as he told me good night. I was surprised when he arrived before noon.

"Morning, Allie Pally," he said, throwing his hat and coat on a nearby chair. "Got anything to eat?"

I racked my brain, for I had eaten the last piece of lunch meat for breakfast, and the only bread left were the two heels.

"Do you like peanut butter?"

"Love it."

I went into the back and made him my last sandwich. "Sorry, but heels are all I have left," I told him as I sat the paper plate in front of him on the counter.

"Happy, happy! Heels are my favorite." He poured himself a cup of coffee, then carried the cup and plate to the small table. "Sell anything this morning?"

I told him about Madam Kay. "I don't think she even recognized me."

"Probably not. People like her seem to live in their own little world."

I thought about my own little world that I had escaped. "Guess there are different kinds of having your own little world."

"Some are worse than others." He closed the book he was writing in. "Bugly ugly. One of these days, when I have time, I'm going to put all our inventory on the computer."

"I'll help you if I can.," I said, laughing at his expression.

"Good. Next Saturday, maybe you and I can get started, and you can work on it as you have time during the week."

"I'd like that. Do you remember my asking you about a website? Do you think you'd have time to help me this afternoon?"

"We can do it now."

At the computer, he clicked on a few icons. "Here's my site. It's hosted by a company that lets me build what I want, and I don't have to know how to program."

"Does it cost anything?"

"They have a free site. All you have to pay for is your site's name."

"I don't have any money right now," I said, the heat rising to my cheeks.

"Tell you what. I'll give you a page on my site. When you have the money, you can start your own. How's that?"

"Wonderful."

"What do you want to call it?"

"*Scenes from Nature*."

"Okay, now all we need to do is show your art. We'll start with the one in our window." He took a picture of my mountain scene with his phone camera. "Guess you don't have email, do you?" I started to shake my head, but he had already sent it to his own.

"Boy, you're fast."

"You will be some day. Now, what else do you have to put up here?"

"Nothing. I've sold all my work except the one in the window." I was ashamed to tell him I couldn't afford the canvas or paper for more paintings.

"Then I'll expect something from you by next Saturday. Deal?"

I nodded, not knowing where I was going to find the money to buy the supplies.

"I need to run some errands. Would you mind staying here for the next few hours and closing?"

"Guess not." I needed to go grocery shopping, but I could do it after the store closed.

"Thanks, Allie Girl. I owe you one."

A few customers came in after he left, but I didn't sell anything expensive. I spent most of the next two hours looking at art supplies—painting paper, stretched canvas, painting boards, acrylic paints, and oils. It was all too expensive. Looking down, I noticed that the hole in the toe of my tennis shoe was growing larger.

The bells on the door jangled as it flew open, and a police officer walked in. "Are you Allison Cooper?" he asked.

"Yes."

"Do you know Harriet Gray at this address?" He showed me a piece of paper with Trag's address.

"Yes."

"I'm sorry to have to tell you. She was killed this morning."

"How? What happened?" I felt like someone just kicked a hole in my stomach, and the room swayed around me.

"The man she was living with, a Simon Traggart, shot her. He claims it was an accident. Said he was cleaning his gun when it went off and hit her."

"No, no! I don't believe it! She was leaving this morning to move to her own apartment, and I'm sure he didn't want her to go. Officer, you've got to find out what happened!"

"I don't live there, miss, and it's not my jurisdiction. I'm sure the Chicago police are investigating."

My body crumpled, and grabbing the counter top with both my hands, I lay my head on my arms and sobbed.

"Can I call someone for you?" he asked.

"No," I said, raising my head. "I'll…I'll manage."

"Would you give me your phone number so the Chicago police can get hold of you if they need to?"

I wrote it down and handed him the paper. After he left, I followed him out the door and locked it, and gripping my stomach, staggered up the street toward Gertie's house.

CHAPTER 31

MORE ABOUT DAVID

GERTIE WAS IN HER PAJAMAS and robe when she answered my knock. I collapsed into her arms and sobbed.

"What is it, Allie?" She ran her hand down my hair, then wrapped her arms around me. I couldn't stop crying, and she held me without asking again.

"My Aunt Harriet's dead!" I sobbed. "She's gone! Trag shot her! On purpose!"

"I'm so sorry, dear." She guided me to her overstuffed sofa, and I sank into it. "Tell me what happened."

"She was living with him, but she planned to move into her own apartment today." I wiped my nose with the back of my hand, and she handed me a tissue, then two more. "She did his housework, cooked for him, and paid the bills, and somehow he found out she was moving out. He told the police it was an accident, but I know he did it on purpose. He's so mean." The thought of everything Aunt Harriet must have gone through overwhelmed me, and my body shook with sobs.

Gertie sat beside me and stroked my back. "I'm so sorry, so sorry," she murmured over and over while I cried.

I cried until I was too tired to cry more, and totally exhausted and feeling weak, I lay my head down on the arm of the sofa. My ribs ached from my wrenching sobs, and my stomach did somersaults.

"Tell me about your aunt," Gertie said.

"She and Uncle Deb adopted me when my mama died, and they were my parents, and Aunt Harriet was smart, and she taught me so much before I started school, and she made me clothes, and she loved me." At this I started crying again. "Now she's gone, and I'm an orphan, and oh..." I sat there feeling helpless, for I couldn't think, and I couldn't find the right words.

"We're all orphans, Allie." Gertie put her arm around my shoulders. "Until we find God, our heavenly Father, we're all orphans."

"Why do you say we're all orphans? You weren't an orphan. David and Laura aren't orphans."

"No, dear, they have parents. But in one true sense, we're all orphans until we get to know God and His love for us."

I sniffed. "I don't know God."

"We'll have to talk about God, you and me."

I didn't feel like talking about God, and I stood to say goodbye, but my body had other notions. The room spun around me. Strength left my legs, my whole body shook, and I fell back onto the sofa.

"What have you had to eat today?" Gertie asked.

"A sandwich this morning."

"Is that all? No wonder you can't stand. I just made some vegetable beef soup. Let's go have some."

I followed her to the kitchen and watched as she ladled steaming soup into two bowls and cut slices from a loaf of French bread. She thanked God for the food. Spreading butter onto a piece of bread, I dipped it into my soup and let the broth soak in.

"Feel better?" she asked when our bowls were empty.

"Yes." I picked up our dishes and eating utensils, rinsed them, and put them in the dishwasher. "Tell me more about David. Where are his parents? Where is Nancy's mother?"

She stood with the help of her walker and led the way into her living room. Easing herself into her chair, she thought for a minute as if deciding what to tell me or whether to tell me anything. "They were just kids, seniors in high school, when Marty got pregnant. They were too young to marry. She had a little girl, as you know, and Marty and the baby stayed with her parents."

"But David got to see her?"

"Yes, he was there a lot. He loved that baby." She sighed and fingered the edging on the afghan covering the chair. "When Nancy was nearly three, she became sickly, and the doctors diagnosed her with leukemia. The doctors did everything they could, but when she was almost five, her little body couldn't take any more treatments and blood transfusions. We lost her."

I got up and put my arm around her shoulders while she wiped tears from her eyes. "You saw her portrait David painted. She was a beautiful child."

"And what happened to Marty? Is she still living here?"

"She is studying to be a teacher at a university in Texas." She wrapped the afghan around herself. "I don't think David is ready for a relationship. Don't know if he ever will be, but certainly not now. It hasn't even been a year since Nancy died."

I nodded, feeling my hopes dashed. It helped explain why David acted friendly, but that was all. At times my whole body ached to be in his arms, and I wished he would take me and kiss me. But he was aloof, and he didn't act toward me like I wanted him to. "Where are his parents?"

"Doug and Linda are missionaries in Honduras. They've been there three years, but they come back to the States once a year. Would you like me to read you why they went to help others?"

"Yes."

She picked up her Bible, turned the pages, and started reading, "Whosoever will call on the name of the Lord will be saved. How then will they call on Him in whom they have not believed? How will they believe in Him whom they have not heard?"

I tried to pay attention, but I felt myself slipping down into the soft cushions. I awoke in the morning lying on Gertie's couch, her afghan tucked around me. I could hear her in her kitchen, and laying the afghan over her chair, I joined her.

"I was just about to wake you," she said, putting two waffles into her toaster. "I hope you don't mind frozen waffles. They're convenient." She took a plate of cooked bacon from the microwave and set it on the table. "Would you prefer coffee or orange juice?"

We sat down to eat, and after giving thanks, she said, "Laura and her family will be here in about an hour to pick me up for church. You're welcome to come."

I looked down at the clothes I had slept in and shook my head. "Thanks, but maybe some other time. Does David go?"

"Not anymore. He and Marty used to take Nancy all the time. But not since..."

"I understand," I said, helping her clean up the dishes. "Thanks for letting me sleep over, and also for the wonderful breakfast. I'd better go home and get cleaned up."

"Come anytime," she said as I left. "I love you like you are my own."

I trudged up the street thinking about everything she had told me about David. Were his happy face and funny words a way to cover the sadness that must lurk within his heart? Did he love Marty? Nancy's illness and death surely left an unfillable hole in his life. All that brought me back to the realization that Aunt Harriet was gone, and by the time I reached Artistic Horizons, my face was wet with tears.

CHAPTER 32

GOOD NEWS

ONE OF LAURA'S CHILDREN WAS ill Tuesday and Wednesday, so I worked all day those days. After doing my laundry and buying some groceries Sunday, I had only eleven dollars. I know I promised David I would paint something new for my website page, but I was afraid to spend the money for paints and canvases. That morning was cold and raining, and we'd had very few customers. What should I do?

David was supposed to come at one, and since I had a half hour to fill and had not really examined the bookcase, I decided to familiarize myself with the books. On the bottom shelf was a set of books. I couldn't tell what they were until I pulled one out, and to my surprise, found the set contained twenty books, one for each year of the McCabbock State Young Artist's Competition.

Holding my breath, I found the book for the first year I had won. My first-place painting of Wee Ears, Rumple Tail, and my forest friends made the front cover. Opening it, I discovered my painting on page one with *Grand Prize Winner by Artist Allison Bainsworth Cooper* written in gold letters above it. A small paragraph about me spanned the bottom of the page. A thrill rippled through my body, sending chills down my spine. I was an artist. Someone called me an artist, and I didn't even know it.

"Hey, hey! I didn't know you won the McCabbock." David stood behind me, peering over my shoulder.

"Three times in a row." I held up the next two books for him to see.

He took the books and studied the covers. "You improved each year. Who was your teacher?"

"Teacher? I didn't have one."

"Master was correct, Allie. You are very talented. What did you do for your web page this week?"

"Nothing." The word came out so softly I could barely hear it, but David did.

"Nothing? How come?" A puzzled look crossed his face.

"Because," I said as the blush crept onto my cheeks again, and I hated it, but I couldn't stop it. "Because I don't have any canvas or paper or paints, and I don't have any money."

He eyed me for a minute. "Then you just get yourself over to the art supply aisle and pick out whatever you need. They're yours."

"I couldn't take anything without paying for it."

"You worked for me last Saturday, and you worked two whole days this week. Now go get what you need, at least a hundred dollars' worth."

How many hours this week had I spent drooling over everything in that aisle? I knew exactly what I wanted. Two pieces of canvas, each sixteen by twenty inches, a set of six tubes of acrylic paint, and a set of different sized paint brushes filled my arms as I walked to the check-out counter.

David rang them up. "That's only seventy dollars and twenty-five cents." He walked over to the paint supplies and returned with two more pieces of canvas and a can of primer, which he put in my bag. "You've earned it. Now go paint. Next Saturday, I'm hoping you'll have something to put on your web page."

I was trying to find the words to thank him when the mailman came in. "A letter for Miss Cooper," he said, handing it to me.

The return address read George Benton, 4040 Stanton Court. I thrust it into my bag and headed for the door leading to the hallway to my apartment.

"Wait a minute!" David yelled, stopping me. He stepped over to me and hugged me. "We couldn't get along without you, Allie. I want you to know you are very important to me and my family. Mom's not doing well this week. If you can spare the time, please check in on her."

"You're important to me, too," I said, gazing up into his blue eyes. My heart beat quickened and my breathing almost stopped as I walked through the doorway. *You are very important to me,* he had said. How was I supposed to interpret that? More and more, I was feeling like one of the Hammond family. Someday, I hoped to be married to David.

I set my bag down on my small table, turned on the light, and tore open George's letter. A crisp twenty-dollar bill and a piece of paper with a phone number fell out. I laid them on the table and pulled out the letter:

Dear Allison,

Remember that I told you I was interviewing for a new job? I don't know how, being a student right out of high school with only one semester of college (almost), but I have been hired as the media representative for the Puttersville Environmental Committee. City officials formed this committee to fight the encroachment of the Puron Oil Company on our land. They want to buy up the beautiful woodlands around Puttersville to drill for oil and to frack if they find oil.

Fracking and drilling for oil will tear up the beautiful forests here. Yes, even the woods beside the house where you lived with your aunt and uncle will be trampled by machinery and devastated by water waste. Fracking also destabilizes the ground and can cause the destruction of house foundations.

The Environmental Committee wants me to find someone to paint a picture of what will happen if fracking happens. They will pay someone $500 for the picture. I thought of you and your love for the forests and the animals that live in them. Could you take on this project? I need the picture in two weeks. Please call me and let me know.

Your friend,
George Benton

Five hundred dollars! Of course I would do it. George was right. I loved those woods and the animals, and I would do it for free even if they didn't offer to pay me. But I was glad they did. I picked up my phone to call, then checked. Only five minutes left on my card, and I didn't want to be cut off in the middle of a sentence. Tomorrow I'd take the bus to Walmart and buy more minutes for my phone.

The rest of the evening I thought about Wee Ears and Rumple Tail and the expressions on their faces when they find their forest homes trampled and destroyed. This painting would have to be my best, even better than the ones I did for the McCabbock.

CHAPTER 33

ALL MY HEART

MONDAY MORNING, I CALLED GEORGE and talked to him about what he needed for the environmental committee. I gave him several ideas, and he told me he liked my thought of a squirrel, a raccoon, and a robin sitting in the top of a tall tree, the only tree left in a field. Underneath the tree, a rabbit peeks from its hole. All the animals have tears in their eyes as they survey the destruction of the forest. Since he liked my concept, I started working on it as soon as I got home that evening, and I had it about halfway finished.

David had come in that afternoon and showed me how to use and update the inventory system he had set up on the computer. I entered the contents of most of the boxes of supplies in the store room. Having something to do made the time go so much faster. Of course I had to enter everything I sold, too. But I loved this place, and I poured all my heart into my work. I had learned so much. Maybe someday I would have an art shop. Or—dare I think it—be married to David and call this one my own.

"Mr. and Mrs. Hank, the older couple who buy a lot of our art, came in this morning," Laura said when I came in Wednesday. "They showed me a piece of art they purchased at a gallery in Colorado Springs. It was a copy of one of those hanging on our wall, and I had to contact the artist and tell him, and I had to call the police again, so I didn't get much else accomplished. Then at noon a local television station ran a story about the illegal copying of artwork in several galleries and shops, but they used a picture of the front of Artistic Horizons. If artists saw the story, they will be afraid to sell their work here." She buried her face in her hands. "I'm so frustrated."

"I'm sorry. Wish I could do something."

"Keep watching. And please finish entering this inventory for me. I guess I'd better go get the girls." She picked up her purse and left.

Just as I finished the inventory, David called. "Howdy, ho! Grandma asked me to bring her a hamburger for dinner, and I wonder... Would you like to go along?"

Would I! I had thought of Gertie every day this week, but I was so busy. And was this a date? I tried to keep my emotions at a low key and answered, "I owe Gertie a visit, and I would love to see her."

He parked in front of Artistic Horizons at six just as I was closing, and he jumped out and opened the car door for me as I approached.

"I already picked up the burgers as Grandma likes to eat early. Hope you like everything on yours."

"Sounds good to me." I was hungry. I had spent the twenty dollars George sent me on minutes for my phone, and I was trying to make the little money I had last.

Gertie hugged both of us as we entered her house. "I'm so glad you came, Allie. Haven't seen you for a while."

We gathered around the table, and David gave thanks and passed everyone a burger and a box of fries. I ate while they talked about how she was feeling and what David was doing at his job. Gertie's eyes shined when he told her about his latest art project, a drawing of a snowy mountain scene and how it would look like a Christmas card with glistening snow and pine trees.

"Speaking of Christmas," he said, turning to me. "This is almost the middle of November, and it will soon be here. We need to keep the shop open longer to accommodate Christmas shoppers. Would you be willing to work until eight Monday through Friday, and Saturday if we need you? It would be just through the end of December."

"I'm terribly busy right now," I said, thinking of my unfinished project.

"What if I paid you two hundred a month for the extra work?"

"David, can we afford it?" Gertie asked. "Sorry, Allie, but I know sales have not been strong."

"Yes, we can afford it. Mrs. and Mrs. Hank came in last Saturday and asked me to paint some of their favorite Colorado scenes."

"What places?"

"Oh, Red Rocks, Rocky Mountain National Park, Garden of the Gods, and a few others. They're paying me well, so I have a little extra."

I added the amount. One hundred dollars for the rest of November, and two hundred for December. "Okay, I'll do it."

"Thanks." His blue eyes met mine, and my heart skipped a beat. "I usually work extra holidays, but with this commission, I doubt I can find the time. And Laura is so busy with the girls right now, helping them practice for their Thanksgiving program at school."

"I'll be glad to help."

"Thanks, Allie. I told you. You're indispensable to this family."

I brooded on his words as we cleaned up the table. *Was I indispensable because of my work at the shop, or did he really like me, even just a tiny bit?* That thought continued to nag me as we retired to the living room. I scooted Gertie's walker to the side of her chair, and she sat down and tucked the afghan over her swollen legs.

"Laura tells me you have a commission yourself," Gertie said, patting my arm. "Tell me about it."

"I grew up in the woods," I said. "Well, practically. The animals were my friends, and they came near me and sat still while I drew them. Someone from my hometown wrote and told me an oil company wants to drill for oil in the forest. He's on a committee to try and stop this oil company from drilling and fracking, and they're paying me to illustrate the destruction of the forest."

"I want to see your painting as soon as you get it done," she said.

"Me too, Allie, me too. Will you have it finished by this Saturday?"

I looked up into his blue eyes and laughed. "You repeat yourself all the time?"

"Guess so. It's just my way. Maybe I should try to stop."

"No, no. I like you like that." The words flew out of my mouth, and the moment they did, that unwanted blush crept over my face.

"Thanks." Laugh lines appeared around his eyes. "I have enough work to do without trying to change."

We visited for a little while more, then left. The drive back to Artistic Horizons was far too short. David nosed his car in front of the store, and instead of getting out to open my door, he reached for my hand.

"Are you free Sunday, Allie?"

"I think so."

"Good." He squeezed my hand. "I have to travel to one of my sites Saturday, so Laura will be here Saturday afternoon. But I'm free Sunday, and I was wondering. Would you like to go out to eat with me Sunday for lunch and then to an art show?"

"To an art show? Yes, that would be fun."

"Great. How about I come by around eleven? That way we can beat the crowd."

"Okay, I'll see you then," I said, opening the door and stepping out. I turned and waved before shutting the door, and my feet didn't touch the ground as I walked to my apartment.

CHAPTER 34

AN ACCIDENTAL FIND

FRIDAY, THE RINGING OF MY phone wakened me a little after seven. Groggy and half asleep, I was confused at hearing a strange male voice.

"Miss Allison Cooper?"

"Yes."

"This is the Cook County Medical Examiner's Office. The police have confirmed Mr. Traggart's story that your aunt's death was an accident. Do you want a copy of the death certificate?"

"Yes."

"It will cost fifty dollars. You can pay by credit card or money order. When we receive payment, we'll send your copy. What do you want us to do with the body, send it to an area funeral home?"

My mind raced through possibilities. "What will it cost to have my aunt cremated?"

"Most funeral homes charge around fifteen hundred. To which funeral home do you want us to send your aunt's body?"

"I...I can't afford that much. Is there anything less expensive?"

"You can have the body donated for educational study."

"What does that mean?"

"We send the body to a university where those studying to be doctors use it for learning how to do surgery."

Aunt Harriet taught me most of what I knew, and I knew she would approve. "Okay, let's do that."

"I'll send you the papers to sign. Please give me your address."

So I made Aunt Harriet's funeral arrangements. No, they weren't for a funeral, and I would never have anything to remember her by. I crawled back under the covers and cried until my pillow case was wet. Growing up, being poor was a problem, but now I understood how living in poverty diminished one's social status and forced one to live without the things one needed and wanted.

I dragged myself out of bed and glanced at my picture for George. I should have sat down and finished the touch-ups it needed, but my heart wasn't there. My whole body ached with an emptiness and a numbness beyond describing. The demon within me, that old habit of hiding in my own world, assailed me, and I fought it back with each step. I plodded through the motions of showering and getting dressed, decided against eating, and walked through the shop door a little after ten.

"I'm glad you're here early," Laura said as I entered. "My younger daughter, Lilah, forgot her lunch and I need to run it over to her school. Would you mind?"

"No, go ahead."

"Thanks," she said, and then she was gone.

I yearned for someone to talk to. Helping myself to a cup of coffee, I let its steaming vapors soak into my body. Its warmth didn't penetrate my soul, hidden in a dark, cold cave.

Laura didn't return until almost noon. She bustled through the door carrying two bags and a drink tray with two drinks.

"Sorry to be gone so long, but as long as I was out, I figured I'd get us some lunch. Hope you like tacos. Sell anything?"

"No."

"It's starting to rain. Weather forecast says it could change into snow by this evening. Hope not."

"Me too." I looked down at my holey shoes. Thanks to George, I had enough money for a few groceries and laundry money, but that was all.

The doorbell jangled, and a woman came in. "I need something cheerful to remind me of summer. I saw that painting of the sunlight streaming through the mountains in your window, and it is perfect for my new house."

Laura rang up the sale, and when the woman left, she handed me one hundred dollars. "Congratulations."

"Here's your thirty percent," I said, giving her back thirty dollars.

"No, no, you're one of us. You don't pay to sell here."

I cuddled the money to my chest as I made my way to put it in my bag. It would buy new boots and Aunt Harriet's death certificate. A shower of warmth and happiness bathed my soul as her words echoed in my mind. *You're one of us.*

After lunch, I went to the bank and bought the money order, which cost an extra five dollars just for getting it. But I still had forty-five left for boots, and I hoped that would be enough.

Laura left as soon as I got back to Artistic Horizons, and no customers came in, so I counted my money. Besides my boot money, I had twenty-eight dollars. It would have to do until I got my money from George. Then I realized I had to send him my painting. How much would that cost?

"Hi, Allison."

Lettie stood behind me. "I didn't hear you come in," I said. "You off for the week?"

"I'm never off," she said, laughing. "Just here to buy more acrylics. The students go through them fast. I need twenty-four of your big jars, four each of blue, yellow, red, green, brown, and black."

"Don't think we have that many on the shelf. Hold on and I'll see what we have in storage." I ran into the back room and filled two boxes with her order. After she paid, I helped her carry them out to her car. It was sleeting, and back in the store, I looked on the counter for some paper towels to wipe my face. There on the counter, right where Lettie had been standing, was her phone.

I grabbed it and dashed through the door. Her car was gone. I could have, should have, called the school and let her know she left it. But no, I looked at the screen, and what came up made me gasp. David's portrait of Nancy. I thumbed through her other pictures, and to my surprise, found photos of many other paintings, including the ones academy students had done.

What to do? Call the police? No, I called Laura, but she didn't answer, so I called David.

"I'll dismiss my students and be there as soon as I can," he said when I told him what I'd found. In a half hour he burst through the door. "Holy moly!" he said as he stared at Lettie's file of photos. "I can't believe she would do this. I always thought she was a sweet, hard-working woman."

"She helped me when I was at the academy. What are you going to do?"

"Take this down to the police station. We have to stop her."

"Let me know what happens," I said as he hurried out the door.

He gave me his thumbs up. The store walls closed in on me as if to force me back into my self-made prison. Too bad I couldn't have gone with David to the police station. It was almost eight o'clock when he called to say the police had obtained a warrant to search Lettie's apartment.

My heart ached for her. She was on call night and day to the students and staff. Instead of Master praising her, he ordered her around like she was his slave. Even though she was busy, she had found time to show me around and advise me. What could have made her copy and sell paintings?

CHAPTER 35

DATE WITH DAVID

SATURDAY MORNING, I MAILED THE money for Aunt Harriet's death certificate and my precious painting to George, which cost fifteen dollars with insurance, then took the bus to Walmart. Their boots were on sale, twenty percent off, and I found a pair that went up my leg about ten inches. They were black, with faux fur around the top and a sole made for traction, and they would keep me warm through the cold and snow. I had enough money left over to buy a package of socks.

Laura had her coat on when I arrived at the store Saturday afternoon. "I hope you don't mind my leaving a bit early," she said. "I have to get my daughter Diana to piano practice at three. She's just starting, and I need to go buy her a music book." She grabbed her purse and headed for the door. "Oh, there's a letter for you on the counter."

It was from George, and I tore it open, hoping he wasn't telling me they had obtained a picture from another artist. No, George wouldn't do that to me. Out tumbled two twenty-dollar bills and a short, hand-written note saying he had his first pay check, only for a week, but he would share as he had promised, and he hoped I had the picture ready to send.

Woo-hoo! I had enough money to buy groceries for a couple weeks. I tucked the bills into my bag and thought about Laura. She was getting more and more preoccupied with her children. Strange that she said nothing about Lettie. Maybe David didn't tell her.

My mind turned to my Sunday date with David. What I really wanted to do was to go shopping and buy myself a new dress or maybe I'd try some jeans. And I needed a new coat, but of course I didn't have the money for any of those things. The best I could do was wash my blue skirt, my favorite of the ones Aunt Harriet had made me, and my coat.

Sunday morning I dressed and slipped on my new socks and boots. Their softness cuddled my feet and ankles in warmth, and I danced around my small apartment just to break them in, wishing I had a full-length mirror. As I passed my one window, snowflakes floated into my view. Ten minutes before eleven I went to the store where I could watch for David.

He was right on time. "Mornin', morning glory," he said, getting out and opening the car door for me.

"Beautiful day," I said, slipping into the car seat. "Our first snow."

"Ever go skiing?" he asked. When I shook my head, he said, "We'll have to do that some time."

"How did your painting trip go yesterday? Where was it?"

"Red Rocks. A spectacular outdoor theater." He frowned. "They were preparing for a play, and with so many people getting in the way...well, let's just say I didn't get as much done as I'd hoped. Did you finish your painting? We need to put it on your web page."

"Sorry, but I already sent it. With everything that's been happening, I was afraid to have it online. Have you told Laura about Lettie? She didn't mention it yesterday."

"No. She's had so much with her girls and Grandma lately." He paused. "Grandma seems to be going downhill. You really should get over to see her if you can."

"I've been so busy, but I'll try. By the way, where are we having lunch?"

"Black Eye Pea, our favorite restaurant, and we're here." He pulled into the parking lot and found a spot in front of the door, then came around to open my door. "Miss Cooper." He bowed and swept his hand forward, motioning for me to get out.

I giggled and got out. He held my hand in his as we walked up the steps, and when the waiter led us to a table, he pulled out my chair. It was all so wonderful and grand. I might as well have been a queen with her royal attendants.

Glancing at the menu, I laughed. "Chicken tenderloins? Pigs have tenderloins, not chickens."

"They're tender strips of chicken battered and fried," he said in amusement. "I think you'll like them."

I ordered the chicken tenderloins, a salad, and fried okra, which I had never eaten, but it's become a favorite. All my food was delicious, including the cup of peach cobbler topped with ice cream David ordered for each of us.

After eating, we drove to a large art studio. David whisked me around the place and showed me some of his favorite pieces, and we met several of the artists and chatted with them about their work. A middle-aged woman spotted David, waved, and we walked over to her booth where huge paintings of vibrant blooms blazed from large canvases. The array of flowers took my breath away.

"Allie, this is Kathryn Bolton, the president of the Denver Art Council," David said. "Kathryn, this is my friend, Allie Cooper. She's a pretty good artist in her own right."

"Nice to meet you," I said, reaching to shake her hand.

"You, too." She didn't shake, and her eyes scrutinized me in one swift glance that passed from my wild, unruly hair down to my worn coat and blue, flowered skirt. Her look said *country bumpkin*. She turned her attention to David and another artist who joined us.

Men don't notice these things. I'm sure David didn't. She might as well have stabbed me with a dagger. She wore a long gray dress that showed off her slender body, and her coif of black curls adorned her head like a crown. Beside her, I looked like an Appalachian hillbilly.

From then on, I pasted a polite smile on my face and followed David around. I met so many people that my head spun, and once in a while someone asked my opinion, which I offered. A little after three David asked if I were ready to go.

"Yes. This has been an exciting day, but I'm getting tired."

Outside, the snow swirled around us. David turned to walk up the street to the parking lot where he had parked his car. Across the street, a flash of brown caught my attention, a small brown dog with white feet. Boots! I dashed into the street to cross over, and the wail of a car horn blasted my ears. The car whizzed past me, brushing against my leg and sending me tumbling back onto the sidewalk.

"Allie!" David rushed to my side, his strong arms lifting me. "Are you okay?"

"I think so. My leg got scratched up." I pulled up my skirt and showed him a scrape going from my knee down to my ankle. Blood seeped from its middle.

"Why did you run into the street?"

"I saw Boots, my little dog. I'm sure it was Boots." My leg hurt, but the tears that spilled down my cheeks sprang from the pain at seeing Boots and thinking about Dee Dee's betrayal.

David scanned the parking lot across the street. "I don't see any dog," he said. "Come, let's get you home."

I dried my eyes on my sleeve, and leaning on David's arm, limped to the car. As I got in, my skirt pulled up, and three inches of my leg showed through a hole in the material. My favorite skirt. Tears again filled my eyes.

"You okay? I shouldn't have let go of you," David said.

"I feel so stupid. I'm sorry for embarrassing you. Dee-Dee must have been at the art show. I know that was Boots."

"It's okay. We all do stupid things sometimes." He reached over and patted my knee.

I knew what I did was stupid. He didn't have to say it. I was sure he meant it in a kind way, but even his pat on my knee made me feel like a little child.

"So what did you think of the art show?"

"I didn't know there were that many artists in Denver. It was great to meet all those people even though I couldn't keep them straight."

"Did you see anything you liked?"

"Kathryn Bolton's flowers. They were so real."

"Yes, she has a large audience and sells a lot."

I could hear a trace of envy in his voice, but said nothing as he pulled in front of Artistic Horizons. I turned to him. "Thanks for taking me to lunch and to the art show. It was a lot of fun."

"You're welcome. I wished it had turned out differently for you." His blue eyes gazed into mine, but I wasn't sure what they were saying. "Do you want me to come in and help with your leg?"

"No, thanks. I'll be alright."

He came around and opened my car door, then unlocked the door of the store for me. He didn't kiss me or anything, just put his arm around me and said, "See you later." As soon as I took care of my leg, I was going to go ask Gertie what was wrong with him that he wouldn't even kiss a girl after a date.

CHAPTER 36

GERTIE'S GIFT

GERTIE USHERED ME INSIDE AFTER I knocked. "How's your day been?" she asked.

"Good and bad."

"Tell me about it." She sat down in her chair and wrapped her afghan around her.

"David took me to Black Eye Pea, and we had the best lunch, and then we went to an art show."

"Oh?" A worried expression flitted across her face, but then she said, "That's nice."

"Part of it was nice. This woman at the art show made me feel like a hick…you know, an unfashionable backwoods person." I sighed. "I wish I had some new clothes, something besides these skirts and blouses that Aunt Harriet made me." *Oh, that sounded terrible!* "I mean, Aunt Harriet did the best she could with what she had…"

"You always look nice, dear. There's nothing wrong with your skirts and blouses. And I see you have some new boots."

"Yes. But I did something really stupid, and I tore my favorite skirt." The thought of Boots and the tear in my skirt choked me up. "And I feel so badly about putting David through all that."

She reached over to the sofa and patted my arm. "Tell me what happened."

"I saw Boots. He was my little dog, and someone stole him. I forgot where I was and ran out into the street, and well, a car almost ran over me, but all it did was knock me down." I pulled up my skirt and showed her my leg. "I tore my skirt."

"Bring it over, and I'll see what I can do to sew it up," she said. "Is there something else bothering you?"

"David." I gathered my courage. "He acts like he wants me for a girlfriend. Once he kissed my forehead, and twice he's held my hand, and he's always kind, but that's all. He takes me out, but he never…you know."

"Kisses you."

"Yes, that's it."

"He suffered a terrible loss when Nancy died. And I hate to tell you this, but he asked Marty to marry him, and she ran off to college instead. You'll have to give him some time."

"I see." It all made sense, but what she told me did nothing to ease my mind. He was probably still in love with Marty.

"I wish David had taken you to church. We have such a sweet little congregation, and I'm sure you would make friends. And you need to know God and Jesus and what they did for you."

"My aunt and uncle never took me to church. I wouldn't know what to do."

"You listen, Allie, and you let God's words sink into your heart. And you talk to Him in prayer, and you sing songs of praise and love to our God and Father for all His wonderful gifts. That's what you do."

"I don't know," I said, squirming. Our conversation made me think about Uncle Deb and his not letting me read his Bible, and thinking about Uncle Deb made me sad.

"Would you like to go with us some time?" She reached over and put her hand on my shoulder. "Don and Laura have a big car, and I'm sure there'd be room for all of us."

"Maybe. When I have time. I'm working extra at the store through Christmas, and I need to paint and sell more pictures, and I have to go grocery shopping and do laundry. Sunday's my only day off."

"I want to give you something." She pushed herself up from her chair, grasped one side of her walker and turned it around, then headed down the hall. When she returned, she handed me a book.

The words *Holy Bible* adorned its front. Some of the gold lettering had flaked off, but what was left shimmered on the worn black leather cover. Inside on the first page I read:

> *To my wife, Gertie Hammond, with all my love. May our love for God and His commandments bind us together always. Much love, Arno, December 25, 1955.*

"I can't take this." I gave it back to her, stunned that she would give me such a precious family heirloom. "What would David and Laura say? What would Doug and Linda think?"

"They have Bibles, and you don't. Besides, it doesn't belong to them. It belongs to me, and I want you to have it." She placed it on my lap. "Please take it."

I turned its brittle pages, some torn around the edges, others coming loose from the binding, but most marked with notes and scriptures written in a tiny, neat hand around the margins of the page. My hands trembled as I realized what lay in my lap. This Bible was the story of Gertie's lifelong study and labor.

"I don't even know where to start," I said, closing the book and caressing its cover.

"Start from the beginning, the first book, Genesis. It tells about God creating our world. Or if that is too overwhelming, start with the book of Luke, my favorite gospel that tells about Jesus."

She reached over and turned the pages forward, so familiar with the Bible she could find her place even with it a distance from her and upside down. Flipping to the inside of the front cover, she pulled out a gold cord and put it where Luke started.

"Do me a favor. Promise me you'll read at least one chapter from Luke every night. That's all I ask."

"I'll try." I thought about Aunt Harriet. "Aunt Harriet wasn't buried or anything. I donated her body to medical study."

"From what you've told me, I'm sure that would be fine with her."

I think she suspected the reason I did it. But ever since that terrible morning when I gave her body to medical study, an idea had been troubling me. "Aunt Harriet probably got all cut up. Do you think she can still go to heaven?"

"My dear Allie, this body is not what goes to heaven. God gives our soul a new, glorious body, with no pain, no sickness, no dying. We live forever with Him."

"Is that in the Bible too?"

"Yes. I'll show you where." She tore two strips of paper from an envelope. "I'm going to put one here in 1 Corinthians 15," she said, finding a spot, "and another here." She went to the back of the Bible. "Right here in Revelation. You go home and read those places, too, and you'll see how wonderful it is to be a child of God and look forward to the resurrection and being in heaven with God."

It was almost eight o'clock. I said goodbye, and as I went out the door, Gertie said, "Call me if you have any questions. I hope you come back to talk about Luke and these other passages as soon as you read them."

"I will." I hugged her and left, but on the walk home, many questions about God tormented me.

CHAPTER 37

ART THIEVES

THE NEXT FRIDAY, DAVID CALLED. "Howdy, howdy! News about Lettie. The police searched her apartment. No evidence she was painting copies. Her phone held a clue, though. She sent the images of the copied works to Madam Kay. They obtained a search warrant for Madam Kay's room. Further evidence led them to Master's bedroom and office. Madam Kay was the one painting the copies and selling them at art studios and on her website. She split the money with Master. Can you believe it?"

"Wow! Sounds like a movie!"

"Yes. And guess what? The state is shutting down the academy while the police do a complete investigation. Master, Madam Kay, and Lettie made bond and will have a trial next April."

"I can't believe it. But now we won't have students shopping at Artistic Horizons."

"True. But my portrait of Nancy would have been the next on the illegal market. I need to take you out for dinner sometime for a reward."

As a reward? *Why not because you like me and want to be with me?*

"See you later," he said and hung up.

Then George called. "The environmental committee met this morning. I showed them your painting, and they fell in love with it. Allison, you have such a talent. Your animals look like they could walk and fly off the canvas. When are you going to open your own studio or art shop?"

"When I have a million dollars," I said with a chuckle.

"Oh, I bet it wouldn't take that much. Think about it." Before I had a chance to reply, he said, "Did I tell you that I started taking a course so I can get my real estate license? My dad just opened his own firm, and he wants me to join him."

"In Puttersville? Come on now, in the little town of Puttersville? Where are you going to find anything to sell?"

"Puttersville is growing. People are building homes here and driving into nearby larger cities to work. That's another reason we don't want the environment messed up. By the way, you should be getting your check in a week to ten days."

A couple young men came in to buy paint brushes. I told George I had to go, but his call elated me. The environmental committee loved my painting. They would pay me five hundred dollars, money to put in a checking account. And when November was over, David and Laura would owe me one hundred. Someday soon I hope to be earning a living with my art.

Last night, I mulled over the idea of starting a line of wild life and animal paintings that would be my specialty, something like Kathryn Dolton did with her flower art. Only mine would be for children. Of course the first one I planned to do was of Boots.

Gertie called. "I have some cookies and tea to share. Could we have a short visit tonight?"

"I can come for a little while." Then I remembered. I had not been reading in the Bible she gave me.

She greeted me with a smile. "Sorry for such short notice. I've been thinking about you all day. I was hoping Laura and the girls would come, but they're practicing for a Thanksgiving program at school. Want to help me get the tea?"

I placed the cups on a tray, added the bag of cookies she got from the counter, and carried them into the living room coffee table. Wrapping her afghan around her lap and legs, she reached for a cup of tea.

"Doug and Linda called today. They're coming home for Christmas. I just had to tell someone." She picked up a photo from the table and handed it to me. "Here they are when they came for Nancy's funeral a year ago."

Doug's sandy hair was thinning, and a bald spot showed through the hair on the top of his head. Linda's long brown hair curled onto her dark coat. A haunting sadness filled both their eyes.

"Their faith is so strong," Gertie said. "Anyone else might have given up their faith at losing a grandchild." Tears filled her eyes. "I thought I was a strong Christian, but I struggled for several months. Why would a good God take away such an innocent child? We prayed so hard."

"Maybe God didn't hear you."

"God always hears our prayers." She sighed. "I think He knows something about the future we don't. Who knows? Perhaps He knew that Nancy's life would be miserable. Or maybe He was sparing her from a more agonizing death by taking her."

"Or maybe He couldn't heal her."

"No, no, Allie, don't say that. God is all-powerful. All things are possible with God. Someday, though, we'll understand."

I wanted to know why now. Uncle Deb's death I could comprehend, but I didn't know why God let Trag kill Aunt Harriet when she helped him so much. It wasn't fair. Nancy's cruel disease and death weren't fair either.

"You look troubled, child."

"It's cruel that innocent people die. Why does God let that happen?"

"I think God sees death differently than we do. The Bible says that the death of God's saints is precious in His sight. He wants us to be with Him."

"I would rather have Aunt Harriet and Uncle Deb here. Not there."

"Yes, me too. But I'm not God to know why He took Nancy."

Part of me, no, all of me rebelled against what she said. If God were all-powerful, He could have made Nancy well. He could have stopped Uncle Deb from falling, and He would have prevented Trag from shooting Aunt Harriet. What happened makes no sense.

"It's late. I'd better get home and start painting."

"Thanks for coming," Gertie said as I carried the tray back into her kitchen. "When you read more in your Bible, maybe God's way of thinking will be clearer."

"Maybe." I gave her a hug. "Thanks for the tea and cookies."

Walking home, my mind was too tired to think any more of what God could and would do. My thoughts turned to my line of animal paintings for children and the expressions I could draw on each face. I couldn't wait to finish my new painting of Boots and put it in the window display.

CHAPTER 38

RED ROCKS

AFTER DAVID PAID ME FOR my evening work, I ran down to Little Miss and bought my first pair of jeans. I put them on that morning and wished I had a mirror to see how I looked. David invited me to go with him to Red Rocks, a giant outdoor amphitheater.

He picked me up at ten. When I stepped outside, he got out to open the car door, but stopped and whistled. "Love your jeans, Allie Pally." I giggled, and he said, "Want to take your art bag? There's some mighty beautiful scenery up there. I'm going to finish my painting for Mr. and Mrs. Hank."

I went back after my bag, and we headed out of town and onto C-470 that took us to Morrison. From there we took another road up into the mountains. Soon we pulled into a parking lot, and David put on his backpack. We grabbed our art bags and walked up a steep flight of steps onto a road that led to the upper level of the Red Rocks Amphitheatre.

With almost every step, I paused to gaze at the giant red boulders that jutted their craggy heads toward heaven. Their sheer sides plummeted earthward, and as I turned, another rose in front of us.

David led the way through the door. We stopped to read some plaques inside telling a little about Red Rock's history and showing fossils of a fern and some dinosaur tracks.

"You're going to be wowed by this," David said as we came to an entrance with *Red Rock Performers Hall of Fame* written above it. The walls showcased the names and pictures of dozens of famous musicians who had performed there from the time it opened in 1941 until the present.

"Look, the Beatles. Willie Nelson. The Bee Gees. John Denver." David pointed to each as I walked by his side, my head swirling. "Which one would you like to see?"

"I...I don't know. I've heard of the Beatles, but who are the rest of these people?"

"You don't know who Willie Nelson is? Never heard of John Denver?"

"No. We didn't have a radio or a television."

"Surely you heard about them at school."

"Guess music wasn't my focus, and I didn't talk much to the other students."

He turned to gaze at me with a look of disbelief, his forehead wrinkled in puzzlement. "Where did you live, in a cave somewhere? The Grateful Dead, Joe Bonamassa, Barenaked Ladies, Rebelution, and many more have been here. But I suppose you never heard of them, either."

I shook my head. How could I explain my escape from reality? Perhaps it wasn't an escape, but I had my world and he had his.

"Well, I guess all this means nothing to you, so we might as well eat."

We entered the Ship Rock Grille, and the waitress led us to a table near the window overlooking the terrace. I couldn't take my eyes from the view of the mountain outside.

We ordered sandwiches, fruit, and iced tea. While we ate, I gazed at the breathtaking scenery.

"Beautiful, isn't it?" he said. "I'd like to eat on the terrace, but they're working on the building, and we'd be in the way."

I nodded. He again stared at me as if I were from outer space. "I can't believe you've never heard of those performers. You seem so naïve, so childlike at times. I think you need an education in many ways."

Was he the one who would give me such an education? If so, I would gladly allow his tutoring and protection, but that wasn't what his face was telling me. Maybe I was a curiosity to him, not someone he would care for and fix. "I think you're a little strange too," I said.

"Oh, you do, do you?" The old sparkle and tease, the David I loved, was back. "In what way?"

"You never talk about your parents. Gertie told me they were missionaries in Honduras. You should be proud. But you've never said a word about them."

"Proud that they left my senior year in high school, just left me with Laura and Don to run off and help some poor little foreign kids, and didn't even go to my high school graduation?" His face was hard. "Proud that when Nancy was so sick they were thousands of miles away and not here for us?"

"Gertie said they've been there three years, and they came back for Nancy's funeral."

"Her memory isn't great. It's been six years. And they came back, yes, but by then it was too late."

"I'm sorry. I didn't realize. I hear they're coming home for Christmas."

"Let's go paint."

We picked up our bags and took the steps down to the level that opened onto a large plaza above the amphitheater. At each side of the plaza, broad steps curved as they descended down into the seating area. About thirty feet down the rows of seats, David took a thick blanket from his backpack and spread on one of the concrete seats. Reaching into his bag, he pulled out a pair of binoculars and focused them.

"Look," he said, putting the binoculars to my eyes. "Can you see Denver? The whole downtown area?"

"Yes, and it's beautiful."

"This is one of the few places where you can see all of downtown Denver, and it's what I'm painting for the Hanks." He settled down with his canvas and paints and got to work, every once in a while holding the binoculars up to his eyes. "What are you going to paint?"

"That boulder." I pointed to a huge boulder towering over the side of the theater. "See the small tree clinging to its side, holding on for dear life? It reminds me of me. That's how I feel in this world."

"Guess we all do. Think of the winds that have howled around that little tree, doing their best to rip it from its roots, but it has held fast. That's what we have to do, just hold on."

I smiled and began working, every once in a while peeking over his shoulder to see his progress. He didn't notice, so deep into his work I think he forgot I was there. After two hours, I put the last touches on my eight-by-ten canvas. "I'm finished," I said.

"I've finished enough for today, but I'll add some small touches at home," he said. "We're going to go back a different way. There's some place I want to take you." His grin was impish.

It took us ten minutes to get back down the road and steps to his car. We left the parking lot and turned onto a highway that wound and turned through the countryside.

"Have you been following the news about Master, Madam Kay, and Lettie?" he asked.

"No. I don't have a television, and I can't afford the newspaper."

"Right. You're the girl living in her own world."

"I'm the girl working overtime at your store and trying to get her own line of artwork started," I snapped. "I don't have time for television and newspapers."

"Sorry. What I said was mean, and I'm going to make it up to you." He turned up the hill to a small shopping center and parked. "You're in for a treat," he said, getting out and opening my door. We walked into a small store with McGill's painted on the sign above the door.

"Pick two," he said, pointing to a long counter fronted by glass.

"So many hard choices." I scanned the rows of round containers holding different flavors of ice cream and frozen yogurt. "I'll take seven-layer coconut and fudgy peanut butter," I told the woman behind the counter.

She handed me a small slip of paper. "Circle any toppings you want."

I chose hot chocolate syrup, peanut chocolate crunch candy, marshmallow topping, and a cherry. We carried our sundaes to a table and sat down, and I dipped my spoon into the chocolaty lava spilling down the side of the mound of ice cream and sending whiffs of rich chocolate to my nose.

"This is the best place to buy ice cream," David said. "And about our art thieves. Master and Madam Kay pled guilty, so they won't have a trial. They'll be sentenced next week. Lettie said Master threatened her with the loss of her job if she didn't help them. She's pleading not guilty, so her trial is still on this April."

"How can she say she's not guilty when she's just said they made her do it?"

"Good question. If there is a trial, you may be called to testify."

"I hope not. I always liked Lettie."

"Me too." He was scraping the last spoonful of ice cream from the sides of his bowl.

We left, and the ride to Artistic Horizons was too short. David parked in his usual spot in front of the shop, then came around to open my door. "I'd come in and talk awhile, but I've got to finish this painting. I hope you had a good time."

"I had a wonderful time." I found my keys and opened the door to Artistic Horizons as he got into his car, backed out, and roared down the street. I stood there, staring after him in disbelief. He didn't even wave goodbye.

CHAPTER 39

SWEET THINGS

MONDAY, I RECEIVED MY CHECK from the Puttersville Environmental Committee. Five hundred dollars, the biggest check I ever received for selling my art. After depositing it in my checking account Tuesday morning, I had the urge to run down to the clothing store and buy more jeans and a new coat, but I squelched it. Who knows what needs I might have in the future?

Wednesday, Laura told me that Master and Madam Kay had each been sentenced to five years in prison with the possibility of parole after three years, plus they could never operate an art school in Colorado. I don't feel a bit ashamed that my heart rejoiced.

Thursday night I finished my second painting for my new line of animal art. The first painting was of Boots and the second of a little gold-striped kitten I saw that week. They were not coloring book animals, but perhaps neither are they entirely realistic. I hid my initials in both paintings. I was going to call my art ABC Designs until I learned another art store in Denver was called ABC Art. So I realized I might have to reconsider the name.

Friday, as soon as I got to work, I called Gertie and asked if I could bring my pictures over for her appraisal.

"I'd love to see them," she said. She was becoming more and more like a mother to me, the only one I had to share secrets with and ask for advice.

My little dog and cat paintings were not framed, so after the store closed, I tucked them into my bag, locked up, and headed for Gertie's house. She opened the door at my first touch of her doorbell.

"Come in, dear. Let's have a spot of tea and a cookie."

I followed her into her kitchen and helped her load the cups and cookies onto the tray, then carried them into the living room where we took our customary seats. "Give me your honest opinion," I said, handing her my paintings.

She studied them for a few moments. Smiling, she said, "I see your signature in the picture of the kitten," and she pointed out the *A*, *B*, and *C*.

"So what do you think?"

"I like them, and I think most children would, since that is your audience. But…" and she pointed to a spot on my drawing of the kitten, "you must have been in a hurry here. See how the brown paint runs over the gold?"

"Oops." She was right. I was in a hurry to get them done. "I can fix it. Thanks for finding that mistake." That's all she found, but it taught me a lesson. Children might not notice little things, but parents and other relatives do.

"I told you Doug and Linda are coming for Christmas."

"Yes. I bet you're excited."

"I am, and Laura and Don and their girls are happy, but David's not. I don't know what's wrong with that boy. He won't go to church anymore, and he's angry and upset with his parents."

"I think he believes they abandoned him," I said gently. "I'm sure he feels that way about God, too."

"God doesn't abandon us. Troubles come, but He sees us through them."

"God didn't heal Nancy."

"No, and we don't know why." She sighed. "We just have to trust Him."

The door opened and David strode in. "Hey, hey, hey! I brought something sweet, you're in for a treat." Laughing, he put a drink tray holding three domed paper cups onto the coffee table. "Who wants a chocolate mint swirl?"

"Thanks, but will you put mine in the freezer? It's almost bedtime."

"Sure, Grandma." He headed to the kitchen with a cup.

"How'd he know I was here?" I whispered to Gertie.

He was back before she answered. Handing me a cup, he sat down beside me. "Someone told me you finished your paintings. May I see them?"

I wished he wouldn't see them until I fixed the mistake Gertie found, but I pulled them out of my bag. "Gertie found a little oopsie here, but I can fix it," I said, pointing it out.

"Not bad, not bad at all," he said, holding them out at arm's length. "Tomorrow afternoon I'll help you frame them, and then I'll take photos and put them on your web page."

"Thanks." I tucked them into my bag.

"Another matter," David said. "Thanksgiving will be here soon." He took my hand. "Laura asked me to invite you. We want you to eat with us Thanksgiving Day."

"Yes, Allie," Gertie said. "We all gather at Laura's house. Please come."

"I'd like that." My heart pounded as David clasped my hand in his warm one.

"Good. It's settled then. I'll come pick you up around eleven." He let go of my hand. "It's getting late. Can I offer you a ride home?"

"That would be nice." I hugged Gertie, then picked up my bag and the drink I had barely touched.

"Bye, Grandma. See you soon." David said as we walked out the door. He held my swirl while I got into the car, and I held his.

Instead of turning toward Artistic Horizons, he turned down another street. "Do you mind if we go for a little drive?"

"Not at all. Where to?"

"Oh, just around." Turning off the road, we entered a well-lit park. "Care to walk?"

"Okay." I put down the cup and got out when he opened the door. I let him lead me to a bench under a light a little distance into the park.

"Have a seat. Can we talk?"

"Of course." I sat down and he sat beside me.

He took my hand. "Allie, I feel we are developing a…a friendship. Know what I mean?"

I hoped I knew what he meant, but I wasn't sure, so I nodded.

"We've been out together a few times. Let's call them what they were, dates. At least that's what I wanted them to be. Do you feel that way?"

"I think so."

"Okay, so dates. Yet I've never kissed you, never told you how I feel." He sighed. "That's because I don't know how I feel. I can't right now. You see—"

"You're still in love with Marty."

"I wish I knew. I wanted to marry her, to give Nancy a home with two parents, but she said that wasn't a good reason to get married. So she's off to some college now trying to make up her mind. Contrary to the old saying, absence does not make the heart grow fonder."

"I see."

"Allie, I like you a lot, but I'm still so hurt I don't know how to fall in love again. Can you give me some time?"

"So I'm supposed to sit around, just waiting to see what happens with you and Marty?"

"No. I didn't mean it that way." He put his hands on my shoulders and turned me toward him. "Allie, look at me. All I want is some time for my heart to heal and learn to love again. Can you give me that?"

Part of me shouted *No! I want a man wholly committed to me.* The other part of me longed to be his, to give him that time, so I whispered, "I'll try."

"Thank you." He stood. "Let's go. I'm getting cold." Then he wrapped his arm around my shoulders, and we walked back to the car.

We drove to Artistic Horizons, and he got out and opened my door, then got my bag out of the back seat. "I want to keep seeing you," he said, handing me my bag. "I mean, outside of work."

"I would like that too."

"Happy, happy, joy, joy. See you tomorrow." He turned to get into his car.

I unlocked the shop door and waved at him as he pulled out. That night I tossed in bed for over an hour, wondering if I should shout for happiness or cry because after all he said and did, he still hadn't even kissed me.

CHAPTER 40

THANKSGIVING

AS I GOT READY FOR Thanksgiving with David's family, trepidation filled me. We hadn't had a date since that night at the park. I saw him at work, where he made frames for my dog and cat paintings, took photos of them for my web page, and we displayed them in the shop window. He said he had too much work to do, even though I'd finished the inventory and stayed a couple hours over last Saturday so he could build frames for his paintings for the Hanks. Sunday he said he had to finish the last painting, and he was working on it at home, so we did nothing.

My painting of Boots sold, and after work, I ran to the bank and then to Little Miss and purchased a dress for Thanksgiving. I chose something different from my schoolgirl skirts and blouses–a medium brown dress with short sleeves and a straight skirt that narrowed to just below my knees. The neckline, adorned with tan and ivory roses, complemented the belt with an ivory and tan buckle.

Of course I couldn't show up in a new dress and my old coat, so I splurged on a short sweater in the same ivory. Staring at my face in the small mirror in the bathroom, I pulled my hair back and pinned it up behind my ears, but let it flow down my neck and back. *If I had a pretty comb like Aunt Harriet's, it would complete my new look. What happened to her things and her truck, especially the truck? I could get my driver's license and use it. How I wish I could have her things.* I didn't even have any makeup, so after fixing my hair, I put on my sweater and went out front to wait for David.

He arrived on time. He let out a low whistle as he opened the car door for me and said, "Is this my Allie Pally I see?"

"Just Allie," I said, getting in. The "Allie Pally" thing was starting to irk me. I didn't want to be his "Pally," but his girlfriend.

"Okay." He shrugged and got in. I feared I had offended him, but he turned and smiled. "You look very nice today. Is that a new dress?"

"Yes. I wanted something different."

"Well, it suits you, and I like it…and you," he said with a chuckle. "I was at Laura's this morning helping with a few last-minute details. The house smelled delicious. What did your family do for Thanksgiving?"

"One time Aunt Harriet's friend came, and Uncle Deb shot a wild turkey. We decorated the house with leaves and dried flowers." That was the only time I can remember Thanksgiving being special, and I hoped he didn't ask anything else. Looking back, I couldn't recall Thanksgiving as a celebrated day most years. No big meals, no family coming to visit, just work as usual.

"I'm glad grocery stores have turkeys and we don't have to go out and shoot one," he said, laughing.

"Did you get all your pictures for the Hanks finished?"

"Yes, just about done. That reminds me. They live in Colorado Springs, and I'm going to take them down this Sunday. Want to go?"

"I'd love to."

"Good. They'll pay me, and we can take in the town." His eyes laughed as he parked in front of Laura's house. "On second thought, some sweet thing has been working so hard, I'll owe it all to her."

We got out and walked into the house. David introduced me to Laura's husband Don, who shook my hand and welcomed me. "The girls are in the kitchen," he said.

Gertie was heating rolls in the toaster oven, and Laura was carrying dishes laden with food into the dining room. Following her cue, I picked up a salad and took it to the table.

"So glad you could come," Laura said. "I want you to meet my girls. They're downstairs playing in the family room." Turning the corner, she stood at the top of a staircase that led to the basement and yelled, "Diana, Lilah, come up and meet Allie."

Two little girls with light brown hair ran up the stairs, their giggles bouncing off the walls. "I'm Diana," the one in front said. "I'm nine."

"I'm Lilah," the younger girl said. "Seven." She held up seven fingers.

"Allie helps us at the store," Laura said. "Say 'hi' to her."

"Hi, Allie," they chimed in unison.

"It's time for lunch, so please go wash your hands," Laura said, and giggling, they disappeared down a hallway.

"Let's go ahead and get seated," Laura said. She pointed to the dining table. "Allie, you and David are on the front with Gertie. The girls can sit in the back, and Don and I are on the ends.

We all took our seats. I stared at the fancy dishes and tall stemmed glasses, embroidered napkins surrounding the polished eating utensils, and the array of food covering the table. Don gave thanks for all the food, their blessings, their family, then added David, Gertie, and me, then the store, his job, and their house. I sat there like a little kid, my stomach growling and my impatience growing as steam from mashed potatoes, gravy, and green bean casserole wafted up my nose.

Don cut slices off the turkey resting in a decorated platter on his end of the table while Laura spooned food onto the girls' plates and passed the bowls to us. I put a spoonful of each offering on my plate and began eating, savoring the cranberry sauce and dressing, foods I had never tasted.

"Good, huh?" David asked between bites.

"Delicious, wonderful," I said. "Thank you, Don and Laura. I don't think I've eaten food this tasty."

"You're welcome," Don said. "Enjoy."

After all that food, came pumpkin pie with whipped topping, and even though I already was full to the top of my throat, I had a slice and hoped my belt wouldn't be too tight.

"Want to watch the games with me and Don?" David asked when we finished.

I wasn't sure which games he meant, and he saw the question on my face and laughed. "Football games on TV. They're on all day."

"Thanks, but I'll help clean up," I said.

"Okay." He followed Don into the living room.

"I think I'll join them," Gertie said, holding to the table and pulling herself up.

I pushed her walker over to her, then joined Laura in rinsing the dishes and putting them in the dishwasher. As soon as we finished, we heard the girls calling from downstairs.

"They probably want us to play with them," Laura said. "Let's go see."

We spent the next hour in the family room downstairs playing house and dress-up and doctor with Diana being the doctor and Lilah the patient. Laura and I were nurses. Inside an hour they were calling me "Aunt Allie." Someday maybe I will be their aunt.

Laura put a DVD of a children's show on for the girls, and we sat and talked on the other end of the long room.

"I took Gertie to the doctor yesterday. Her heart is getting weaker." She sighed. "She'll be eighty-five in January. We've been fortunate that her health has been good this long."

"Yes. Gertie has been so kind to me. She's almost like my own mother."

"You mean a lot to her, too. Thanks for keeping her company when we can't."

"Christmas is coming. What can I get her?"

Laura walked over to a small table and picked up a photo of Diana and Lilah sitting together, taken from the side. "She wants a copy of this picture to hang in her bedroom. Could you paint one for her?"

"Of course. What size?"

"Eight by ten would be nice."

"Thanks, I'll do it," I said, wishing I had brought my bag.

"One other thing would make her very happy. Can you go to church with us Christmas Day?"

"She has asked me several times. I'll try."

"Good. We'll pick you up at nine Christmas morning. Let's go see how the guys are doing."

Upstairs, we found Gertie and Don asleep in their chairs. David was stretched out on the couch with his feet on its arm. As we entered the room, he sat up.

"Ready to go home? I mean, you don't have to go now, but if you're ready, I'll take you."

"I'm ready, if you don't mind missing your ballgame."

"Just college stuff." He laughed. "Now if the Broncos were playing, you'd have to stay until the game ended."

Laura came from the kitchen carrying a rectangular plastic container with a lid. "Here's a few leftovers for your dinner," she said. "Hope you had a good time. We enjoyed having you."

"I had a wonderful time. Thanks so much, Laura. And thank Don for me, and please tell Gertie and your girls good-bye."

After we pulled onto the street, David grinned. "You fit in our family just fine," he said. "But then I knew you would." Unexpectedly, he pulled into a parking lot, bent toward me, and kissed me on the lips.

Tears sprang to my eyes as I looked into his face. "What was that for?"

"To show you that you're mine, and I appreciate your helping Laura today and being there for Gertie."

He pulled out onto the street and headed for Artistic Horizons. Once there, he helped me out of the car. "Thanks for being with us today, Allie. Oh, since tomorrow is Black Friday, we open the store at eight o'clock instead of nine. Think you can go in an hour early? Laura has an appointment."

"It'll cost you double," I said.

"In cold cash or kisses?"

"Both. And I'm holding you to it." With that I unlocked the door, and heart beating out of my chest, turned to wave goodbye. His car was already down the street.

CHAPTER 41

COLORADO SPRINGS

SUNDAY, I BOUNCED OUT OF bed and peeked out my window at a world wrapped in a blanket of snow. After putting on my jeans, I microwaved two frozen sausage patties, made some toast and instant coffee, and sat down to a warm breakfast. My shabby coat hung over a chair in the corner, and I stared at it with loathing. I couldn't wear it, not when David was taking me to Colorado Springs. I wanted to look nice.

Just before ten, I walked down the hall and opened the door. A gust of wind caught the door and tore it from my hands as I stepped out. Shivering, I bolted back inside and dashed back to my apartment to retrieve my coat.

When I returned to the shop, David's car waited out front. I ran to the door he was holding open and climbed in. The glistening snow reminded me of the time I made animal statues of snow for Uncle Deb and Aunt Harriet, and I laughed.

"What's funny?" David asked as he got behind the wheel.

"Memories of my snow animals. And I'd rather laugh than cry." Sometimes the strangest little things could bring tears to my eyes. I still missed them.

"CDOT reports that I-25 is in pretty good shape," he said after studying me a moment.

"CDOT?"

"CDOT is the Colorado Department of Transportation. And I-25 is the highway we're taking to Colorado Springs," he said, a teasing smile on his face.

He's making fun of me. I shrank down in my seat and struggled to keep my monsters shut in, to remain affable and smiling, the kind of person he would want to be around. *You're not a schoolgirl anymore.* "I've never been to Colorado Springs," I said, a smile pasted on my face.

"I know. I'm just trying to be helpful." He reached over to take my hand.

He wasn't the type to put me down. The heaviness pressing on me like a lead cloak slid off, and my love deepened. I realized that to rid myself of the demons that threatened to take over my life, I needed someone to envelop me in love and guide me through life's hazards.

Not that I was a weak woman. I could tell I wasn't, not because of all the hardships and suffering I had survived, but I believed there was a limit to the number of hits my soul could take before it was completely worn down, pounded into the ground like so much mud, and there was no more me. I didn't want to go there.

"How far is it to Colorado Springs?"

"About an hour, depending on traffic and road conditions. We pass through a couple smaller cities first, Castle Rock and Monument. And we'll go past the Air Force Academy. We turn off to the Hanks' house soon after."

He let go of my hand as he merged onto I-25 and eased the car into the left lane. The time flew as we chatted about painting and the techniques he used in the pictures he did for the Hanks. I learned more from him than I did during the few weeks I was at the academy.

We pulled off the freeway onto a street heading east, then turned right onto a different street. Two-story stone houses with three-car garages and expansive driveways lined the streets. It was a world I could see, yet for me, a universe away.

"I'll just sit in the car while you deliver your paintings," I said as he pulled up the driveway of one of the larger homes.

"No, no, you have to see their art collection," he said, coming around and opening my door. "Besides, I need you to help me carry these in."

I got out, and he handed me two paintings wrapped in brown paper, then picked up three larger ones. As I followed him up the steps to the porch, I noticed flower urns holding Christmas greens lining the steps. The doorbell chimed a soft melody when he touched it.

"David, so glad to see you. Come in." A tall man with black hair and beard speckled with gray opened the door. His wife stood behind him, her short black hair tucked behind her ears. I recognized them as the couple who had stopped to watch me paint Boots that desperate day.

"Allie, let me introduce you to Gene and Jeanette Hank. This is my friend Allie Cooper," he said as I shook their hands.

"Yes, we've seen her at your shop," Jeanette said. "Come see our art. We don't have some of our recent purchases up, but I'd like you to see what we have."

She led the way into a large living area. Two walls held probably fifty paintings, and built-in shelves holding smaller works covered a third wall. Their tastes included wilderness and mountain scenes, wild animals, and views of cities.

"Someday we're going to have a book made," she said.

"I'm sure a book full of all these paintings would be treasured," I said.

Gene and David joined us. "What do you think?" Gene asked.

"You have a wonderful collection," I said.

"Oh, you haven't seen them all. The upstairs showroom is in a mess as we're redoing it."

Why would they want so many pictures?

"Will you have some coffee or tea with us?" Jeanette asked.

"Thanks, but we'd better go," David said. "I want to show Allie some of Colorado Springs."

We said our goodbyes and left. As David got behind the wheel, he turned to me. "What did you think of their art?"

"I'd like to have an art gallery but not in my house."

"True, true. Hungry?"

"Yes."

"Let's have Chinese for lunch. I know a good buffet."

I'd never been to a buffet. So many different foods in one place. I had to shop for groceries and do laundry after we got home, and I wouldn't have time for dinner, so I filled two plates.

After leaving the restaurant, David turned onto another street and drove slowly past large brick homes. "Just thought you'd like to see some homes in another part of the Springs," he said, driving down the street, and at one point almost stopping in front of one of the houses.

I didn't care about looking at houses, but I smiled and nodded. It wasn't long before he got on I-25 and headed north toward home.

"I really enjoyed Thanksgiving at Don and Laura's. And Diana and Lilah are so sweet. You're lucky to have family."

"I think they're getting more mischievous as they get older." He laughed, then grew serious. "The demise of the academy has hurt our sales. I wish we could move the shop to a better neighborhood. Somewhere like the Santa Fe Art District or maybe the Navajo Street Art District."

His wish jolted me out of my comfort zone. "That would be great, but what would happen to me? Where would I live?"

"You'd have to find an apartment." He looked down at me with a twinkle in his eyes. "And we'd have to pay you enough to afford one."

The thought of having an apartment that I could decorate and buy furniture for excited me, but I knew David and Laura would have to pay me a lot more. "Do you think you could afford me?"

"I have a friend who works at a shop at the Santa Fe Art District. He says their business has been booming and sales have tripled the last two months. Of course, this is the holiday season. So maybe."

An hour later we left the freeway and were nearly home when I remembered what Laura told me. "Gertie wants me to go to church with her on Christmas Day. I hope you can go with us."

His face soured. "I don't think so."

"Why not?"

"I'm not into church. Not since—" He stopped talking and pulled in front of Artistic Horizons.

I know he was thinking about Nancy's death, so all I said was, "Thanks for taking me with you and for the great lunch. I enjoyed our day."

He leaned over and gave me a quick kiss, then got out to open my door. As I unlocked the door, he climbed into his car and waved as he backed up.

Something was missing. David seemed only too eager to speed away once he dropped me off. Is that a sign of love?

CHAPTER 42

WHAT IS LOVE?

THE FIRST FRIDAY IN DECEMBER I received another letter from George. I tore it open and pulled out the contents. A letter and a check for two hundred dollars! Disbelief filled me, and tears blurred my vision as I read:

Dear Allison,

I received my first full monthly paycheck today, and I'm sending you a part. I have few expenses since I live with my father. I know Denver is cold, and I can imagine you shivering without a coat as I never saw you wear one. Also, you should see the billboards springing up around here, all showing off your drawing and begging people to vote "NO" against allowing Puron Oil to drill and frack. Our special election is in February. I truly wish you could come see the billboards, but I suppose you can't.

I hope you are well and will say good-bye for now.

Your friend,
George

George was right. In the coldest weather, my old coat was not warm enough. So tomorrow before work I planned to go to the bank and then to Little Miss, where I saw a coat I wanted to try on last week but didn't because I didn't want to spend the money. I hoped it was still there.

That afternoon Gertie called and asked if I could come for a visit after work. She had some chili and cornbread, which I love. I couldn't wait to close the shop and walk the few blocks to her house.

"I hope you don't mind canned chili and store-bought cornbread," she said when she opened her door. She turned her walker toward the kitchen and scooted her feet along behind it. She already had the chili in the pan heating on the stove, and she stirred while I set the table and warmed the cornbread in the microwave.

"Laura invited me to go to church with you Christmas Day," I said after she asked the blessing. "I would like to go."

"I wish David would go with us. It breaks my heart that he won't stick his head in a church door. And his father will be preaching the sermon Christmas morning."

"I asked him last Sunday when we were coming back from Colorado Springs. He said no, but I'm going to keep working on him."

"He used to go to the Springs a lot," she said. "Marty's parents live there, you know."

My mind flashed back to the houses he showed me, the street he drove down, and the home we nearly stopped in front of. *It was her parents' house, and he was hoping to see her! That's why he went there!*

"Something wrong, dear? You look upset."

"I'm okay."

"Are you in love with David?"

I stared into my chili. "I don't know. I've never been in love with anybody, so I don't know what it feels like. How am I supposed to feel?"

"Does your heart give a leap when you hear his name? Do you think of him all the time? Does his touch send shivers through your body? Do his kisses make you want to melt into him? But most of all, do you believe in him, what he does, how he thinks, and what he wants to become? Do you want to go where he goes and do what he does? Do you feel like you could spend your whole life with him and never wish for someone else?"

"Is that how I'm supposed to feel?"

"You see, I remember when I was your age and met Arno. I couldn't wait to be with him when he got off work, and I thought about him every second he was away from me. We thought the same way about everything. It was like I had found my soul mate, and the better half of me was missing when we weren't together."

"I don't know," I said after thinking about our last few dates. "At first it was like that, at least a bit. He took my breath away when he first kissed me, even though it was on my forehead, and I trembled when he touched me. And he was so kind and understanding, but I never knew if it was because he wanted me to work at the shop or because he really liked me. Not long ago, when he was taking me home, he stopped in a parking lot and kissed me. He said it meant I was his. I don't want to be owned by him. I don't like it when he calls me 'Allie Pally.' I want to be his girlfriend, but he seems to keep me at arm's length." Tears gathered in my eyes.

"Well, it's like I said," she reached over and patted my hand, "he has been through some traumatic experiences with Nancy and Marty, and I think it's going to take him a while to get his head on straight." Then she asked a question that sent me reeling. "Allie, do you ever pray for David?"

"Pray for him? No, I guess not." I mumbled.

"You ought to, you know. God can change people and circumstances. I pray for David and all my family every day. And you."

I stewed on what she said as I finished my chili. Maybe I had been self-centered, looking at our relationship only from my point of view. Did David think me selfish? Was he afraid to show me how deeply he hurt? Evidently, for it appeared he was afraid to get too close to me. Maybe he was afraid to even try.

After we ate, I cleaned up the dishes and then joined Gertie in her living room. She had an open Bible on her lap.

"Please sit down. Would you like to hear the Christmas story? I'll read it to you out of Luke."

I think she knew I hadn't touched the Bible she gave me since I got it home. "Sure," I said, making myself comfortable on her sofa. Her gentle voice soothed my spirit, and as I listened, images of Uncle Deb reading his Bible flashed through my mind. *Why had he never read the story of Jesus' birth to me? Why didn't we celebrate Christmas?*

"There, I've read through chapter two, verse thirty-nine," Gertie said, closing her Bible and putting it on the coffee table. "What do you think?"

"It was interesting. I've never heard it before."

"Didn't your aunt and uncle have a Bible?"

"Yes, and sometimes Uncle Deb read it to me, but he never read that."

"You never picked up the Bible to read it for yourself?"

"No." My cheeks and neck grew warm as I thought about the time I tried to read his Bible. "But I liked what you read."

"Good. Go home and read it again. I marked Luke in the Bible I gave you, remember?"

"Thanks for everything, Gertie. I enjoyed the chili and cornbread. Guess I'd better get going." I hugged her and walked back to my apartment. Then I took the Bible down and reread the first two chapters of Luke.

That night, I tossed in bed for more than an hour, recalling how she defined love before I drifted off to sleep. Was I really in love with David or did I only want to be in love with David? Did he think about me all the time? Did he miss me when we were apart? Did my kisses thrill him? Did he want what I wanted for our lives, and did he pray for my happiness and well-being? I didn't think so.

CHAPTER 43

IN MY PRAYERS

SUNDAY, DAVID'S CALL WAKENED ME. "Have you looked outside?"

"No. Why?"

"It must've snowed all night. At least a foot. I'm afraid we won't be going to lunch today. Road's too dangerous."

"I'll miss being with you," I said, swallowing my disappointment.

"Me too. Later." He hung up.

The snowplows would've been working all night, and by lunch time, the roads would've been fine. Every time David and I went on a date, he provided the ride, the food, the fun. Maybe he was bored with that routine. I vowed that when I saw him next Saturday, I was going to ask him over for dinner. I saw a lasagna in the freezer section at the grocery that cooks in the microwave. That, a salad and a loaf of French bread would be good. And I'd buy a lemon pie for dessert.

The day before, an elderly woman bought my painting of the gold kitten, so after work, I went to Little Miss to try on that coat. It was gone. I bought gloves for Laura, and hats and gloves for Lilah and Dinah. I'd have to shop somewhere else for Don and David. What should I get David? Shirt and tie? I'd never seen him wear a dress shirt and tie. Painting supplies? He owned a store full. I'd have to think about his gift.

I put on my boots and coat, gathered my laundry, and trudged through the snow to the nearby laundromat. As I pushed quarters into slots in the washers, a surge of thanksgiving filled my heart. The first week living in my little apartment, I did my underwear by hand in the sink and hung it in the bathroom to dry. "Thank you, God," I said to myself, "for the money to buy food, gifts, and to put in these washers and dryers."

After getting home and putting away my clothes, I tackled some housekeeping that I wouldn't have time to do during the week, things like dusting, mopping the linoleum floor, and cleaning off the kitchen counter. I would have loved new curtains for the windows and some pillows for the couch, but these were things I couldn't afford with my limited funds.

"God, I'm surviving. I have a place to live and basic needs. But I'd like a place of my own. I need a car. And God...." I threw my hands toward the heavens. "I want David to love me. To not make excuses to not see me. To act like he cares for me. How am I going to find a better job? How can I open my own art shop and let my art support me? How does a girl make someone love her?" Tears slid down my cheeks.

Crying wouldn't get anything done, so I settled down to my painting, finishing my portrait of Diana and Lilah for Gertie's Christmas present. I had already purchased a mat to go around it, a frame, and non-reflective glass. Tomorrow I would put the portrait in the frame when I was sure it was dry.

The day before, I bought more minutes for my phone. How I wish I could call Aunt Harriet and tell her everything I was doing. This would be my first Christmas without her and Uncle Deb. I poured myself a glass of water, but my hand was shaking so much I put it down before taking a drink. I shoved thoughts of them out of my mind and drank the whole glass without stopping, as if it would fill the empty hole left by their deaths.

After I ate lunch, my phone rang.

"Hi Allison, it's George. How are you?"

"Fine," I said, wondering why he was calling. "How are you doing?"

"Just fine. Did you get my note and check?"

"Yes, thank you." I had put it in the bank, and he should have seen that I'd cashed it. Then it hit me. I was so wrapped up in me, the art store, and David, that I hadn't even bothered to thank him. Shame and guilt flitted through my mind. "I'm sorry. I should have let you know. Thanks for sending it."

"Did you get a coat? Are you warm enough?"

"I'm plenty warm, George. What's up with you?"

"This week I'm finishing my real estate course, and Friday I plan to take the test to get my license. Will you keep me in your prayers?"

My mind skidded to a halt at his request, and after regrouping, I managed to say, "I guess so. Of course."

"Thanks, I keep you in mine." Several moments of silence followed. "Well, I guess I'll go now. Glad I caught you. Bye."

He hung up. I sat there, lost in thought. George kept me in his prayers. I'd known him nearly all my life, but did I really know him? The last time I saw him, he was a chubby man in a rumpled suit, broke and trying to explain to me why I had no money left. He seemed so different now, not at all the man I thought he was.

Falling snow swirled outside my window, and I laid down on the couch and pulled the blanket over me. Again my heart bounded in thankfulness. I could be homeless in the snow, living under a bridge or under a cardboard box. I might be hungry. Maybe I wouldn't have a job, maybe no friends.

I must have drifted off to sleep, for when I wakened, my phone was ringing. It was Gertie.

"Since we can't meet tonight, I thought you might like to read some more of Jesus's story," she said. "Do you have time?"

"I do."

"Why don't you get your Bible so we can read it together?"

I found my Bible and opened it. "What are we reading?"

"Let's start where we left off with Luke chapter two, verse forty. Can you find it?"

"I think so." It took me a minute. "Got it."

She read five verses, then let me read five, and we alternated until we ended the third chapter.

"Do you have any questions?" she asked.

"Did Jesus do any miracles when he was a child?"

"We don't have a record of any in the Bible."

"Can you remind me who John the Baptist was?"

"He was Jesus's cousin, and he was a special messenger sent from God to prepare the way for Christ and His kingdom."

"Gertie, thanks for reading with me tonight. Can we do this every weekend?"

"Any time you like."

I bid her good night, and as I got ready for bed, I thought of how much I had missed out on growing up. I saw Uncle Deb and Aunt Harriet in a different light. Others surely thought them strange when they isolated themselves and me. How I wish they had taken me to church. No wonder I had no friends in school.

Uncle Deb wanted to live isolated from everyone else. Maybe it was his PTSD. But I have learned that living in isolation makes life meaningless. Where would I be without David, Gertie, and their family.

CHAPTER 44

DINNER AT MY PLACE

THE SUNDAY BEFORE CHRISTMAS I awoke excited. David was coming for dinner. At church I prayed, "God, please help me understand him. Don't let me do or say anything stupid. God, I want him to love me so badly. Please help him love me."

A knock on my door announced David's presence a few minutes before six. "Howdy, howdy," he said as he came through the door I held open. He looked around the apartment. "Ah, I can see a woman's touch. Looks so much better than when I stayed here."

"Everything's done. We can eat now if you're hungry."

"I am. Smells good." He sat down at the table, and I scooped out a square of lasagna onto his plate while he poured dressing on his salad.

"Will you ask the blessing?" I asked as I took my seat. "You did the time we first met and you gave me the sandwich." I meant it to bring back good memories, but he frowned.

"Grandma was there. I had to." Then he took my hand and said it.

I opened my eyes and looked into his face. "Lately my heart has been thanking God for all the good things I have. I could be out on the street, hungry and cold. But I found Artistic Horizons, and you and Gertie, and the rest of your family. I feel so blessed."

"Dad and Mom will be flying in this Wednesday. I have to pick them up at the airport." He shrugged. "They don't feel much like family."

"I'm sorry."

"You're invited, by the way. Next Saturday is Christmas Eve." He smiled. "But you probably know that. Anyway, we'll close the shop early, probably around two. We'll all meet at Laura and Don's for an early dinner, and then we'll open gifts."

"And Sunday we'll go to church."

His eyes narrowed and he stared at me. "You'll all go to church. There's something I have to do."

"Oh? Gertie said your father will be speaking at church Christmas morning. What's more important than hearing your father?"

"I'd rather not talk about it. But I'll be with the family Christmas Eve and later for dinner on Christmas Day. I hope everyone understands."

He might as well have said, "I hope *you* understand." I certainly didn't understand. One glance at his obstinate eyes, and his puckered brow told me to leave it alone. I smiled as I served the pie, but a blanket of sadness settled over me. It wouldn't be the same without him at church. Gertie's words, "I couldn't wait to be with him" as she talked about when she and her husband were courting echoed in my mind. Is love so different than it was in her time?

"Good pie. Are you giving out seconds?" he asked, back to his old self, a twinkle in his eyes.

"Sure. Cut whatever size you want." I placed the pie near him, and he helped himself to a two-inch piece.

"I forgot to tell you," I said between bites. "The environmental committee is exhibiting my picture on billboards all over Puttersville. In fact, all over the county."

"I'm proud of you." He reached for my hand. "My little artist is becoming famous."

"If you knew the little hick town of Puttersville, you would know I'm not that famous." I laughed. "Everyone has to start somewhere."

"It's a good start. And I got another commission."

"You did? What for?"

"A local business asked me to paint a picture of their headquarters to display in their foyer. They're paying me a thousand dollars."

"That's wonderful! See, you're becoming so well known that customers are coming to you."

"I'll have to stand out in the cold on the hill above the building to at least sketch the outline. The company website doesn't have a picture of their building. They want it in two weeks."

"You can do it, David. You're good."

"Since the art school where I teach is closed for the next two weeks for the holidays, I can. Otherwise, I wouldn't have time." He rested his head in his hands for a minute, then sighed. "Do you mind if we just hang out here and talk for a while? I'm tired."

"Of course not," I said, throwing our plates and plastic utensils into the trashcan. After covering the leftovers and putting them into the refrigerator, I joined him on the couch, but I sat on the opposite end.

"Come over here," he said, laughing and patting the cushion beside him.

I snuggled against his side, and he put his arm around me. Leaning his head on my shoulder, he said, "Allie, what are your plans for your future? What do you want out of life?"

"To be a famous artist and have my high-priced paintings hanging in galleries in large cities so I can have my own house with a backyard. And I want a dog. I miss Boots. What about you?"

"I want to be famous enough I can rely on my art for an income and don't have to teach in some art school. I want a house of my own too, but I'd like to afford a nice condo or loft in some downtown building with a parking garage near shops and good coffee." He tilted my face up and kissed me. "Now tell me what you really want."

Taking his hand, I said, "I told you. At least I told you some things. Here's the rest. To be loved, really loved by someone who will help me and I can love and help. Someone who understands all my silly quirks and moods. And I'm searching for…for God. I want someone who at least knows what that's like."

"I searched, and I thought I'd found Him, but then… Let me know if you discover Him."

We sat there for maybe twenty minutes, just holding hands and enjoying each other's company, talking. His remark about my letting him know if I found God hung in the back of my mind, overshadowing everything.

"Remember when we talked about moving Artistic Horizons?" he asked, seriousness edging tone.

"I think you said something about it a while back."

"It's still on my mind. Last month was the first time we didn't make enough money to pay the bills."

"I'm sorry. Laura didn't tell me."

"She's been so busy with the girls I don't think she knows, but I've been thinking about it a lot. We need a new start in a different place. One thing that keeps us here is that it's close to where Grandma lives, and if she needs help, Laura can close shop for a few minutes and be there quickly."

"I can see that."

"Well, I'd better go. Lots to do tomorrow." He pushed himself up from the couch and reached for his coat before wrapping his arms around me. "Thanks for the good food and just letting me talk. You're a good listener." Then he kissed me and left.

I stood there for at least five minutes, enjoying the lingering scent of his cologne and the feel of his arms around me. I guess love is more complicated these days. We had a good evening, but it lasted only until seven thirty.

CHAPTER 45

CHRISTMAS EVE

I WOKE UP EARLY CHRISTMAS EVE and packed all my gifts into a large box so they would be ready to take to Laura's house. In the bottom, I placed a large tin of chocolate chip cookies Gertie helped me bake for David and the light blue shirt and matching tie set I had bought him, then piled the rest of the packages on top, all wrapped in pretty paper. Knowing how he liked sweets, I thought he'd be pleased.

I put on the new red blouse and black velvet pants I bought the day before, wishing I had a full-length mirror. I spent more than I should have on clothes, but I still hadn't bought myself a new coat. And I still didn't have any combs for my hair.

At ten minutes until nine I picked up my old coat, ashamed to take it, yet not wanting to freeze. I laid it on top of my box of gifts and managed to carry the whole thing down the hallway into the store, where I placed it against the wall at the back of the store. The morning was quiet with few customers. I emptied trash cans and dusted shelves. At eleven o'clock Gene and Jeanette Hank came in.

Gene eyed me. "Allie, you look like Christmas."

"We're buying ourselves a Christmas gift today," Jeanette said. She walked over to David's portrait of Nancy. "There's no price on this painting. How much is it?"

"I'm sorry, I don't know. David is the artist, and he'll be here soon, at least by one. Could you come back then?"

"We could go get a bite to eat," Gene said. "Then we'll come back."

After they left, I updated our inventory records. No other customers came in. I don't know which was worse, the boredom or the butterflies in my stomach as I thought about the coming Christmas party at Laura's. I was glad when David showed up at eleven thirty.

"Happy, happy, Christmas Eve Day," he said, closing the door. "Any sales?"

"No. But the Hanks came in. They wanted to buy your painting of Nancy, but it doesn't have a price tag on it. They're coming back at one."

A look of panic crossed his face. He walked over to the portrait, took it down, and carried it into the back room. "It's not for sale," he said when he returned. "I hope they understand. And you, too."

"I sold my painting of Boots to you," I said. "I know how you feel."

"Not quite the same. You'll never understand until you have a child."

The Hanks returned shortly before one. I listened as David explained why he could not sell the portrait. "It's the last portrait I did of her before she got so sick she was bed-ridden. I want to remember her like that." He pulled a tissue out and blew his nose.

"Let's get out of here," he said after the Hanks left. "I need some happiness."

I put on my coat, and he picked up my box and carried it to his car, and when we arrived he took it into the house. David introduced his parents, Doug and Linda, and they hugged me. I wanted to talk to them, but Diana and Lilah danced around singing "Santa Claus Is Coming to Town" as we added my gifts to the pile around the Christmas tree.

"Aunt Allie, Uncle David, come downstairs and play a game with us," Diana said. She took my hand, and Lilah grabbed onto David's.

I glanced at Laura. "Do you need some help in the kitchen?"

"The best help you can give us is to get the girls out from under our feet," she said as she returned to the kitchen with Gertie and Linda.

We played Old Maid and Tiddly Winks until Laura called us to lunch at one-thirty. I had never played either, and Diana and Lilah took great pleasure in teaching me. As we ascended the steps, Diana took my hand, and with the most innocent look, asked, "Aunt Allie, are you and Uncle David getting married?"

"Married? Uh…"

"Marry me, marry me, but don't tell me now," David said, laughing.

Laura was standing at the top of the stairs, her face red. "Little ones will say anything. I'm sorry."

"No problem," David said, still laughing. "We didn't think a thing about it."

He might not have, but I did.

I held hands with David and Gertie as Don asked the blessing, then heaped my plate with ham, candied yam casserole, fruit salad, asparagus, and rolls. Laura fixed three plates, two for the girls and one for Gertie, cutting up her ham just like she did for the girls. After eating a slice of chocolate cake for dessert, I helped rinse the dishes and put the food away.

"Mommy, hurry! Time for presents!" Lilah grabbed Laura's arm and pulled her toward the living room, where the rest gathered around the tree. I followed them and sat in the last empty chair beside Gertie.

Doug handed Gertie the portrait of the girls I painted for her.

"What pretty paper," she said as she unwrapped it. "Oh my! Did you paint this, Allie?"

"Yes. Just for you."

"I love it," she said, pressing it to her front. It didn't leave her lap.

"Thanks, Aunt Allie," Diana and Lilah chorused after opening the glove and hat sets I gave them.

I held my breath as David opened my gift to him.

"Just what I need," he said as he examined the blue shirt and matching striped tie. "My favorite color, too. Thanks, Allie." He slid the opened package beneath his chair.

"You're welcome. It matches your eyes." The minute the words came out of my mouth, I wished I hadn't said them.

Doug handed me a small bag tied with a red bow. I undid the bow and pulled out a sheet of red tissue paper, then reached my hand into the bottom. My mouth flew open in surprise as I took out two silver hair combs set with sparkling blue stones.

"I thought you needed some pretty combs for your beautiful hair," Gertie said.

"Oh, I love them. They're just what I've always wanted." I turned to her and gave her a hug. "Thank you so much."

Diana and Lilah shouted whoops of joy as they unwrapped the dollhouse Don had made them, complete with small furniture and dolls. *Oh, everyone is having so much fun. Too bad Uncle Deb and Aunt Harriet never did anything like this for Christmas.*

All the presents were opened except one, a fairly large box covered in blue foil. It was from David and Laura to me. My hands trembled as I unfastened the bow and unwrapped it, and I gasped as it came into view—the three McCabbock State Young Artist Competition books with my paintings on their front covers.

"Do you like them?" Laura asked.

"Oh, yes. Thanks to both of you." I smiled at David, then at Laura. "I appreciate being here for Thanksgiving, and now for Christmas, and for all you've done for me."

I would always treasure the books, but they looked back at my life, not forward. They were personal, but not the kind of gift from David that would give me hope that our relationship was going somewhere. And he had probably asked Laura to wrap them. I was hoping for a necklace with a heart pendant. Or a book of love poems, something sentimental.

"It's great for us to be here with family," Doug said. "In Honduras, we share a meal with our Christian family. The little children love the candy and cookies we give them."

Linda told us the story of a young woman who was expecting and had no husband and no place to go. "Right before we came, we opened *La Casa de la Esperanza,* The House of Hope, for young mothers like her."

David rose from his chair and walked out the front door. I could see him through the living room window, pacing back and forth, talking on his phone. The look on his face shifted from worry to happiness. Was he talking to Marty?

CHAPTER 46

CHRISTMAS DAY

I SLEPT IN THE NEXT morning until eight. In spite of getting to bed early the previous night, I lay awake until after midnight, just thinking about the day. I couldn't understand David. He was the one who told me how important it was to be kind to others, yet I didn't think he was kind to his parents. Church meant so much to them. How could he not come and hear his father speak on Christmas Day?

"I'm going to be busy" was the excuse he gave them. I saw Linda sigh and look at Doug as we headed out the door when David took me home. He climbed behind the wheel with that steel-bound look on his face. I knew all the pleading I could do would not change his mind. We didn't speak on the way to Artistic Horizons.

"Good night, Allie," he said, opening the car door for me. "I hope you've had a good day."

"A wonderful day," I lied. It would have been wonderful, it could have been, if he had understood what a girl wants. "Thank you again for the books." I walked slowly to the door, hoping he would at least kiss me goodbye. He held my packages while I unlocked the door, and then he gave them back and waved as he headed for his car. My mind replayed every scene, each second of the day after I went to bed.

One thing life had taught me was that I couldn't live in the past, even if the past were only yesterday. Christmas morning I made up my mind to be happy and enjoy Gertie's company and church. I had to decide what to wear. I put on my blue skirt that Gertie had fixed and a matching blouse. My new blue combs held my hair back. I admired myself in the small mirror and saw that my hair had formed a halo of tiny curls around my forehead.

"You look nice," Laura said when they stopped to pick me up. "I love those combs."

"They're very special." I slid into the back seat beside the girls. "Isn't Gertie coming?"

"Dad and Mom are bringing her," Laura said.

It wasn't long before we pulled into the parking lot at the side of a gray stone church. Doug, Linda, and Gertie were getting out of a car, and when Gertie turned and saw me, she smiled.

"You look pretty today. Happy Christmas."

"Merry Christmas to you," I said, walking over and giving her a hug. I unfolded her walker and stayed by her side all the way as we went into the church building behind the rest of the family. Inside the sanctuary, she shuffled up the center aisle.

"My seat," she said, handing me the walker. "Can you fold it up and lean it against the side of the pew?"

I did as she asked and Gertie looked up at me, then patted the pew cushion, indicating that I would sit beside her.

"I'm so glad you came," she said. "This is the best present you could give me."

Don, Laura, and their girls filled up the rest of the pew. I wondered where Doug and Linda were, and Gertie must have guessed my question, for she pointed forward to a front pew where they were sitting. As if on cue, they turned around and waved at us. Several people stopped where we were sitting, and Gertie introduced me like I was her granddaughter.

What was going to happen? The buzz of whispers stopped as a man walked up the steps to the pulpit area with a book in his hands. "Let's all sing joyfully to the Lord," he said.

We sang "Silent Night," then "O Little Town of Bethlehem," "O Come, All Ye Faithful," and several more I had never heard. The beauty of the blended voices of over two hundred people took my breath away. I sang the hymns I had heard, but listened and followed along in the hymnal when I didn't know the melodies.

A man introduced Doug. "Brother Hammond has spent the last six years as our missionary in Honduras. His Christmas message today is about the work he and his wife Linda do there."

Doug stepped up to the pulpit with his Bible in his hand. "I will be reading from the book of Luke, chapter two, verse sixteen. 'And they came with haste, and found both Mary and Joseph, and the babe lying in the manger,'" he read. "Now we all know the story of the birth of the Baby Jesus. Maybe what you have never noticed are the words 'And they came with haste.' They were eager to meet and worship the Christ child. They hurried to see Him. Just like we should all do. Just like the people of Honduras whom we serve."

He told about several of the people in their small Honduran church. Antonio was an alcoholic who used all his money for *cerveza*, beer, and did not support his wife and children. After he found Christ, he became the best husband and father. Luis, a teenager, was living on the streets until Doug found a church family to take him in. Now he is bringing friends from school to church and several have become Christians.

Doug's words opened up a whole new world to me. I had read about the poor peoples of other nations in my history textbooks, but it never made an impact on me. Doug told stories of living people helped by Christians.

"These people and many more in similar circumstances were lost," Doug said. "They were lost because of the problems they faced in this world. More so, they were lost eternally. They may have never known the end to their problems if it hadn't been for the love and kindness of God. Their biggest loss would have been not getting to know God, the sacrifice Jesus made for them, and the opportunity Jesus gives us all to live eternally with Him in heaven."

His words jolted me. I had known the love and kindness of Gertie and her family and all the help they had given me. Now I understood the love of God and Jesus. Here was the *more* I had been searching for.

"Let us be like those shepherds who heard the angels tell about Baby Jesus," Doug said. "May we make haste to come to Him, for He stands with open arms waiting for every man, woman, and child. If you want to know more about God and His plan for you, come now. If you need God and Jesus in your life, bring your life to Him right now. Won't you come as we stand and sing?"

The hymn tugged at my heart. I was an orphan, just like Gertie said. I didn't have God as my Father. I almost walked up that center aisle. Almost, but I didn't. It was all so new to me, and I still didn't understand what I should do. My hands trembled as the people sang the last words of the hymn and I put the hymnal back in its place in the rack.

Gertie noticed. "It's okay, dear. We'll talk later," she said, patting my arm.

All I could do was nod and whisper, "Yes, I'd like that."

After the last prayer, I unfolded Gertie's walker and handed it to her. Several members gathered around us and introduced themselves. Of course I couldn't remember any of their names, but they made me feel a part of them. I would love to have belonged to a church like this one. I needed a family of friends and fellow Christians to help and encourage me. If only I knew how to get there.

CHAPTER 47

GREAT PLANS

I WAS SO DISAPPOINTED THAT David did not come for lunch at Laura's house Christmas Day.

"I wonder why David isn't with us," I whispered to Laura as we sat down at the table.

"He must be busy with his art projects," she said as others reached for hands, a signal that Doug was about to give thanks.

"I'm dying to show him my newest portrait of Boots and the one I am working on now, a small dog I saw walking its owner in front of Artistic Horizons yesterday," I said after the prayer.

"I'd like to see them," Gertie said.

"You have such a gift, Allie," she said when I took them to show her one evening. She held my Boots picture at arm's length and studied it. "Your animals are cute enough for us to love them, yet they look real."

"Thanks, Gertie." I hugged her. "I can always count on you to tell me if my work is good or it lacks something. You really think children will like this picture?"

"I'm not a child, but I like it. I know Diana and Lilah would."

"I'm eager to get more animals drawn. What can I do with my pictures besides sell them as paintings for people to enjoy?"

"Lots. With your abilities, you could illustrate children's books. Card companies would love your art."

"Thanks. I need to get my art out there. My uncle and aunt believed in me. I've been thinking about them and what Doug said in his sermon. Aunt Harriet and Uncle Deb never went to church. I don't know what they believed. Do you think they're in heaven?"

"Only God knows." She placed a wrinkled hand on my arm. "We all worry about our relatives who didn't go to church while they were alive. I worry about David. But God is the judge of all people. We have to leave it up to Him."

"What does the Bible say about those who don't believe in God?"

"It says those who don't believe and don't accept Christ will not be with them in heaven."

I knew it was her nice way of saying they would go to hell, a place of torment and separation from God. I'd heard about hell and the devil somewhere, and I tried to remember where. It certainly wasn't from Uncle Deb and Aunt Harriet. I thanked her and left, but all the way home, images of fire and brimstone raged through my mind, and I lay in bed thinking about God. I hoped Uncle Deb and Aunt Harriet are living in paradise with God.

That day I took some time to redo our window display. I couldn't find much to work with in the back room, but I removed the Christmas decorations and replaced them with some false pieces of evergreen branches and green and white candles.

"What a great look for the new year," Laura said when she came in. "I appreciate your initiative and the extras you do."

Her comment raised my spirits all day. As soon as I returned to my apartment after work, my phone rang. I answered, hoping it was David.

"Hello, Allison, this is George. I have some exciting news."

"Hi George, what's happening?"

"Our local television station, KPSV, wants to interview you. The committee thinks hearing your story will give our cause a much-needed boost, and they're willing to pay for your airplane ticket. Would you like to come?"

"Well…I have a job here and responsibilities. I'd have to ask my boss, and…"

"Surely he will let you off for a few days. Wouldn't you like to see your hometown and your picture on all the billboards?"

When I left Puttersville, I didn't care if I ever returned, but being away made me recall the things I liked most. My secret place in the woods where I met my animal friends might not be there or it might have changed, but a small yearning had been growing inside me ever since I began my art for children. A part of me wanted to be there again.

"I'll ask. But I don't know. When would I come and for how long?"

"They want you to be on their nightly news Friday, January six, so please let me know tomorrow. I'll buy the airline tickets as soon as I hear from you."

After saying goodbye to George, I sat down, stunned. Interviewed on television. The girl from Puttersville no one in school would talk to, who they now wanted to be on television. Maybe it would be good to go back to the only place I'd ever called home. I picked up my phone to call Laura, then decided to call David instead.

"Hello, Allie Pally, what's up?"

"I'm going to be on television," I blurted. "If I can get a few days off from my work." I explained George's call.

"I don't see any reason why not. I'll talk to Laura. Surely we can arrange for someone to help with the shop while you're gone. You need to do this. It may be just what you need to help launch your new line of art."

My excitement started growing the minute I hung up. Suddenly, Artistic Horizons wasn't the only reason for my being and working. I began making a list of all the things I would need for the trip, a used suitcase from Little Miss, a pair or two of jeans, some new shoes dressier than my boots, and a new purse. What would I wear for the interview? My brown dress? Probably not. I added *new dress* to the list. Luckily, I had the extra money from working in the store and the money the committee paid me, so I could afford a few accessories.

While I pondered my needs and a few wants, David called. He had talked with Laura, and they both thought I should go. His teaching didn't start until the middle of January, so he would take me to the airport and pick me up when I returned.

"You are coming back, right?" he asked. I could hear the chuckle in his voice.

"Yes, of course."

"Great. The airport's about an hour's drive. Let me know when your flight is as soon as you can."

"Thanks." My head spun with ideas as soon as he said goodbye. Maybe he would pick me up early and we could stop for lunch somewhere. Silly me. I didn't even know what time my flight was. But a girl can dream of all the possibilities. Hmm...maybe he would kiss me goodbye or give me a kiss when I got back.

CHAPTER 48

TO PUTTERSVILLE

THIS WEEK HAD BEEN A whirl as I got ready for my trip. I bought a blue suit matching my hair combs and black dress shoes with a low heel, plus a brand new black purse. Two new pairs of jeans, a flowered blouse, and a pink turtleneck sweater fill my new suitcase. Not wanting to wear my boots, I bought a pair of comfortable leather tie shoes.

David and Laura hired Jenny Lou to help with the shop while I was gone. We had great fun while she worked with me Tuesday and Wednesday while I showed her how to do everything.

George called to say I could pick up my tickets at the airport. I was disappointed my flight left at eleven Thursday morning, giving me and David no time to stop for lunch.

He made a face when I told him. "So much for my plans for sleeping in." Then he laughed. "I don't do that anyway."

Thursday morning the temperature was sixty-six degrees, unusually warm for winter. I donned my ivory sweater and hauled my suitcase into the shop to wait for David. He pulled up in front of Artistic Horizons at eight. Laura wished me a good trip as David put my suitcase into the back seat of his car and opened the door for me. While we drove to the airport, we talked about my animal paintings, his latest projects, and the future of Artistic Horizons.

"Laura and I are serious about moving the shop," he said. "As soon as we can find an affordable place in a better location." He looked at me and grinned. "Don't worry. We'll take care of you."

"Thanks." I looked out the window at white tent-like structures looming in the distance. "What are those?"

"Denver International Airport. It does look different, doesn't it?"

We parked, and he carried my suitcase into the building and up the escalator. We found the ticket counter and checked in my suitcase, then walked to the security gate. "I can't go in there with you," he said. "Who did you say is going to meet you in Pittsburgh?"

"George, the public relations guy with the environmental committee. He's made all the arrangements."

"Well, be careful. I'll pick you up when you return Monday."

"At four thirty," I reminded him.

"See you then." He hugged me, and I passed through the gate. I followed the signs to my boarding gate and sat down. Had Puttersville changed as much as George said? Would he be different than when I last saw him? Would he know the questions the interviewers from the television station planned to ask me? Would I be able to answer them?

"First-class passengers can now board," the loudspeaker said. I looked at my boarding pass. I was flying business class, and after a few minutes, they announced that business class could board. I handed the airline worker my boarding pass, which she checked. My heart pounded as I passed through the door and walked up a long, narrow hallway leading to the plane's door.

"Welcome aboard," the flight attendant said as he looked at my boarding pass. "You're in seat ten-A by the window."

Some minutes later I stared in fascination as the plane taxied to the runway, sat there a few moments, then began its journey skyward. For the first few moments, I gripped the seat arms but then relaxed. The houses and cars grew smaller and smaller and became mere specks as we passed through layers of clouds and sunshine. The pilot told us where to look to see the Rocky Mountains as we circled and headed east.

A few minutes later, a flight attendant came by with a cart of drinks. I asked for iced tea, and she handed me a can of tea and a straw. The two men sitting next to me in seats *B* and *C* got out their laptops and worked. They hadn't said much to me, so I looked out my tiny window and adjusted the shade to keep the sun out of my eyes. I think I nodded off for a while.

"We're approaching Pittsburg International Airport," the captain announced. "It is snowing and the temperature is twenty-four degrees." I fastened my seatbelt and listened to his instructions about deplaning, then looked out the window. As the plane descended, I could see a blanket of snow covering the fields and roofs of buildings.

How stupid of me! It's the first week of January, and I hadn't bothered to check the weather in Pittsburg. I'd been too busy to think about it. Snowflakes from a leaden sky stuck to the outside of the plane window.

The plane landed with a soft bump and taxied down the runway, then made a U-turn and crept down a shorter runway, finally coming to a stop in front of a gate. I waited for the passengers in the seats ahead of me, then stood and followed the line out the door. Even though I was still inside, as I stepped down into a small room that led down a hallway, a blast of cold air hit me in the face, and I shivered and buttoned my sweater all the way down.

I followed the arrows to the baggage claim area. The carousel was empty, and I looked anxiously through the crowd for George. He wasn't there. I stood with the gathering crowd waiting for the baggage. In a few minutes, the carousel began turning, picking up suitcases spilling from a hole. My bag landed on the carousel, and I stepped forward and picked it up just as it almost passed me. I pulled it to a row of chairs and sat down, all the while scanning the area for George.

George knew my plane was to land at three-forty. I hadn't heard my phone ring, but I pulled it out. No calls, and it was four-twenty. The crowd had dissipated, making it easier to see, so I sat there and waited. I would give him a few more minutes before calling him.

"Allison, I'm sorry to be so late."

I turned, and there he was, so out of breath that he was panting, snow dripping off his hair and jacket. He came around the row of chairs and handed me one red rose.

"The traffic was horrible, and the snow is really coming down. I didn't think I would ever get here. And it took me ten minutes to find a place to park."

"It's okay," I said. "I knew you would be here." I held the rose up to my nose and sniffed its delicate fragrance, its velvety petals brushing my cheek.

"I hope you brought your coat. It's very cold, and the snow and wind are howling."

"I didn't bring one." My neck and face burned as the blush crept up my cheeks. "Sorry. It was so warm in Denver when I left, and I didn't think about checking the weather here."

"We're not far from my car." He took off his jacket and wrapped it around me. "The sooner we head out, the better." He grabbed my suitcase and led the way.

A barrage of huge snowflakes slammed into my face as we walked out the door, blinding me. George put his free hand on my arm and headed toward the parking lot.

CHAPTER 49

GEORGE

WHILE WE WALKED TO THE car, I noticed George was just an inch or so taller than I. Trying not to be too obvious, I studied him. His blue jeans and blue plaid flannel shirt fit loosely. His green eyes searched the parking lot, looking for a path through the slush. I had known him nearly all my life, but I didn't know him at all.

"I hoped this storm was not going to be as bad as the weather station forecast," George said when we reached his car. Snow plastered his brown hair, and my red rose sported a white crown. He opened the door for me, then put my suitcase in the trunk.

"Why didn't you just tell me not to come? I hate that you are going to so much trouble," I said when he got in.

"No trouble. Your career needs this boost, and so does our campaign against Puron Oil. We're fighting the old battle of environment versus jobs and money, and I want the environment to win. And Puttersville."

He guided the car out of the parking lot and inched along the highway through the pelting snow. A truck had skidded off the road and flipped onto its side. Police cars and an ambulance surrounded the accident, closing the lane we were in.

"I hope we don't see any more accidents and the roads are open," George said. He eased his car into the right lane. "Did I tell you I sold my first house? I was able to put a down payment on this Forester. She's not new, but she has all-wheel drive, which I need in this weather."

I nodded, but my thoughts were elsewhere. "Remember when I saw you at the bus station in Denver? Why wasn't your father the one trying to get money to repay those who invested with him?"

He blushed and shook his head. "No one understood what Dad was going through when that happened. He didn't know that the investment company was one of those multi-level schemes. When the government discovered what its leaders were doing, they shut them down." He thought a minute. "He flew to Dallas to talk to friends and ask for money. Some of his investment clients threatened to sue him for much more than they lost if he couldn't pay them back."

"Did he get any help?"

"Some. He also refinanced our house. He paid them back every cent."

"Then why didn't he give me back my money?" The thought rushed into my mind and out of my mouth before I could stop it.

"Two reasons. One, he ran out of money after he paid those threatening to sue him. He even used my college fund and took out another loan. Two, you didn't threaten to sue him. That's why I'm determined to give you back every cent we owe you."

That night at the bus station, his news had plunged me into the depths of despair. It must have been more terrible for him. All that week he had tried to find me, even though he had horrible news. Doing that took a ton of courage. "Does your mother work?" I asked.

He frowned. "My dad and mom never got along. They were always quarreling. When I was thirteen, she ran off with another man."

Maybe that's why he was crying that day in eighth grade. "Do you ever see her? Talk to her? Where does she live?"

"She died last year of cancer."

"I'm so sorry." A scene flashed through my mind. Snotty Georgie. Little Georgie sitting and picking his nose when he couldn't figure out a math problem. I wonder what his home life had been like. Probably miserable.

"It's okay." The snow stopped, and he turned off the windshield wipers. "Hungry? I am, and I know a good restaurant ahead if you want to stop."

"I am hungry. Let's stop."

"I was hoping you'd say that." A half smile curved his mouth, and he winked at me.

I wore his jacket into the restaurant. The wind howled around us, but he didn't complain. After we sat down and ordered, he looked into my eyes.

"Allison, are you okay? For money, I mean."

"I have the money you sent me. And I've sold a few pictures. So I can eat." I told him about my job and little apartment.

"I notice you don't have a coat."

"I do. Only it's old and grubby. I didn't want to wear it." I looked down. "I know you mentioned buying a coat, but I was very busy and ran out of time."

"I want to buy you a coat. Let's do that as soon as we eat."

"George, you're not responsible for my not buying a coat."

"I'm responsible for you're not having much money. I'm not rich, but I want to take care of you. Please let me."

I felt secure with him and at ease while we talked. I didn't worry about doing or saying something wrong, and I didn't struggle to think of something funny to say. He was just plain George from Puttersville.

Our hamburgers and fries arrived, but before George took one bite, he reached for my hand. "Would you mind if I give thanks?"

I shook my head. I kept my eyes open, glued to his face, as he prayed. He talked to God like he knew Him.

"Thank you for this food, dear Heavenly Father. And please help us to get to Puttersville safely. In Jesus' name. Amen." After, he asked, "Would you like to go to church with me Sunday?"

"You go to church? With your father?"

"Dad doesn't go. I'm working on him." He smiled. "I would be honored if you'd go with me."

"I'll go." I studied him. So different. I had begged David to go with me, but he refused. George asked *me* to go with *him*.

We ate in silence. George was dipping his last three fries in a pile of ketchup when he said, "I have a confession to make."

"Oh? What do you want to confess?"

"The television station wants to interview you tomorrow for their five o'clock news report. You could have gone back to Denver Saturday, and if you insist on doing that after you hear what I have to say, I will pay the extra money to change your ticket. But I wanted to get to know you better. I hope you don't mind being here until Monday so we can have some time together." He blushed. "Will you stay?"

Surprised, I asked, "The committee paid for me to stay in the hotel through Sunday night?"

"No." He fidgeted with his napkin and spoke so quietly I could barely hear him. "I'm hoping you will stay with me and Dad Saturday and Sunday. We have a guest bedroom and bath."

After a few moments of awkward silence, I said, "I'll stay, but don't expect too much."

His eyes lit up. "I'm so glad. There's a mall around the corner. Let's go look for you a coat before the stores close."

CHAPTER 50

PUTTERSVILLE

GEORGE CAME TO PICK ME up at nine Friday morning in spite of the dunes of sparkling snow that crunched under our feet as we loaded my things into his car. "You look nice in your new coat," he said.

"Thanks." I liked the detachable hood and double row of black flower buttons on the front, and it covered my thighs and kept them warm. And the black fur around the collar and sleeves kept the wind out.

"What do you want to do today? What do you want to see?" he asked as we left the hotel parking lot.

"Judy's Special Occasion Dress Shop."

"Any reason?"

"Just memories. See how things have changed."

He drove the mile and a half to downtown and parked. "Let's get out and walk."

"Lots of new buildings," I said as we strolled past shops I didn't remember. "I don't recall this restaurant being here."

"It wasn't. Neither was the new bank across the street."

"I don't see the blue dress," I said as we stopped in front of the dress shop.

"Want to go in? I hear the owner may be retiring."

"I don't think so. Aunt Harriet said the dresses in that shop are frivolous. I think she was right."

"I could tell she was practical by the clothes you wore at school."

"It would be a neat place for an art shop. I'd get rid of those ugly brown walls, paint them a sunny yellow. Stand vases of flowers among my animal pictures."

"Why don't I see what I can find out? I could see how much it costs. Maybe you can buy it."

"No, don't. I'd never come up with enough money."

"Don't give up on your dreams," he said, taking my arm in his.

"I'm nervous about the interview. Do you know what they're going to ask me?"

"They said one of the questions would be where you got the idea for your painting. What experiences you had growing up that led to your love for nature and animals. Just things like that."

"I can answer those questions."

"I know you can. Now, where to?"

"Do you think we could go look at where I used to live with Uncle Deb and Aunt Harriet?"

"It won't bring back too many bad memories?"

"I don't think so. I'd really like to go there." Tears filled my eyes. "My uncle and aunt, our livestock, all gone. But I want to see it."

"We'll go see," he said as we walked back to the car.

George pointed out several billboards displaying my painting after we hit the highway.

"I'm proud of them," I said.

"You should be. Those billboards mean a lot to many of the folks around here. A few people held a rally and waved signs demanding the billboards not be put up, but as you can see, they lost."

Fifteen minutes later, we turned off the highway onto the snow-covered gravel road leading to the house. We parked in front of a new white wooden fence surrounding the yard. A car and a Jeep sat in front of the fence.

"Someone is living there," I said. "I wanted to see the spot in the woods where I painted my animals, but maybe we better not."

"I'm sorry," he said as he turned the car around. "We'll come back later."

I blinked back the tears filling my eyes. Should I tell him about Aunt Harriet's death? No. He didn't know her.

We took a back road into town, and George drove into a new area where high-rise apartments dotted the hills. Then he showed me a subdivision where a company was building two-story stucco homes. "These are the most expensive new homes in town," he said. "I hope Dad and I win the contract to sell them."

After having lunch at Wendy's, we headed back to his home. "Ah, Dad's here," he said, parking beside a newer Forester in the driveway. "He's anxious to meet you."

"What do you think of the changes in Puttersville?" John Benton asked after George introduced me. Mr. Benton's face was creased, whether with worry or laugh lines I couldn't tell.

"They're good and bad. If too many people move here, the schools and hospitals will have a hard time accommodating everyone."

"Smart girl. They're already working on those problems," John said. "I'm proud of George for taking a positive stance for the environment, and of you, too, Allison. You're quite the artist." He wrapped one arm around my shoulders and hugged me.

"Thanks, Mr. Benton. You're too kind," I said, a blush tingling my cheeks.

"I have some work to do," George said. "Would you like to rest in your room for a little while? We need to be at the radio station at four-thirty."

"Or you can watch television or whatever you want. Please make yourself at home," John said.

"Thanks. I think I will rest a while." George showed me to my room. "Please knock on my door at three-fifteen," I said. "I might fall asleep."

The room wrapped me in warmth. A comforter with purple and pink flowers covered the bed. It looked new. Solid white drapes hung from the window, and a vase of pink and purple flowers adorned the top of the dresser. I removed my shoes and stretched out on the bed, flipping the comforter over my body.

I didn't want to go to sleep, didn't mean to, but I did. A gentle tapping on the door wakened me, and I sat up suddenly, confused, until I remembered where I was. "Thanks! I'm awake!" I said.

Opening my suitcase, I extracted my blue suit, glad it was made of a material that didn't wrinkle. After putting it on and changing my shoes, I spent twenty minutes experimenting with my makeup, which was still new to me. Then I combed my hair and inserted the sparkling blue combs Gertie had given me.

At four I walked into the living room. George turned from his computer. He said nothing, but his eyes gave away his thoughts.

"You look perfect, Allison," John said. "I'll be glued to the television, watching every second of your interview."

I smiled, but my stomach did somersaults. I turned to George. "What're you doing?"

"Studying the market. Reviewing some of the things I learned in my classes. I won't have my notes in front of me when I'm talking to clients, and I have to know what to say." He glanced at his watch. "We'd better go. It won't hurt to be a few minutes early." He helped me put on my coat, then waved to his dad as we were leaving. "We'll come back and pick you up, and we'll all go out to celebrate."

We climbed into his car, and I fastened my seatbelt, then sat there, fidgeting with my fingers in my lap.

"Nervous?" George asked.

"Of course. I've never spoken on television before."

"Don't worry. Mike Tappas is the newsman talking to you. He goes to church where I go, and he's very nice."

George drove two more blocks, then made a right and pulled into the parking lot of a long building topped by several large, round antennas. Opening my door, he walked with me up the steps and into the station.

A short, chubby man with black hair came around the corner. "Hi, George. This must be Miss Cooper, our famous artist." He took my hands in his and said, "Hi, I'm Mike Tappas. Thanks for coming all the way from Denver and being part of our broadcast."

"I'm glad to," I said as my stomach did another flip-flop.

"Come in and make yourselves comfortable. Have a cup of coffee. I'll go round up Patty, our make-up gal."

I sat down in an overstuffed chair, clasping my purse tightly, while George poured two cups of coffee.

CHAPTER 51

QUESTIONS

PATTY, THE STATION'S MAKEUP ARTIST, dabbed a little blush to my cheeks and applied some brighter lipstick. "With your beautiful blond hair, we want you to stand out," she said.

I handed my coat to George and walked onto the set with Mike. The heat of the bright lights above us warmed me, as did what Mike said when he introduced me.

"We are so proud to have Allison Cooper with us today. Not many of you know Allison painted the picture you see on our billboards, and she grew up right here in Puttersville. Allison, can you tell us what made you paint such a picture?"

"Those animals were my best friends and companions when I was younger. I love them. When I learned Puron Oil planned to ruin their habitat with fracking, I had to do something."

"Did you take classes to learn to paint with such finesse? Or does your painting come naturally?"

"Naturally, I suppose," I said with a chuckle. "Maybe people here remember I won the McCabbock State Young Artist Competition three times. But even before then, I was drawing pictures of my animals and sculpting them in snow."

"What are your hopes and wishes for Puttersville?"

That question surprised me, and I had to think. "I know that Puttersville is growing. Many new homes and industries are springing up. I just hope we can preserve the natural beauty we see everywhere around us."

"Thank you, Allison. I know many of our citizens wish for the same. Surely all of us will do everything we can to make that happen. Let's vote against letting Puron Oil drill near our beautiful city."

Mike ushered me back to where George was waiting, watching on a monitor.

"You did great," he said. "I'm proud of you."

"I came all this way for three questions?"

"We have so much to cover, no one gets much air time," Mike said. "We'll replay your interview on the news tomorrow. I hope when people see it, it will help persuade them to vote against Puron Oil."

We left and picked up George's father. "I watched your interview," John said. "George didn't tell me about your winning awards for your art."

"It was in the Puttersville newspaper, and the first year I won, they announced it at school," I said.

"Do you remember that, George?" John asked.

"I think so. Come to think of it, you won more than once, right?"

"Three times. Then I was too old to enter."

"Congratulations," John said. "Let's go to Larry's Steakhouse and celebrate."

We had a wonderful dinner. While we were eating, several people stopped by to say they had just seen me on the news and they were going to vote against Puron Oil. I thanked them for saving my animals and their habitats. When we arrived back at George's house, I was so pumped it took me an hour to fall asleep.

In the morning George made bacon and waffles for a late breakfast. He needed a flash drive for work, so we went shopping. We walked past Judy's Special Occasion Dress Shop. *Life is crazy. Almost a year ago, I dreamed of swirling through the streets of Puttersville in that blue dress with George admiring me, and here I am, walking by his side.*

"Dad still owns the old bank building," George said, bringing me back to the present. "That's where our real estate business is. We've been working for the last two months, cleaning it up and getting the office set up on the first floor. Would you like to see it?" His eyes shined.

"Yes."

We walked a couple blocks up the street. George had the key out of his pocket before we reached the door, but it was unlocked. John sat at a desk inside a reception room, talking to a young couple.

John stood. "This is George, my son and partner," he said. "And his friend, Allison."

"I'd like to show Allison around," George said after acknowledging them. He opened a door and turned on the light. "Here's the new bathroom dad and I built."

"I like the gray tile and the pedestal sink," I said. "You did a good job."

"Thanks." He opened another door. "Here's the large office where we'll do our work. It's bare except for our desks and computers. Let me show you our kitchenette."

As we rounded the corner, we entered a galley kitchen. The odor of fresh coffee and toast permeated the room.

"Dad sometimes has breakfast here. At least he cleaned up. What do you think?"

"I like it. I can't believe you both got your real estate licenses and did all this. You and your dad have worked hard."

"Dad has already sold three houses, and I told you I've sold one." He pointed up a flight of stairs. "More office space up there, but we haven't had time to refurbish those rooms. Dad hopes to rent them out to a couple more agents. He has his broker's license."

We stopped in a small diner and ordered soup and a salad. Of course George offered thanks. When I opened my eyes, he was staring at me. "Do you have a Bible?"

"Yes."

"Did you bring it?"

"No." My face burned as the telltale blush crept up my cheeks.

"I'm so excited that you're going to church with me tomorrow. I'll loan you one of mine. And there's something else I want to talk to you about."

"Oh?"

"You told me once that your phone minutes were running out. You have one of those phones that uses a monthly card with a limited amount of minutes on it, don't you?"

I nodded.

"So…" He reached into his jacket pocket and pulled out a small bag and handed it to me. "I want you to have this."

A smartphone slid into my hand. "George! I can't take this. It's too much money." I noticed the protective case showing wild animals peeking from a forest.

"I can afford it. It's only twenty-five dollars a month on our plan. It even has your number on it." His eyes fixed onto mine, pleading. "I want to feel free to call you anytime without you worrying about minutes." His face blushed. "Please take it."

"It's very nice," I said, turning it over in my hand. "Thank you."

"I want us to be friends, someone I can talk to. Is that okay?"

"I guess so." He must be lonely if he needed me to talk to.

"After we eat, will you go to a movie with me?"

"That sounds like fun."

"Great." His face broke into a smile. "Our first date."

What about David? How could I go back to Denver and date David and be George's girlfriend at the same time? I bit my lip and glanced at him as he ate his soup, his face aglow.

CHAPTER 52

ANOTHER CONFESSION

"THE PEOPLE AT YOUR CHURCH liked me, didn't they?" I asked George as we drove home after the worship service Sunday.

"Of course. Why wouldn't they?"

"They welcomed me like I was one of them. I learned a lot from the sermon about how Jesus has power over disease, demons, and the weather, as He showed in His miracles. And the potluck hit the spot."

"Do you believe Jesus is the Son of God and died for your sins?"

"Uncle Deb read the Bible, but we never went to church. I didn't learn much about Jesus until Gertie told me."

"Who's Gertie?"

"My friend who gave me my Bible. It has all her study notes in it. I wish I had brought it so I could show it to you." I sighed. "I promised her I would read it every day, but I got busy, and I haven't. We talk about God sometimes. And I plan to read it when I get back."

"I hope you can." He thought a minute. "I wish I could get Dad to go to church with me. Maybe someday."

When we arrived at his house, George said, "I have something to show you. If you promise you won't be angry at me, that is."

"How can I promise I won't be angry if I don't know what it is? I'll let you know after you show it to me."

"Sit on the couch a minute, and I'll be right back." He disappeared into his bedroom and returned with a large box that he put on the sofa between us. It was taped shut. He reached into his pocket for his penknife, opened a blade, and cut down the middle of the tape. "Open it."

I folded back the flaps and gasped as I spied dozens of my drawings from elementary school. "Where did you get these?"

"You thought the teachers confiscated them, didn't you? No, it was little Georgie, the one who has always admired your drawings, the one who has always loved you." His words ended in a whisper, and when he looked up at me, his eyes were brimming with tears. He took my hands. "Allison, I have loved you since kindergarten. Can you find a little love in your heart for me?"

Thoughts tumbled through my brain as I grabbed a handful of my smudgy drawings. I sorted through them, remembering the little brown-haired boy who watched me, wanted to talk to me and play with me. Had he been as lonely as I had been?

"George, it's not that simple."

"You love someone else, don't you?"

I put the pictures back in the box. Gathering my courage, I looked into his eyes. "You are so frank and honest with me, it's the least I can do to be honest with you. Yes, there is someone."

His face fell.

"But I don't know if it will work out or not," I said. "I would like to be friends with you if you don't want the phone back."

"No, keep it. I hope we can still talk. Would you mind if I call you once a week? To see how you're doing?"

"I would like that. We both go to church, and we can talk about God and Jesus."

"Thank you" came his whisper. He let go of my hands. "My hopes aren't completely dashed."

His dad came in. "Can I have a minute?" he asked George.

"I think I'll go rest a little while," I told them. I lay on the bed, but I couldn't sleep. Too many thoughts were spinning through my head.

That night, George ordered a large pizza. It did nothing to ease me. Visions of my night eating pizza with Gertie and David flashed through my mind, David's hands chopping the tomatoes for salad, serving me another slice, then our doing the dishes together, feeling like a team. *Had he missed me?*

After dinner, I joined George at his computer in the living room.

"Dad heard a rumor that we're going to get the contract for selling Waterpond Estates," he said. "Seventy-five homes with six different plans. If it happens, we'll both be very busy."

"How exciting. I hope you get it." I pulled a chair up to his. "Show me the pictures." I oohed and ahed as he scrolled through the pictures of the models.

"Great family homes. See what big back yards they have? And amenities, too, right beside a park with areas for children to play with swings and slides, a pretty fountain, and on the other end, a pool. I'd love for us to someday have a home like one of these."

I don't believe he realizes what he just said. His words tingled my ears. I glanced at him, so animated about what he was doing. "What are you and your father calling your real estate company?"

"Benton Real Estate. Original, right? But people know us, and they think of Dad as an honest man."

"I don't know what I would have done if you had not sent me money, especially at first. I had a place to live, but nothing to eat."

He faced me and took both my hands in his. "Allison, promise me you will never get that hard up without calling me. I am building up my credit, and if need be, I will borrow money to send you. Promise me."

"Okay. I promise."

The next morning at the airport, George stayed with me until I passed through the security gate, and as I checked my bag, I could see him standing behind the gate looking my way, waving goodbye.

I boarded the plane, my head still spinning from his declaration of love. How his tear-filled eyes pleaded as he begged for me to care. My heart ached for him, yet I couldn't love him and David at the same time.

I buckled my seatbelt and watched the landscape whiz by as the plane taxied. David would be waiting to pick me up at the Denver Airport. Tomorrow I would be back at Artistic Horizons, and tomorrow night I would visit Gertie and tell her all about my trip.

The flight back seemed much shorter. David was at luggage claim, waiting for me. I pointed to my bag as it tumbled onto the carousel, and he grabbed it.

"Grandma had a stroke," he said. "She's in the hospital."

CHAPTER 53

PLANS

LAURA AND I VISITED GERTIE at the rehab center shortly after I returned. She lay there, almost as white as the sheets, unable to move much. One side of her mouth sagged. She couldn't talk. Her eyes followed us when we moved, and sometimes she nodded when we spoke.

Saturday after work I braved the sharp wind to catch the bus for the long ride to the rehab center. Gertie's eyes brightened as I sat down beside her and held her hand. Drool came from the droopy part of her mouth, and I wiped it off with a tissue and smoothed her long, gray hair from her face. Her good hand grasped my hand and put it against her cheek where a tear had escaped from her eye.

"I love you," I whispered, struggling to hold back the tears that brimmed in my eyes. "My friends wanted to know all about my life here, and I told them about you. I went to church with a friend on Sunday."

She tried to smile. "And I have to tell you about my interview. Everyone said I did a good job."

I pulled my latest drawing out of my bag, a picture of a mouse sitting and nibbling on a grain of corn he held in his paws. Gertie's eyes darted from my picture to my face, and she nodded. "I'm calling my company Enchanted Art, and some day, I'll have my own studio and shop."

After talking to her a little while, I kissed her goodbye and took the bus back home. I loved her, but visiting with her wasn't the same. It was difficult to talk with someone who couldn't respond. Still, I planned go see her as often as I could.

Wednesday, Jennie Lou came in to work, not David. She showed me her new painting of Dillon Reservoir. Behind the lake rose a majestic, snow-covered mountain with pine trees scattered at its base.

"I went up there with my family a couple weeks ago," she said. "The view was so gorgeous, I couldn't help but paint it. Laura said I could display it here." She placed it in the window and wrote out a label for it.

"It's beautiful," I said. "I hope it sells quickly."

"David been around?"

"Not today."

"Why don't you call him?"

"Maybe I will tonight." I left and walked to the grocery store, where a carton of strawberry ice cream and a package of cookies found my shopping cart. There's nothing better than a full bowl of ice cream to drown the sorrow in one's heart.

But as soon as I got home, George called. "Hello, Allison, how are you?"

"Fine, George, how about you?"

"A little down, I guess. Dad and I didn't get the Waterpond Estates after all. They hired a company from out of town. What do they know about Puttersville? Oh well. The other new development I showed you, Magic Forest, will have nearly two hundred new homes, and Dad is sure we'll get it."

"I hope so."

"So how's your weather?"

"Probably warmer than yours. At least it's not snowing."

"Yeah, we had another round of the white stuff this week. Hey, I'd like to send you a book. Is that okay?"

"What kind of book?"

"It's called *The Case for Christ* by Lee Strobel. I just finished it and really enjoyed it, and I think you will, too."

"I don't have a lot of time to read," I said, remembering that I hadn't read a thing in my Bible since I'd returned.

"I think once you read the first chapter, you won't be able to let go of it. Do me a favor though. Can you write this down?

John, Chapter One. Make sure you read that before you start Strobel's book."

He said goodbye. Guess I'm not much of a conversationalist. Or maybe I don't enjoy talking about real estate and books. I feel sorry for him as he sounds lonely, but other than church, I don't think we have much in common.

I was adding a few touch-ups to my mouse picture when David called. "Howdy hey! I'm out front. Can I come in and talk for a while?"

"Sure. Come on in." My heart pounding with excitement, I scurried around, picking up plastic bags from the grocery store and hanging up my coat.

"Got anything to eat?" he said as he came through the door.

"I was about to have some cookies and ice cream. How does that sound?"

"Perfect."

I filled two paper bowls, stuck a plastic spoon in each, and set out the cookies. "I went to see Gertie last night. She knew I was there, but it was a one-way conversation."

"No, not much fun. That's why I haven't been yet. I'm the one who found her. She was on her bedroom floor, unable to move, for who knows how long."

Tears filled my eyes at the thought of what Gertie must have gone through. "I'm sorry."

"Me too. I just have to get over there to see her soon. Laura says she's not making much progress." He finished his ice cream and set the bowl down. "It's been a busy week. I searched all day yesterday and today for a new place for Artistic Horizons, and I found something. Not at the Santa Fe Art District or the Navajo Street Art District, though."

"Where is it?"

"Not that far from here, actually. Down on Wazee and Eighteenth. It has double the space we have now. There's another art shop not too far away. Expensive art, but people will be in the area shopping for art, and we will be a second choice."

"So you think it's a pretty sure thing?"

"I told Laura about it, and she agreed. It won't be available until the first of April, and by then, I'll have enough from the sale of my extra projects to pay first and last month's rent. I've already told their real estate company that I want it. They said they would send me a contract."

"But it doesn't have an apartment attached."

"No, but there are apartments nearby. Jenny Lou said something to me about wanting to move. Since she's working for us too, maybe you could share a two-bedroom. You could probably sell enough of your art to make a go of it."

"You think so?"

"Sure. We'll pay you for helping us move, of course. And we'll all sell more art there. Well, thanks for the ice cream and cookies. I need to get home and finish my new winter painting. It goes with the forest one I did last month. A client is paying me eight hundred for both."

He hugged me, and as soon as the door clicked shut, I sank into a chair and buried my head in my hands. "You could probably sell enough of your art to make a go of it" kept going through my mind. I'd checked on the shop computer, and rent was expensive downtown. Around a thousand a month for a two-bedroom. Even if Jenny Lou wanted to share an apartment, we'd have utilities to pay. What if I couldn't sell enough art? Would I have enough money for food? If I couldn't buy art supplies, how was I going to have enough art to sell? How was I ever going to be an artist and have my own shop? Tears slid down my face as a wave of hopelessness washed over me.

CHAPTER 54

GERTIE

SATURDAY, LAURA CAME INTO THE shop as soon as I opened. "Grandma slipped away from us last night," she said.

"I'm so sorry." A flood of loss and sadness poured over me.

"I'm not. Her body was worn out. She would have spent the rest of her life helpless and not able to live in her own home. She wouldn't have wanted that."

"I know, but..." Tears escaped my eyes and slid down my face. "I'll miss her."

"We all will. But she's happy, at home with God," Laura said, hugging me. "I have a favor to ask. David and I have to make funeral plans, get Dad and Mom home, and do a thousand other things. Jenny Lou is out of town. Could you work all day today and all day during next week? We'll pay you extra."

"Sure. Anything I can do."

"You're a big help." She hugged me again. "I'll let you know about the funeral plans as soon as I can. Please call if you need me."

She left. Gertie had taken the empty spot Aunt Harriet left in my heart, and once again, I felt like an orphan. Maybe it was because I was so unsure about God. Gertie said we were all orphans until we know Him as our Father. I needed to know Him now more than ever, but sometimes I was so angry at Him, and I didn't know where to start looking. Maybe I would ask Laura and Don to pick me up for church tomorrow. If only I could call David and ask him to take me, but I knew his answer.

Several customers came in. I sold my mouse painting, but not before taking a photo of it with my phone. I never did get it on my website. Like David said, one of these days I'll have my own computer and website.

That afternoon, I sold Jenny Lou's painting of Dillon Reservoir. I called her and left a message. We received a shipment of art supplies, and I lugged them into the storage room and added them to our inventory on the spreadsheet David had set up. Other customers came in to browse or buy paints and brushes. A package came from George, and I could tell it was the book he'd said he would send. I put it on the counter to take to my apartment after I closed for the night.

I was proud of myself. I knew how to run the store. Laura and David trusted me to handle everything by myself. Working for them had given me the experience and knowledge I would need when I had my own shop, and I was saving money every month. Even though it might take me several years, one day I would have enough saved to make it.

At six, I locked up and grabbed the still-wrapped package from George, ready for dinner and some time to work on my new painting of two chipmunks sitting on a log by a pond. It would show a frog on the bank of the pond staring at them with his bulging eyes, and his mouth smiling as if he were bidding them welcome.

Time and the world disappeared when I painted. I didn't know how long I had been working when my phone rang, and I picked it up.

"Hi Allison, how's it going?"

"Hi, George. I'm fine. How are you?"

"Excited. Dad and I got the Magic Forest account. They want us to start next week."

"That's wonderful. I'm happy for you."

"Thanks. You sound a little down tonight."

"My friend Gertie died."

"Who?"

"My friend Gertie. Remember I told you how she gave me her Bible and we talked about God and she took me to church? She's gone." Tears stung my eyes as I explained.

"But she was a Christian, right? Then she's in heaven."

I wanted to scream at him, "But I have no one!" I didn't because I still had David and Laura. "Yes," I said half-heartedly. "George, why do people get sick? Why do they die? Even little innocent children, and good people who do right, and they suffer, and sometimes bad things happen, like someone kills them. Why, George? Why?" By the time I reached the last *why*, I was yelling, and I broke into sobs.

"Allison, everyone has to die. It's the curse sin brings to man. The Bible says the wages of sin is death. It's not just our physical bodies that die, but our souls can too, if we don't believe in God and live for Him. But Jesus overcame death. The gift of God is eternal life through Jesus."

"But God could have made Gertie well, and He could have saved little Nancy, and He could have kept Trag from killing Aunt Harriet. Why didn't He, George?"

He didn't answer at first. Then he said, "I don't know about Nancy, and I'm sorry to hear about your Aunt Harriet. I wish I was there to wrap my arms around you and tell you things will be okay."

"But they're not okay. Right now I hate God. He took away everyone I love."

"Please don't say that. God loves you more than you can know."

"How can He love me and let everyone I love die? How? Is He a good God or not? If He's all powerful and good, how can He let such bad things happen?"

George sighed. "Christians believe that God is all powerful. Someday, He will do away with temptation, sin, diseases, natural disasters, suffering, sadness, and death. But that time is not yet. We must have faith in Him and wait for heaven. Or for Jesus to come back and take us there, whichever happens first."

"That's not fair. If God can do all those things, why doesn't He do them now? Why does He let bad people do horrible things? Why didn't He make everyone good?"

"God gives us free will. Would you like to be a puppet on God's strings doing only what He wants? Would you like to have no choices?"

"No." I could see his point. "But why did God create evil if He is so good?"

"God didn't create evil. Evil comes from inside us."

"But why? Why can't everyone be good?"

"Don't blame everything on God. Satan plays a huge part in getting people to sin. Jesus overcame Satan and death, the separation from God that sin brings. Did you get the book I sent?"

"Yes, it came today."

"Then please read it. And read the Bible Gertie gave you. The Bible will help you understand God and what He does. Please read it."

"What should I read? Which part?"

"First Corinthians, chapter fifteen. It's rather long, but the last part is best, and you can understand it better if you read the whole chapter."

After I said goodbye, I found my Bible, now more precious because Gertie gave it to me. The passage George mentioned was one of those where she had inserted a piece of paper, so I found it easily. I didn't understand some of the things in the first half of the chapter. I came to the verses starting with forty-two.

> *So also is the resurrection of the dead. It is sown a perishable* body, *it is raised an imperishable* body; *it is sown in dishonor, it is raised in glory; it is sown in weakness, it is raised in power; it is sown a natural body, it is raised a spiritual* body.

Then I saw verses forty-nine through fifty-two.

> *Just as we have borne the image of the earthy, we will also bear the image of the heavenly. Now I say this, brethren, that flesh and blood cannot inherit the kingdom of God; nor does the perishable inherit the imperishable. Behold, I tell you a mystery; we will not all sleep, but we will all be changed, in a moment, in the twinkling of an eye, at the last trumpet; for the trumpet will sound, and the dead will be raised imperishable, and we shall be changed.*

Then at the end of verse 54 including verse 55.

> *"DEATH IS SWALLOWED UP IN VICTORY. O DEATH, WHERE IS YOUR VICTORY? O DEATH, WHERE IS YOUR STING?*

It was as if the writer were shouting for joy. Gertie, thank you for telling me about this passage. George, without you I would never have read it.

CHAPTER 55

ALONE

MONDAY, JENNY LOU CALLED, EXCITED that her painting of Dillon Reservoir sold. "I have some great news to tell you," she said. "I got engaged Sunday. We're getting married in May."

"Engaged? Really? I didn't even know you had a boyfriend."

"I did, but he went away to college, and for a while, it was off and on. I didn't tell you because I wasn't sure. Mike's here at Vail with us, and we're having a wonderful time skiing. Yesterday he said he had really missed me. He asked me to marry him last night. We were all standing around the fire pit at the hotel. The stars were out, and oh, Allie, it was so romantic! He has moved back to Denver and will go to college here. I'm so happy, still on cloud nine."

"Congratulations. I'm happy for you." A twinge of envy hit me. *Why can't it work out for me and David?* Since Jenny Lou wouldn't be rooming with me, how could I afford a downtown apartment by myself?

Laura called. "Gertie's funeral will be Saturday afternoon at two at the church where she has been a member for thirty years. Doug and Linda are flying in tomorrow from Honduras, and Don's brother and his wife are coming from Dallas. I'm super busy getting everything set up. Really appreciate your working so hard."

"Can I—" The line clicked as I started to ask her if someone would pick me up for the funeral. A bucket full of sadness drenched me. *Hadn't Laura said I was part of their family? Or did she say so because I kept the store going when she couldn't? Why doesn't*

David call to see how I'm doing? He's teaching again, so I won't bother him during the day. I'll call him this evening and see if he will take me to Gertie's funeral.

Gene and Jeanette Hank came in. "Allie, did you know that there's a company in Colorado Springs that sells cards, gifts, and stationery?"

"No. Is it a good place to shop?"

"We think so," Jeanette said. "It's called Harmony Cards. We are friends with the owners, Ted and Cindy Fallon. We were there yesterday, and they told us they're looking for someone talented in drawing animals. They want to start a new line of cards with animals on them, and we thought of you." She handed me a business card. "Give them a call if you'd like."

"Thanks." I tucked the card into my pocket.

"We were hoping Laura or David would be here," Gene said. "We heard about Gertie's passing."

"They're busy with family and arrangements."

"Please give them our condolences," Jeannette said. "Gertie was a fine woman. We wish we could come to her funeral, but we have to be out of town Saturday."

"I'll tell them."

After they left, I looked up Harmony Cards on the Internet. "Are we looking for you? Can you draw or paint animals?" their home page asked. Underneath in smaller letters I read, "We need an artist to help us with a new line of cards. Work from home. Get paid for original artwork and earn a residual with every card we sell with your design." The ad gave an email address and phone number for sending sample pictures and a letter of application.

My mind buzzed with excitement. What do I have that I can send? I have a photo of my mouse painting, and I can finish the chipmunks and frog I'm working on. A sense of urgency overtook me, and I set up our little eating and work table in a back corner where I could paint. My work will be out of the way and handy in my spare time.

A few young people came in to buy supplies, and after updating the inventory record, I secluded myself in my corner and nearly finished my picture before the bells on the door jangled.

"Lettie, I'm glad to see you. How can I help you?"

"I came to apologize," she said. "It has taken me this long to find the courage. Are Laura and David here?"

"No. Gertie died. You know, the older woman who used to work here? She was their grandmother."

"I'm sorry. After all the trouble I caused them. Do you think they can forgive me?"

"I'm sure they will."

"Please tell them I'm sorry. What I did wasn't right. I knew it, but you don't understand the pressure Master and Madame Kay put on me. They said if I didn't find some good art to copy, they would fire me. I should have let them."

I hugged her. "We all make mistakes, Lettie. I appreciated your help while I was at the academy. You were kind to me, and I think you're a good person."

"Thank you. My lawyer said I can take a plea bargain. He thinks the judge will give me a hundred hours of community service. After finishing that, I plan to move to New Mexico and live with my sister. I can start over again."

"Good luck. I hope things go well with you." She left, and I watched her from the window as she got in her car and drove away.

I worked some more on my chipmunks and frog. Every time I did a painting, I got new ideas for signing. I sketched the *A* in the cattails at the edge of the pond, the *B* in a knot on the log the chipmunks are sitting on, and the *C* in the curve of the lily pad by the frog.

I locked the shop door and carried my painting to my apartment. Opening a can of chili, I heated it and sat down at my little table. Nights alone in the apartment got to me. Working in the shop was lonely except for when customers came in, and at night I had no one, not even a television. Thinking of David's visit almost two weeks ago, I sighed. Why couldn't he come visit me, take me out a bit, or at least call me? As if my phone read my mind, it rang.

"Hi Allison. This is George."

"I can see it's George. And what does George want?" I said, laughing.

"Just to tell you that Dad and I sold our first houses at Magic Forest today. We both sold one. A lot of people are coming to look before our grand opening this coming Saturday."

"That's wonderful."

"How about you? How did your day go?"

"Pretty well." I told him about the Hanks and the job at Harmony Cards.

"You would be perfect for the job. I'm so proud of you and your talent. Go for it. Well, Dad and I didn't have time to cook, so we're going out. Talk to you later," he said and hung up.

I rinsed out my bowl, picked up my phone, and called David.

"Hello, hello. What's up, Allie?"

"Hi, David. How are you doing?"

"I'm okay, thanks. Did Laura tell you that Gertie's funeral is this Saturday at two?"

"She did. Would you mind picking me up and taking me?"

"Uh…taking you? Sorry, but no can do."

"Oh? Any reason?"

"I'm too busy that day. I have to do other things. Why don't you take the bus? It runs right past the church."

I wanted to scream at him, "What other things?" I managed to stay calm. "Okay, I'll take the bus." As soon as he hung up, I burst into tears.

CHAPTER 56

GERTIE'S FUNERAL

I HAD BEEN SICK IN bed for three days, but that night I felt well enough to get up a bit. Saturday, the day of Gertie's funeral was a gray, snowy day. I kept the shop open until noon, then closed. On the door I hung a sign—"Closed due to the death of a family member"—then I ate a hurried lunch. Wanting to look my best, I perused my clothes. I thought most people wore black to funerals, but I didn't own anything black except slacks. My brown Thanksgiving dress? No, I wanted to wear the hair combs Gertie gave me, so I picked my new blue suit. My boots seemed too clunky to wear. Out came my black heels. After dressing, I fussed with my unruly hair for some minutes, trying to get the combs just the way I wanted. Desiring to be there early, I walked out the door at one fifteen.

A gust of cold wind hit my face and sent my hair swirling. Thankful for my warm coat, I pulled the hood up, lowered my head, and plowed through the falling snow to the bus stop. My feet morphed into blocks of ice and my legs into icicles by the time I arrived. I climbed on and settled into a seat behind the driver.

After making four stops, the bus pulled to a stop in front of the church twenty minutes later. I got off and faced an empty parking lot. Strange that no one would be here. When I arrived at the front of the church, I saw a sign tacked to the door. "Due to a plumbing problem, the funeral for Gertrude Hammond has been moved to Bethel Community Church." It gave the address. I looked it up on my phone. It was ten blocks away, and another bus wouldn't come for twenty-five minutes, so I decided to walk.

The wet, slushy snowflakes slammed against my coat and face as I walked up the hill. I hunkered against the wind and wished for my boots as every step propelled me into a precipitous slide on the packed snow. A large truck veered toward the sidewalk as it passed a snow plow. Muddy, icy slush flew from under the truck tires onto my coat and skirt.

I looked down at the damage. Quickening my steps, I made it to the church at two, and I dodged into a restroom and washed my skirt off as best I could. After signing the guest book in the foyer, I slipped into the last pew. Cold water dripped from my skirt onto my legs and ran down into my shoes, sending a shiver through my body. It didn't compare to the anger and hurt surging through me like a storm. *How many times had Laura and David told me I was a part of them and they needed me? It wasn't true. They hadn't even bothered to tell me that the funeral had been moved.*

Doug was speaking, giving the highlights of Gertie's life. Behind him on a large screen flashed pictures of Gertie as a child, as a young woman, getting married, with Doug and Linda when they were a young couple, at Laura and Don's wedding, at Artistic Horizons, and at church. When Doug sat down, the people sang several hymns.

Two large people in front of me obscured my view of Gertie's family sitting in the front two rows. I could see a little of Gertie's casket in front of the pews and some of the flowers surrounding it.

Doug got up and spoke again. "Gertie was a woman who loved God. She preached to us through the life she lived. It was her desire that all her family and friends go to heaven, and she worked tirelessly, telling others about Christ. We found this note on her coffee table. 'To my dear friend, my adopted granddaughter, I feel your loneliness and emptiness. My prayer is that you will find God and accept Him as your heavenly Father and believe that His son Jesus died for your sins.' I don't know who this person is, but I know Gertie loved her. But she loved everyone, no matter who they were or where they came from. I wish we could all be like my mother."

The love in Gertie's words supplanted my hurt and anger and replenished my soul. I thought of all the times she had talked to me about God. She gave me her precious Bible, and I had not read it. I vowed to change.

Laura spoke next. "I will miss Grandma, but I will not cry that she is gone. Her eyes always looked toward heaven. After Grandpa died, her heart was there, too. Now God has taken her home. I can imagine the reunion she and Grandpa had. I can see them there, holding each other's hands, walking those golden streets without pain, and talking to Jesus. Grandma, I want to thank you for being the perfect grandmother, for your patience and kindness when I needed you, for all your help as I was growing up, and for your love to me and my family."

David strode to the podium and read a poem he had written about Gertie. It told of some of the things they had done together. I don't know why I thought it was shallow, but that's how it struck me.

Doug stood. "If anyone else would like to talk about Gertie and what she meant to your life, please feel free to come up here and say something."

I had planned to, and that morning had thought about what I would say. But I was shivering uncontrollably, and my head was throbbing. My cold, wet skirt clung to my legs; I decided not to.

"After the viewing, there will be a meal in the fellowship room," Doug said. "We hope you can stay and visit with the family." He said a final prayer, and men came forward and motioned for those in each row to go up front and greet the family members standing beside the casket.

I rose and made my way to the front. Passing Gertie's casket, I looked at her face, her gray hair in a bun, her eyes closed in peace.

David stood on the other end of the casket. "Hello, Allie. I'm glad you made it."

I raised my eyes to his face. He had on the shirt and tie I gave him for Christmas. Beside him stood a young woman. She was tall and slender, and her brown curls cascaded onto an expensive looking, knee-length leather coat that was cinched at the waist. Leather boots covered her legs up to her knees.

"Allie, this is Marty," David said. "Marty, this is Allie. She works at the store."

Marty extended a slender hand, ending in long nails painted with designs of flowers. "David has told me about you," she said, her voice cool as we shook hands. She threw the end of her scarf around her neck, sending a waft of her perfume toward me, and her eyes traveled down my coat onto my wet skirt. "Nice to meet you."

"You too." I smiled, but inside, my heart shattered into pieces as I absorbed the reason for David's excuse. I should have known.

"Allie, I didn't think you made it," Laura said, pulling my attention away from David and Marty. "I didn't see you come in."

"I took the bus. When I found out the funeral was here, I walked from Gertie's church. And I got splashed by icy water."

"I'm sorry, I forgot to call you about the change. It happened this morning, and I lost track of time. Are you staying for lunch?"

"I'm not feeling well, so I think I'll go home and rest." A sharp knife sliced my throat every time I talked and my head throbbed. I nodded to Don, and on the way out of the church, I grabbed a small brochure about Gertie and tucked it into my purse.

As I stepped outside, a bitter wind stripped the air from my lungs much the way David had ripped my hopes from my heart. At least the snow had stopped. I caught the bus home, changed clothes, and crawled into bed. I shivered uncontrollably, hurting too much to cry.

CHAPTER 57

HOPE

WHEN I ARRIVED AT WORK the first day of February, Laura was there, and I gave her the message from the Hanks and told her about Lettie. "She seemed truly sorry," I said. "I hope she does okay."

"I do too," Laura said. She stopped what she was doing and looked at me. "I'm sorry you were so sick. Are you doing okay?"

"I'm fine."

"If you're doing okay, I'll go pick up the girls from school," she said as she slipped out the door.

My mind replayed the last four days. When I'd gotten home from Gertie's funeral, my whole being tumbled into a black abyss, falling further into despair than I had ever been. I landed in my secret world, as far away from people and reality as I could get. Sunday I didn't get out of bed until noon, and then only to use the bathroom.

Monday mid-morning I got up and took a shower, had a can of soup and some crackers, and brushed my teeth. Even that little bit seemed like too much of an effort. With trembling legs, I crawled back into bed and drifted into a fitful sleep, not waking up until evening.

By noon Tuesday I felt strong enough to work on my chipmunk painting, and by six I finished it. I put on my coat and started out the door with it in my hands, planning to show it to Gertie. Then I remembered. Gertie could see it from heaven.

Picking up my phone to take a photo, I noticed a voice mail.

"It's Saturday evening," George said. "You're not answering your phone, and I hope you're okay. Please call when you can."

Still half stuck in my own world, I didn't want to talk to anyone. How should I think and feel? Could I work with David? Should I find myself another job and place to live? Do I have enough money? The last notice from my bank said I had $860.

I did another search on the Internet for available apartments in the area where David had applied for the new location for Artistic Horizons. The results frightened me. Even a four hundred-square-foot efficiency cost $900 a month, and that price did not include utilities.

I wrote an application letter to Ted and Cindy Fallon of Harmony Cards and emailed it with the photos of my mouse painting and chipmunks and frog painting. *If I get the job, will what I earn be enough? I'll look for similar positions.*

Laura called. "I received a letter from Lettie, telling me how sorry she was and that someday she hoped to make up for what she had done to us and the reputation of Artistic Horizons."

"Are you going to write her back?"

"I don't know. Maybe it would be better to leave it alone. Maybe I'll drop her a note telling her I forgive her and that I wish her well."

"That would be nice," I said. "It's always good if we can forgive people."

"That's right."

She said goodbye. If she meant I should forgive David, I couldn't. I was looking for revenge.

He came in at five-thirty and didn't say anything to me, but bustled about wrapping his portrait of Nancy in protective paper and putting it in a box. As he carried it to the door, he turned to me. "You're not saying much. Are you okay?"

"Am I supposed to be?"

He stopped with his hand on the doorknob. "What's wrong?"

"I thought you and I had more than an employer-employee relationship. I asked you to take me to Gertie's funeral, and you were too busy. You didn't have the decency to call me and tell me the funeral was somewhere else. Then you showed up with *her*. I could see why you were too busy."

"I'm sorry you feel that way. You should have known that I had to be with the mother of my child at such an important family occasion. Gertie and Marty spent quality time together."

"You've never given up on her, have you? All this time I thought you cared for me, and you were using me to entertain you and sneaking around to be with her."

"Sneaking? How dare you accuse me of sneaking around! If that's all the respect you have for me, we're through!"

"I was through at Gertie's funeral."

"Good!" He slammed the door as he left.

Yes, good. My insides were shaking with anger, and tears filled my eyes. I replayed what had happened several times, each ending with the sight of David's face twisted in anger. *He never loved me.* That's what hurts the most. Tears streamed down my cheeks as I closed the shop and went to my apartment. I threw myself on the couch and cried until I was worn out.

"Gertie, you warned me." I looked heavenward. "You told me he asked her to marry him. You know what? I'm strong enough to live life without him."

I got up, washed my face, and microwaved a frozen dinner. I picked up my Bible and opened it to Luke chapter eleven. "Lord, teach us to pray," the disciples said to Jesus. Yes, I needed to know how to pray, and I read it eagerly. "And forgive us our sins; for we ourselves also forgive every one that is indebted to us."

I closed the Bible. Do I forgive everyone? Forgiving Lettie was easy. She hadn't hurt me. But David had. I felt used. He liked me just enough to use me to make Marty jealous. Or maybe I was a fallback. If it didn't work out with Marty, he still had a girlfriend.

Then I remembered my words to George. "There is someone, but I don't know if it will work out or not." Poor George. I talked to him just enough to keep him hoping. Who had really cared for me? Who had sent me money as he was able? Who saved my grade school drawings and told me of his love for me? Who was a Christian and took me to church? Who bought me a new coat and telephone? Who had even said he wished we had a house like the ones he wanted to sell?

A sense of shame crept through my body as I saw myself, my own motives and selfishness. With tears in my eyes, I picked up my phone and called George.

"Allison, are you okay? I've been so worried about you."

"I'm sorry I didn't return your call. I've been sick. I went to Gertie's funeral and..." I couldn't go on. *Maybe someday I'll tell him about Gertie's funeral. Maybe never.*

"Are you feeling better?"

"Yes. Physically, I am. But..." I didn't want to tell him about the black hole I had fallen into.

"But you're not okay?"

"No." I gathered my courage. "I feel lost. I'll never be the Christian Gertie hoped I would be. I don't even know how to pray."

"The disciples of Jesus didn't either. That's why he told them what to say."

"I know. I just read that in Luke eleven."

"Oh, is your Bible still open there? If it isn't, find it again."

"Hang on." I put down my phone and found the place, then picked my phone up. "Okay, I'm there."

"Read verses nine and ten."

"'So I say to you, Ask, and it will be given to you; seek, and you will find; knock, and it will be opened to you. For every one who asks receives; and he who seeks finds; and to him who knocks it will be opened.'"

"Now I want to read Hebrews 11:6 to you. Listen. 'And without faith it is impossible to please *Him,* for he who comes to God must believe that He is and that He is a rewarder of those who seek Him.' See, God knows what you need. He knows you are seeking Him. All you have to do is ask Him to show you the way. God is good and gracious. He knows we're evil, that we sin. That's why He sent Jesus to die for us."

"Thank you, George. Can we talk about God again?"

"Allison, I was so hoping you'd ask. Any time you want. Oh, I love you."

He said goodbye. He loved me. I bowed my head. "God, George said you would listen and help me. Thank You. Please help me to forgive David. Amen."

Could I learn to love George? Was I worthy of his love?

CHAPTER 58

WHAT COMES AROUND

"MY WORK FOR THE COMMITTEE is almost finished," George said when he called me for the fourth time that week. "I'll soon be working full time with my dad. During our grand opening last week we sold two homes each, and people are coming to look every day. I won't get paid for about a month, but when I do, I'll send you part."

He didn't say how much he would send me. It would be so like George not to know how much he'd get from each house he sold. Whatever he sent me would be fine. I admired him for keeping his promise.

But I remembered two Georges, the chubby, broke guy in a wrinkled suit who had no money, and the George who has lost weight, had a good job, and was interested in me and wanted to take care of me. The George who said he loved me. Which was the real George?

My phone rang, and *Harmony Cards* flashed on the display. My hand shook as I picked it up.

"Allison Cooper?"

"Speaking."

"This is Cindy Fallon. We liked your animal paintings very much, and we'd like to hire you to paint our new animal line for Harmony Cards. Are you still available?"

"Yes," I squeaked.

"Good. We need you to paint six pictures, each showing a different animal scene. We'll pay you two hundred dollars for each painting we accept, and you will earn a ten percent commission on each box of cards we sell. If they sell well, we'll have you do more. Does that sound okay?"

"Sounds great," I said, regaining my voice.

"We'll send you a contract in the mail. If it meets your approval, please sign it and return it in the enclosed stamped envelope."

I told her goodbye and did a happy dance around the office, my heart pounding. Money to rent an apartment. No, wait. Money to add to my savings to start my own art gallery. I picked up the phone to call George when David walked in.

"How are you?" he asked.

"Fine, thank you. I hope you're well."

"I'm going to pick up some of my frames, and then I'll be out of your hair."

He sported a tattoo on his left arm, a red heart with the blue initials *MJ* inside. I wondered what the *J* stood for. My heart hit bottom at the reminder, and I was glad when he left without saying another word. Laura told me he was busy finishing several paintings for a client as they needed the money to set up Artistic Horizons in its new location.

The mail carrier came just before six. "A letter for Miss Allison Cooper," he said, handing me a white envelope.

I thanked him, locked the front door, and hurried back to my apartment to open it. It was from Mr. Albert Thomes, attorney. Tearing open the tape from the end of the envelope, I extracted several sheets of paper. The first was a letter.

Dear Ms. Cooper;

Mr. Simon Traggart passed away on January 30. Mr. Albert Thomes, Esq., is the executor of his will. Mr. Traggart has no other living relatives and named you as his sole heir.

Mr. Thomes has hired a real estate company that valued Mr. Traggart's estate, including his property and his home, the contents of his home, and his truck at $106,000.

> *Mr. Traggart banked at Wells Fargo Bank, where his savings account shows $25,000 and his checking account $3,785.*

Trag left everything to me in his will? Disbelief filled me, but then anger surged through me, making my whole body shake as I recalled how Trag had nothing to eat when we arrived in Chicago, hungry and exhausted. He had handed Aunt Harriet the electric bill to pay when she had very little money. He could afford to buy Boots food, but he had left him without food or water. Trembling, I read the rest of the letter.

> *Please contact Mr. Thomes within thirty days and let him know how you want the estate disposed. You may come to Chicago and dispose of the property yourself. If you prefer, Mr. Thomes will sell Mr. Traggart's estate and have the money wired directly to your bank account. By signing and returning the enclosed documents, you give Mr. Thomes permission to sell the property for you and to wire the money in Mr. Traggart's Wells Fargo account directly to your bank account.*

Sign two documents. Return them in the mail. It all seemed too easy. If I did it, I would never see any of Aunt Harriet's things. Was it worth flying to Chicago just to see if Trag kept any of her personal belongings? He probably hadn't. I sighed as I realized it was the sensible thing to do.

Then it hit me. When I got the money, I'd be rich. I could buy almost anything I wanted. I wouldn't have to depend on my job at Artistic Horizons. I wouldn't have to rely on George. I had learned all there was to learn about running an art store here, and I wanted to move on. I could afford to quit and look for another job. I could afford to attend a real art school. I could do anything I wanted. I could get my hair fixed and styled every week. I could get my nails painted and buy all the shoes and clothes I needed. I could afford a car. I might buy delicious food or eat out in fancy restaurants any time I didn't want to cook.

Would I tell anyone? No, at least not now. Sometime, maybe in early March, I'd tell Laura that I would not be working for

Artistic Horizons when they moved. I could quit right now, but the money wasn't in my bank account yet. And If I quit, what would I do? Where would I go? I needed some time to explore my options.

George called at seven, his regular time for calling on Saturday. "Hi, Allison, how are you today?"

"Just fine, George. And how's it going with you and your father?"

"We're selling homes so fast we can't keep up with the paper work. I can't go to church tomorrow because Dad and I have to catch up in the morning, and Magic Forest is open from one until six."

"I'm sorry. I know how much you love going to church."

"Will you go to church for me tomorrow?"

"What am I supposed to do, inhabit your spirit, take it to church, and leave your body at work?"

"Hey, can you do that? Then we'll be at church together."

"Yes, I'll go. I've been planning to go."

"Good. Will you pray for me that I won't forget God just because I'm making money? And for Dad that someday he will accept Jesus as his Savior? Please?"

"Of course I will. I'll be glad to."

"Okay. Good night, then. I'm tired and need to get to bed."

I said good night and looked through my clothes to see what I could wear to church. My eyes lit upon my blue skirt and blouse that Aunt Harriet made me and Gertie fixed, and I pulled them out. I would go to church feeling wrapped in their love.

CHAPTER 59

GEORGE'S PROBLEM

MR. THOMES TRANSFERRED $25,265 INTO my checking account the next Friday. I couldn't use it for a few days because the bank has some rule about verifying it. I bought myself a new pair of dress shoes to replace the ones that got ruined when I went to Gertie's funeral. They dried, but they didn't fit right. I think they shrank. Then I splurged at the grocery store and bought more fresh fruit and vegetables. I thanked God every day for how He had blessed me.

Sunday, I sat with Laura and Don and their girls at church. "Dear God, please be with George and his father," I prayed. "Help George tell his dad about You. Amen." Gertie said praying for someone is a sign you love them. Did I love George even a little? I liked him, but I wasn't sure it was love.

On Valentine's Day, a dozen red roses from George arrived at the shop. Uncle Deb and Aunt Harriet never did anything for most holidays, and certainly not for Valentine's Day, so I didn't even realize what day it was until the bouquet came. I called him as soon as I got home.

"Allison, what a nice surprise. I've been thinking about you all day," he said.

"Thanks for the roses. They're beautiful. No one has ever given me flowers."

"Then I'm glad I did. You've waited too long. I wanted you to know I'm thinking about you."

"That's nice." After he hung up, I smelled the roses. Their perfume permeated my small apartment. The thought that George cared for me warmed my heart. Would I ever think of him in the same way he sees me?

George called again later that week. "Someone is suing Dad for a hundred thousand dollars," he said. "I can't believe it. He worked so hard to pay everyone back."

"But why?"

"This man, Reb Tully, invested just over a thousand dollars in that firm. Dad paid him back every cent. But he said he was so worried he had a heart attack, and he's suing Dad for payment of medical expenses and pain and suffering."

"Can he prove he had a heart attack because the investment firm was shut down?"

"I don't know. Maybe. If there is a trial and he wins, Dad will have to pay him. Even if we put all our money together, we couldn't pay him that much." He sighed. "We don't know what to do. Lawyers cost a lot, but Dad is thinking of hiring one."

"Mr. Tully must not be very rich. How can he afford a lawyer?"

"If he wins, he can pay from the money we'll have to give him. He's the town drunk. He and Dad were in high school together. They were friends, and both tried out for the football team, and they both made the team. Reb got into some trouble and got kicked off the team. Dad became the star quarterback, and Reb's always held it against him."

"What did Reb do with his life? How did he become the town drunk?"

"After graduating from high school, he went into construction business with his father. His father died a few years after that, and Reb couldn't do the work and went out of business."

"I see." I didn't know what else to say. George said he had to work and hung up.

A hundred thousand dollars. Even if I it was in my bank account, I wouldn't want to give it to George and his father. I've been thinking a lot about a certain dress shop on Main Street in Puttersville. I want to buy it and make it my own art studio and store, and I'm planning on how to decorate it, but most of all, I'm thinking of names for the sign on its front.

After saying good-bye to George, I thought about their dilemma while I painted. Maybe Reb Tully is lying and didn't have a heart attack at all. George and his father should check with the hospital to see if Reb had a heart attack, and if he had one, when. No, that wouldn't work, for the hospital wouldn't give them any information about a patient. If they hired a lawyer, he could find out from the hospital. I decided to do some research to see if there were any lawyers in Puttersville.

Shortly after I arrived at the shop Saturday, David and Marty came in, arms wrapped around each other.

"Hello, Allie," David said. "You remember Marty."

"Of course," I said and greeted her. She nodded as they headed for the art supplies aisle. David gathered an armload of canvases, acrylics, and brushes. "Would you mind entering these on the inventory page?" he asked me.

I put his supplies on the inventory spreadsheet. *What a stupid thing for him to ask me if I remembered Marty, especially after our last conversation.* A ring sparkled from the fourth finger of her left hand. *Well, she's finally agreed to marry him. She can have him.* I might have fainted if I had seen a ring on her finger at Gertie's funeral, but at that moment, the hurt was gone.

"Thanks," David said when I finished. He laid his hand on Marty's arm. "Come on, love, we need to get on the road." She nodded and followed him out the door without glancing my way.

I watched them through the window. Were they going someplace to paint another Colorado scene? I was free of the constant worry of whether I was his girlfriend or just an employee. And I was free of the hurt and pain he caused me. Had I forgiven him, or had I just decided I didn't need him in my life?

The ringing of my phone broke my reverie.

"Miss Cooper? This is Mr. Thomes. I've sold Mr. Traggart's house. The money will be in your account by the end of next week."

"How much?"

"All of it except for the rest of my fee. I think the rest of the fee is one hundred fifty dollars as Mr. Traggard had paid most of it."

I stood there, a jittery feeling flowing through my body. I was rich. I could walk out of Artistic Horizons and never look back. I never had to see David and Marty again if I didn't want to. I could wash the memories of Gertie's funeral out of my mind.

Then I realized all the money in the world could not make me happy. Mixed in with the bad memories were all the good ones—Uncle Deb's and Aunt Harriet's care, Gertie's love and compassion, David's laughing blue eyes and his help, and Jenny Lou's friendship. Aunt Harriet was right. Our existence was not good when we lived in isolation.

CHAPTER 60

GIVING AND SHARING

I WALKED AROUND LIKE A giddy zombie all week. The last Saturday of February, the money was in my bank account—all $135,050. I couldn't wait to tell Laura and David that I wouldn't be working with them after they moved Artistic Horizons.

Last Sunday at church, the preacher talked about giving and sharing. His first story was about the poor widow woman who gave so little, but it was all she had. Then he told us about Mary Magdalene who loved Jesus and poured expensive perfume on His feet and wiped them with her hair. The last half of his sermon was about Jesus and how much God's Son gave for us.

I'd never heard about Jesus's gift the way the preacher told it. I'd never thought about how it must have hurt Jesus to give up His glory and His place in heaven with God. He was treated terribly by others while He was doing good, healing people of their diseases, and preaching to them. I cried when the preacher told what horrible things they did to Him when they crucified Him.

So all week I thought about how much God had done for me. My mind had been set on me, what I needed and wanted, and how mean David was to me. But if I looked at things from David's perspective, I knew I could have and should have done more to understand him. Then George came to mind. While I was growing up, going to school with George for twelve years, all I knew was that he was the little boy who talked to me. I didn't understand that his father's and mother's lack of affection for each other probably made his home life difficult. I'm sure he was lonely and frightened.

My own actions confused me. Jesus had given His life for me, but I couldn't tell George I had some money and would help him and his father. But if I gave them the money I received for Trag's house, how could I afford my art shop? What would I live on until I started making money? Yes, I would still have over $35,000, but would it be enough?

I pondered my present actions and future plans as I painted a picture of two playful kittens that were in the yard across from the shop the day before. One was a gray tiger and the other was black and white. I stood outside in the sun and sketched their outlines and facial features as they frolicked on the porch. I've painted them playing on a lush lawn full of flowers, though. It would be my third picture for Harmony Cards. I'd send all six when I finished them.

George called tonight with some news. "Dad hired a lawyer. He wanted a two thousand dollar retainer to work on our case. We managed to scrape together the money even though Magic Forest isn't paying us until Friday."

"I'm glad he hired a lawyer. Was it Mr. Piersces or Mr. Shelty?"

"Mr. Shelty. How did you know?"

"Oh, I did a little research."

"Mr. Shelty said he would ask the hospital for Mr. Tully's medical records and should have them by next Friday. Then we'll know if Reb had a heart attack. Now for the exciting news. You'll never believe it."

"Believe what?"

"Puttersville wants to change the name of their elementary school to Allison Cooper Elementary School because you helped save the town. What do you think of that?"

"You're right, I can't believe it. They want to name the school after me? The school where I didn't fit and had so many problems? And why didn't they contact me?"

"They asked me for your address and phone number, and I told them I would ask you. I hope that's okay."

"George..."

"I'm sorry. I should have had them call you. Do you want me to?"

"I guess it's okay," I said, even though I wished the school would have called.

"Anyway, your painting on all those billboards did the trick. Our citizens voted against Puron Oil. If that bill hadn't passed, they would be tearing up our forests and our town. They're going to announce the renaming of the school during our spring festival the first weekend in April. They want you to come. Can you?"

Artistic Horizons would be at its new location by then. "I think so."

"Good. I'll buy your plane ticket. No, I'll come and get you. No, I'll—"

"George, slow down," I said. "I don't want you to buy me a plane ticket. Coming after me costs a lot of money. You and your dad have enough expenses."

"So you're not coming?" His voice fell. "I thought you would. I was counting on your coming." He said nothing for a while, then, "The mayor of Puttersville wants you to come."

"I didn't say I'm not coming, but it's a month away. I have to think and plan. I want to see what happens during the next few weeks."

"You're still not sure about me, are you? You still love your boyfriend."

"Let's get some things straight, George," I said, stamping my foot and putting my left hand on my hip. "Number one, I don't have a boyfriend. Number two, I don't like your making plans for me without even telling me. You could have at least called and asked before you told the whole town and the mayor I would come."

"But that's what I'm doing, calling and asking. I haven't told anyone you're coming, not even Dad. But I would like to."

"Okay, but give me some time."

"Before I go, I have some more news. Judy's Special Dress Shop is for sale. I talked to the owner, and she hired me to be her real estate agent."

"But I thought you're working for Magic Forest. Don't you have enough to do?"

"Now you're telling me what to do," he said, laughing. "I thought of what you said when you were here. You said it would make the perfect art shop and studio. Are you interested?"

"How much are they asking for it?"

"Fifty thousand dollars. The twenty percent down payment would be ten thousand dollars. I think when Magic Forest pays Dad and me, my share will be at least ten thousand. I'll make the down payment for you if you want it for an art studio."

My eyes teared up at his words. He remembered everything I told him. "Can I have a few days to think about it?"

"Sure. Let me know by March third so I'll know what to do."

I promised I would and hung up quickly, not because I didn't want to talk to him any longer, but because I couldn't hold back the tears streaming down my face. He cared for me so much he was willing to buy my plane ticket, or drive all the way to Denver to get me, and put the down payment on a site for my art shop, even though he and his father were facing a trial and possibly a payment of $100,000 to Mr. Tully. Maybe the court would decide they would have to pay more than that.

I fell to my knees and buried my face in my hands. "Thank You, God," I cried. "Thank You for George and his love for me. Please forgive me for being so selfish with Your good gifts. Help me know what to do."

CHAPTER 61

FOR LOVE'S SAKE

I WRESTLED FOR HOURS WITH the decision of whether to give George and his father the money from the house if they needed it. I couldn't bear the thought of what would happen to them if they had to pay money they didn't have. How could I be selfish and not help them when God has been so good to me?

George had proven his love for me in so many ways. Looking back, I realized that I had yearned for his love for a long time. His teasing on the playground, his comments about my drawings, his flirting with me in high school, and his asking me to the prom—all should have clued me in. I was so occupied with myself and my world, I couldn't see him.

As my thoughts struggled with each other while I turned and twisted in bed, something knocked some sense into me. Call it sanity, truth, an eye opener. Or call it love. George had always been near my heart. I saw in him as a friend and an understanding listener I could trust. He needed me just as much as I needed him. How could I ever think I didn't need and want him? He had been in the back recesses of my mind since I started school, each year growing on me.

On the first day of March when I went to work, Laura said, "The new site for Artistic Horizons is ours. David signed the contract and paid the security deposit and first month's rent. They are giving us the last week of March free, so we can start moving then."

"What will happen with this place?" I asked.

"We're selling it. Didn't I tell you?"

"If you told me, I didn't hear you," I said, shaking my head. "But I've had a lot to think about this last month. I've decided to do something else and not work at Artistic Horizons after your move."

Her jaw dropped. "Really? When did you make this decision?"

"Like I said, I've been thinking about it for a month, but the last few weeks cemented what I wanted to do."

"What will you do? Where will you go?"

"I have learned so much working here that I hate to leave, but I want to open my own art shop and studio." I told her about the result of the election and how the town wanted to name the school for me. "George found me a place for my art shop, and he's buying it for me, and he's a Christian, and…" Out of breath and feeling a flush covering my face, I stopped.

"And you're in love with him," Laura said. "Oh Allie, I'm so happy for you! Gertie would be, too." She hugged me, then stood back, her eyes fixed on me. "I watched you all the time you wanted David to love you, and I knew that even though he took you places, it would never happen. I watched you suffer, but I couldn't tell you. I'm sorry."

"David was good to me and so were you, and I loved Gertie. I don't know what I would have done without your kindness. I was homeless, and you gave me work and a place to live. Gertie taught me about God and Jesus." My eyes filled with tears as I showed her the Bible Gertie gave me that I now kept in the shop to read in my spare time. "It's probably a family heirloom. If you want it back, I'll be glad to give it to you."

She put her hand on the worn cover, then looked up and smiled at me. "Gertie loved you and wanted you to have it. You keep it. We have others."

"That's what Gertie said. Oh, I have missed her." Tears welled up in my eyes. "But I know she's in heaven looking down and smiling."

"I'm sure she is." She gave me another hug. "When are you leaving?"

"Sometime the last week of March after I help you move. I haven't told George yet. We'll figure it out together."

"You have been such a big help to us, I don't know how we'll replace you. But I'm so happy for you. Well, I have to pick up Diana and Lilah, so I'd better go. May I tell David?"

"Yes, of course. I hope I see him again, though. I want to tell him that I'm happy for him. I saw the ring on Marty's finger."

"Thanks," she said. "I'll save that part for you to tell."

David came in that afternoon. "Have to get some info from the computer for taxes," he said. "It won't take long." He didn't talk while he worked. He printed two pages, picked them up, and headed for the door.

"Do you have a minute?" I said. "I'd like to tell you something."

"Yes?" he said, stopping in front of the door.

"I won't be going with you to your new site."

"Really, Allie? Where are you going?"

After I told him, I said, "I'm happy for you and Marty. Thanks for everything you've done for me."

"I'm happy for you, too. Do you think you'll marry George?"

"I think that's a good possibility. If he has his say."

"And how about your say? Do you love him?"

"Yes, I believe I do, at least by the criteria set down by your grandmother. I'm sure she has had her say in all this."

"I'm sure she has," he said, laughing. "Good luck." Then he walked over and hugged me. "I'll see you again before you leave. I'm happy for you."

All I could think about was George and how I would break my good news.

He called that night, right on schedule. "Hi, Allison, have you been thinking about my offer? Do you know what you're going to do?"

"I want to decorate a little store on Main Street in Puttersville and make it into a lovely art shop. Do you know how I can get such a place?"

"You mean…you really mean, you're coming? You're coming to stay?"

"Yes, George. Do you know why?"

"Why?"

"Because I love you."

"Oh, Allison, will you say that again?"

"I love you, George Benton."

"Oh, Allison. When can you come?"

"The last week of March. Laura and David need me to help them move, but I can come when we're finished. Can you come get me or should I fly?"

"I'm sure you have lots to bring, so I'll come get you. I think Dad can handle Magic Forest for a few days. I'm so excited."

"I'm excited, too. And happy."

"I forgot to tell you the other news," he said. "Mr. Shelty learned that Reb Tully has never been in the hospital. Not in Puttersville, anyway. If Mr. Tully wants to pursue the lawsuit, he will have to provide proof that he's had a heart attack or get a medical test that shows he has had a heart attack. I don't think he'll do it, but we'll see."

"I hope not. George, I have been praying for you and your father. I asked God to please protect you from Mr. Tully's schemes to get your money."

"Thank you. I've been praying for you, asking God to open your eyes to His presence and to help you find Him. I want you to be a Christian."

"I believe in God, George. I know Jesus died for my sins. What else is there to do?"

"I'll tell you when I come because I want to be the one to help you. Good night, dear. I can't wait to tell Dad you're coming."

"Good night," I said. After hanging up, I broke into a song of praise.

CHAPTER 62

HOW IT ALL TURNED OUT

A LITTLE PART OF ME wept as George and I drove away from the old Artistic Horizons shop. David and Laura stood out front and waved until we were too far away to see them. Laura gave me her email address so we could keep in touch when I get a computer, but I could always call her.

What a great time we had traveling together to Puttersville, almost like a honeymoon—except I stayed in a separate room at the hotel. I paid for the rooms, and George paid for our food and gas. Along the way, we enjoyed sharing our thoughts and getting to know each other better.

"I have a confession to make," I told him as soon as we got into the car on our second day.

"You? A confession? Let's hear it," he said, laughing.

"I recently inherited some money."

"Seriously? How much?"

"Enough to buy Judy's Special Dress Shop. And then some. I planned to help you and your dad if Reb Tully's story turned out to be true."

"Instead of buying your shop?"

"If that's what it took."

"Oh, Allison, I love you." He reached over and took my hand, and when I looked into his face, tears filled his eyes. "I know how much having your shop means to you."

"But not as much as having you."

"I know about a cute little house in Magic Forest, the last three-bedroom on the far south end that abuts the woods. The same forest where you spent so much time with your animal friends. Those woods are now a protected park, but anyone can go there."

"So? What about this little house?"

"Let's buy it."

"We're not even engaged."

"We can fix that," he said with a twinkle in his eye. "But there's something I need to tell you. Remember when we talked about you becoming a Christian? That there is something more?"

"More to do?"

"Yes. If you believe that Jesus died for your sins, you must be baptized to receive forgiveness for your sins. That is how you become a Christian. It means that Christ is your Lord and King, and you give your life to Him."

"I want to be baptized. Will you do it?"

"Yes. We'll make it home in time to go to church tonight. I'll baptize you tonight."

After we arrived, George called the preacher and told him my story. That evening, I professed that I believed that Jesus is God's son and died for my sins. George immersed me in the baptistery. When I came up out of the water, the church members sang "A New Creature." I am a new creation, a child of God, and no longer an orphan.

The next Saturday, we went to Puttersville's spring festival and the ceremony for renaming Puttersville Elementary School to Allison B. Cooper Elementary School. I sat on the stage with Mr. Wheyton, who was the principal when I was a student there. It seemed as if everyone in Puttersville attended the ceremony at the high school football stadium, for the crowd filled the bleachers around the football field and covered the grounds inside the field and outside the bleachers.

"Our honoree is Miss Allison Cooper," Mr. Wheyton said. "She was one of our students. She longed to be an artist. I don't think she will mind if I tell you she had many obstacles to overcome. She triumphed over Asperger's Syndrome and made a name for herself and a career. You saw the billboards displaying the charming scene of the animals weeping over the destruction of our forests. That would have happened if Puron Oil had fracked the oil wells in our area. Allison's picture persuaded many to vote against Puron Oil and fracking. Because of Allison's talent and perseverance, Puttersville is a thriving, growing community that attracts businesses. Mayor Hill will present Miss Cooper with our certificate of appreciation."

Mayor Hill stepped to the microphone. "It is the decision of the Puttersville School District Board, the Puttersville City Council, and myself as mayor that Puttersville Elementary School will from now on be Allison B. Cooper Elementary School. Miss Cooper, will you please come and accept this certificate?"

My legs trembled as I rose and walked to Mayor Hill. He handed me the framed certificate, and my heart thumped as I shook his hand.

"Speech! Speech!" roared the sea of people.

"Thank you, Mayor Hill, Puttersville School Board, and Mr. Wheyton," I said. Looking down into the sea of people, I saw a huge sign. The words I longed to hear, *Marry me, Allison,* flashed in front of my eyes. I blinked back tears of happiness and finished my speech before I forgot it.

"To all you students in school, never give up. Your dreams can come true. To all of you who are working hard, keep working and learning. It's the only way to succeed." Then I looked straight at George and his father who were holding up the sign and said. "To Mr. George Benton, my answer is yes."

The crowd broke into thunderous applause, cheering, and whistling. George ran up onto the platform and whisked me off my feet, and right in front of everyone, he kissed me. As the crowd kept cheering, he slipped a gold ring with a large, marquis-cut diamond onto my finger.

"How about June tenth?" he whispered.

That evening I called Laura. "George and I are getting married June tenth. Can you come? I'll send you an invitation, but I want to know now."

"I'd love to, but that's when David and Marty are getting married. What a coincidence!" she said, laughing.

"It is. How differently my life is going than what I had hoped for and dreamed of, but God knows what I need, and I couldn't be happier."

Just a few weeks later, I was perched on a stool at my new Enchanted Art Shop and Studio. I didn't have a sign yet, but that was what I'd name it. I made a list of supplies I needed. Yellow and white paint for the walls and ceiling, flowers and backdrop material for the two windows, carpet, shelves, and later I'd be ordering art supplies.

My ring sparkled in the sunlight streaming through the window, and I gazed at it for the thousandth time since George put it on my finger. Its multifaceted diamond reminded me of everything I'd learned from others. Uncle Deb had said, "God will always take care of you. He has a plan for you." So true, Uncle Deb.

Aunt Harriet had said, "Work hard, and you will succeed. A little work never hurt anyone." She showed me by her example. Enchanted Art needed a ton of fixing up, but I could do it. She'd also said, "Life is no good if you live in isolation. You need friends and love." I had found both.

My dear friend Gertie told me I would always be an orphan until I had God as my heavenly Father. She taught me about God's love. She read to me about the birth of Jesus and told me how He suffered and died for my sins. Thank you, Gertie, for starting me on my way to finding God.

David had said, "Be kind to everyone." He was kind to me, even though he broke my heart. I shuddered. I might have ended up being a street person sleeping under a bridge in cold Denver if he hadn't hired me.

George didn't say it. He'd just done it. He'd sent me money when I was destitute. He loved me when I didn't know how to return his love. He'd kept calling and never gave up on me.

As I sat thinking, he breezed through the door. "Half hour lunch break," he said, handing me a bag holding a sandwich and drink. "Our secretary is holding down the fort."

While we ate, I outlined my plans for my shop and what I needed. "Maybe we can go get these things after dinner."

"We'll do that. I'll tell you something else we're going to do. Get your driver's license and get you a car. Then you can bring me lunch." He wrapped me in his arms and kissed me. I trembled at his touch, and I wanted to melt into him.

I had my art shop. I had George. But most of all, I was a child of God. And that was all I needed.

TO MY READERS

ASPERGER'S SYNDROME is a socially debilitating developmental disorder. The American Psychiatric Association's manual for classifying mental disorders, the *Diagnostic and Statistical Manual of Mental Disorders, Fifth Edition,* puts Asperger's Syndrome in the spectrum of autism disorders.

People who have Asperger's display a number of symptoms. They have a hard time making friends. They often do not understand body language or do not respect interpersonal boundaries. They are inflexible and need routines. They may also have ADHD, a lack of empathy for others, depression, obsessive compulsive disorder, and sensitivity to noises, odors, and touch.

However, some persons who are diagnosed with Asperger's show few of these symptoms and have learned social skills. Many people with Asperger's have a high intelligence quotient and are gifted in one area. Some believe that Einstein and Tesla may have had Asperger's.

Allison's school counselor diagnosed her with Asperger's because she had a difficult time making friends and would rather paint than be with people. But does she have it, or are her personality traits caused by the environment in which she was reared? As she grows and learns without contact with playmates, her social skills are lagging. Her hearing Uncle Deb's viewpoints on the world every day surely tainted her ideas and views.

Do I believe a relationship with God can help people who suffer from Asperger's? Certainly. Knowing how much God loves each one of us imparts self-worth, and the Bible guides us in getting along with others.

The purpose of this book is not to help someone diagnose Asperger's Syndrome in himself or others or to prescribe interventions. This book is for everyone who is shy, lonely, and has a hard time making friends. May you find the courage and help you need to learn to communicate with others and form relationships that will enrich your life. This is my prayer for you.

ABOUT THE AUTHOR

DONNA WITTLIF has a Master's Degree in special education and has taught students with Asperger's Syndrome, a developmental disability that hinders social skills. She and her husband live in Colorado. They enjoy writing, reading, studying and teaching the Bible, and keeping up with their grandchildren.

Other Books By Donna

World Eternal Series

Book 1 World Eternal: Promises

Book 2 World Eternal: Proselytes

Book 3 World Eternal: Perils

Available online at Amazon and Barnes & Noble

Connect with Donna

Website: **www.donnarwittlif.com**

Facebook: **www.facebook.com/authordonnawittlif**

Twitter: **www.twitter.com/DonnaWittlif**

Bublish: **www.bublish.com/author/view/6560**

Book Discounts and Special Deals

Sign up for free to get discounts and special deals on our best-selling books at

www.TCKPublishing.com/bookdeals

CPSIA information can be obtained
at www.ICGtesting.com
Printed in the USA
LVHW081017021118
595731LV00012B/125/P

9 781631 610547